FALLOW'S FIELD

Fallow's Field

A Novel

Dennis McKay

iUniverse, Inc.
New York Lincoln Shanghai

Fallow's Field

iUniverse books may be ordered through booksellers or by contacting:

iUniverse
2021 Pine Lake Road, Suite 100
Lincoln, NE 68512
www.iuniverse.com
1-800-Authors (1-800-288-4677)

Because of the dynamic nature of the Internet, any Web addresses or links contained in this book may have changed since publication and may no longer be valid.

This is a work of fiction. All of the characters, names, incidents, organizations, and dialogue in this novel are either the products of the author's imagination or are used fictitiously.

ISBN: 978-0-595-43652-1 (pbk)
ISBN: 978-0-595-68270-6 (cloth)
ISBN: 978-0-595-87979-3 (ebk)

Printed in the United States of America

This book is dedicated to the old way
and to those who remember.

The author wishes to acknowledge the help
and support of Jim Cotton
and Leo Olivia in making this book possible.

PART 1

▼

CHAPTER 1

KETCHUM, TEXAS
1880

For this land takes more than it gives ...

At first light, the old man stood on the porch and looked out. From the north the clouds came, like black tombstones tumbling out of the gray sky.

"Ye gods, William," he said to himself.

He stepped off the porch and crossed the yard.

At the side of the barn, he pulled out his corncob pipe and tapped it on a pile of stones. Thinking better of it, William O'Connor put the pipe back in his shirt pocket.

He poked his head inside the barn and noticed an empty stall with its gate open. His breath lingered in the cold November air as an old feeling stirred in his stomach.

"Doggone critter," he muttered as he headed back toward the house.

In the distance, a black speck wandered about on this hostile land, which was capable of devouring living things in an instant and a man's dreams over a lifetime.

William clumped onto the porch and into the entryway, where mackinaws, chaps, hats, and overalls hung along the walls.

He peered toward the back of the house where his daughters, Helen Fallow and Lorrayne O'Brien, were serving oatmeal to their husbands and two young sons at the kitchen table. William thought of his deceased wife as he looked at the black cherry table ribboned with ebony. It was a family heirloom and looked out of place in such spare surroundings.

"Jim, Tom, there's a storm comin'." William hollered at his sons-in-law as he entered the kitchen. "We'd better—"

"Don't fret none, William," Jim Fallow said. He stood and downed the last of his tin of coffee. "We'll see to the livestock in the barn."

"Now, one thing," William said, scratching his ear. "The bull's loose in the north pasture, but we best not bother. Crazy critter gets wanderlust at the worst of times."

Jim Fallow strode past his father-in-law, with Thomas O'Brien right behind.

William stepped onto the porch as Jim and Thomas hustled across the yard toward the barn, scattering the chickens with a flurry of protest.

Jim and Tom rode out of the barn in to the yard.

As Jim's frisky sorrel raised its front legs, Jim held the reins close to the bit. "Tom and I will round the bull up and be back before the first flake hits the ground."

William noticed his son-in-law's eyes were like those of mustangs not all the way broke, with some of the wild still in them. "First sign of danger, head on back here." William watched until his sons-in-law disappeared into the sweeping backdrop of land and sky.

William sat down at the kitchen table and dipped his spoon into a bowl of oatmeal but decided against it. He got up to make his bed along the back wall, thinking of a time when he had also had a bit of the mustang in him. It struck him how the women in his family were drawn to daring men.

"Helen, Lorrayne, I'll tend to the barn," William said. He creased his sheet and tucked in the back corners. "I don't want the boys going outside." As he straightened himself, a great whoosh of wind rattled the house.

"Can't we help, Grandpa?" young Ned Fallow asked.

William shot a glance at his grandsons at the kitchen table and caught the glimmer in their eyes. He had seen the same one in their fathers'. "No, boy. I won't be long."

William secured the barn door and turned to face a howling sea of white. He trudged toward the murky silhouette of the house.

With one hand on the porch railing to steady himself against the wild blizzard, he brushed snow off his flannel shirt and denim trousers. He stomped his boots clean and went in the front door.

William entered the kitchen. "Animals fed and tied down; barn is closed up tight."

Little Tom O'Brien strained to look over the windowsill in the front room. "Mama, I can't see the barn."

Lorrayne paused from kneading dough at a small table next to the stove, glanced at her son, and then at William. "Yes, Tom, I see." She shifted her gaze to the seven places set for the noon meal, and then back toward her father.

William went over to the window and stood beside Tom. Somewhere out there, his two sons-in-law were fighting for their lives.

The fading dusk stole the last meager bits of daylight, and dull gray shadows spread through the room. William lit a lamp at the table and sat across from his family. Jim and Tom had been gone for over six hours.

"Grandpa, should someone go lookin'?" Tom asked.

The little boy's eyes, so young to be drowning in such fear, reminded William of a frightened doe.

Helen Fallow stared at the table, her beautiful face aglow in the flickering lamplight. "Dad … please don't go." Her finger repeatedly traced a circular vein on the cherry table.

As the lamplight struggled against the imminent darkness, the storm howled and whooshed against the little house. William noticed only five places set for dinner.

The land was quiet now, its damage done. The scratchy terrain, its knobby-topped buttes spreading over rough, sparse grassland, had swallowed two men and a bull without leaving a trace.

Ned, his family, and a smattering of neighbors gathered on a lonesome hill beyond the barn. The north wind blew easy now, as if trying to atone for its rage of a week before.

William O'Connor rubbed a patch of white stubble on his cheek and cleared his throat. The sadness carved in the lines of his weathered face. "Lord," he said, "we know not why you took them, but forsake us not. Somehow, some way, we'll see it through. They were good and decent men, and it was an honor to have them in the family. In this time of darkness, we will seek the light."

The front door on the Sorenson's porch creaked as it hung ajar. Ned listened to the hushed tones of mourners coming from inside the house. "Don't know how they can make a go of it now." The voice was a rusty whisper. "Gonna be a load on Mr. O'Connor, that's for sure," said another. These voices sounded different to Ned—a happy kind of sad. "We're glad it's not us," they seemed to say.

Ned noticed a slim, red cloud resting on the horizon, trapped between the great, bully sky and the heartless land. Hoping against hope, he searched for his father and uncle to come riding up. Bit by bit, the loss of hope settled in his bones.

He ached to see his dad galloping in. To see those broad shoulders bobbing up and down, to hear his short, choppy laugh from deep inside, making him feel everything was gonna be all right. Ned wanted one more time to see the spark in Jim Fallow's gray eyes when he put his head off to the side a little while pondering a situation. He wanted one more hug from that great chunk of man, one more hug after a day's work smelling of horse, sweat, and earth.

As the mourners departed, Ned peeked through the porch window and saw his grandfather staring into his mug of coffee. It was an empty, hollow stare. Mrs. Sorenson held hands with Ned's mother and aunt, both of whom appeared so alone without their men alongside.

In the waning light, the O'Connor clan departed in silence. They approached their home, and never had its windows looked so cheerless to Ned, or the house so cold and solemn like a giant tombstone anchored in this god-awful little nothing place.

Ned heard the faint sound of his father's laugh off in the distance. He scanned the barren terrain, which greeted him with silence.

CHAPTER 2

▼

AUTUMN 1882

"Grandpa, those red streaks go as far as I can see." Ned pointed his hoe toward the sky.

William O'Connor looked up at the crimson splinters scraping the horizon as though trying to find safe shelter. "Red sky at night, sailor's delight," the old man said. He scratched the stubble under his chin. "Be real good if I was still at sea, but it can't help us now." He stood in a meager garden of okra, potatoes, cabbage, and other wilting plants.

"We gonna be all right, Grandpa?"

"Could get a little lean this winter." William tossed a handful of weeds into a corncrib basket.

"Pa and Uncle Tom would know what to do." A thin tremor ran through Ned's voice.

William kept an eye on a young red-tailed hawk perched on the top branch of a lone mesquite tree. The bird flapped its proud wings in the failing light.

"Lord took your pa and uncle two years ago." William put a hand on Ned's shoulder. "He's got them now, along with your grandma."

"I can't remember what my grandma looked like," Ned said. He turned the hard, dry soil between the okra plants.

"You were just three when she passed. You have her eyes. They were like the sea—strong, with no room for nonsense. Most practical person I ever knew." William motioned for Ned to bring him an empty basket from the next row.

"Wish I'd never laid eyes on this land. But we'll see this through, Ned. Don't you fret none." William nodded at his grandson, took the basket, and placed it up the row they were working.

"I'm gonna be eleven next March, and Tom will be ten." Ned tossed a handful of weeds into the basket. "We'll help you plenty, Grandpa."

"I know you boys will." William moved the basket further up the row. "You're both hard workers and growing like sprouts."

William shuddered as a sudden gust of cool air blew down from the north, whistling across the meager land like it owned it. "Ned, let's get on inside for supper."

Ned kept hoeing.

"Ned," William said with gentle authority. "Suppertime."

"Okay, Grandpa."

As they headed toward the farmhouse, the faint howl of a coyote greeted the settling darkness.

"Grandpa, look!" Ned raced forward, pointing toward the dark purple horizon.

"That's a shooting star, Ned. Indians think it's a good sign."

"Do you think it'll be good for us?"

"Can't hurt none, that's for sure."

"They didn't think it an evil sign, Grandpa?"

"Not the Osage. They're an intelligent people, tall and proud, with a long history. They have two clans, the Sky and Earth."

"What's a clan?"

"A group of people tied by blood and something more—a belief in each other and their virtues."

"Grandpa—"

"Let me finish, Ned, and things will come clear. Now, Black Dog was the great leader of the Earth Clan and a fierce warrior."

"Did you see him fight, Grandpa?"

"No, but I went on a hunting party with him. From a great bluff, we saw thousands upon thousands of buffalo thundering across the Great Plains. Clouds of dust rose from the earth and blackened the sky."

William looked off as if he could see that far-off time. "Old Black Dog wanted to make the first kill. He handed me his rifle, then rode straight and true down the bluff. His long hair sparkled in the sunlight. Then he disappeared into the stampeding cloud of dust, which swallowed up everything in its path. What a sound it was! Like the earth making powerful music. Black Dog broke from the herd in pursuit of a big ole bull heading in our direction. He rode alongside the beast and jumped on its back. He grabbed the buffalo's mane with one hand, took out his long knife with the other, and sunk the blade into the animal's neck. Down the bull went, and Black Dog—so help me, on my mother's grave—stayed on top of the critter as it fell in a heap. He then stood and raised his knife in the air. Never seen a more magnificent sight."

Ned picked up a stone and threw it at a jackrabbit, which scuttled into some brush. "Were you afraid, Grandpa?"

"Can't *ever* show fear to an Indian. It's a great sign of weakness." William stopped and rubbed his left thigh. "You must always keep their respect. The Sky Clan talked often to me about the stars, teaching me some things I never learned at sea." He started toward the house, his bad leg lagging a bit.

"Like what, Grandpa?" Ned picked up another stone and kept an eye on the brush.

"How to find your way from the stars without maps or instruments. It's called 'wayfaring' or, as the Osage called it, one's 'journey with the stars.' I got the hang of it some, but they were masters at it. The sky was very important to the Osage. They looked to it often."

"What were they looking for?" Ned threw the stone into the brush and scanned the horizon for the departed meteor.

"Many things, none more important than finding the true journey of their spirit. That is to say, each individual must temper his desires with what's best for unity in the tribe. Something white men could pay more attention to. A man must have harmony in his life, Ned, or it will be an empty journey. Remember that."

Shafts of light from the December sun, slung low in the west, splintered into William O'Connor's kitchen. He had gathered his family around the old cherry table. "Well, we done eaten just about all there is to eat. We can either start with the Maisie or the chickens."

"Not Maisie!" Ned pleaded. He leaned forward in his chair and stretched his hands out on the table. "I'll catch us some game with the .22."

"Now, Ned," his mother said, "you know you can't go out past the barn in this weather." She reached a hand across the table.

Ned pulled back. "I saw a cottontail just the other day, out back of the barn. If I'd only had the rifle."

"Son, a rabbit isn't going to last us." William placed his palms down on the table. "We need something to get us through to spring, and Maisie appears to be the best candidate."

"Please, Grandpa. Let me and Tom have a chance to hunt us up some game. There might be an elk or deer about."

"Tell you what," William said. "I'll give you two till day after tomorrow to catch something. Keep a safe distance from the house, and be home before nightfall."

The following morning at the first trace of daylight, Ned sat up in bed. Rubbing his eyes, he realized that this was the day he must bring home meat for his family. He jumped down from the top bunk.

Tom sprang up and said, "Let's catch us some game, Ned."

They scurried about the room, putting on their trousers and flannel shirts.

"Ned, have you seen my socks?"

Ned laced up his brogan boots. "Look under the bed."

Tom rooted under the bed, looking like a prairie dog going for cover. "I got 'em." He squirmed back out. "Gonna catch us some game, Ned."

Ned put his breakfast plate in the sink, then took the .22 down from the wall. "Come on, Tom."

Tom took one last bite of flapjacks, grabbed his mackinaw off a peg, and went for the door.

"Thomas O'Brien, you put your jacket on proper," Lorrayne said. She went over and buttoned up her son. "Now, fetch us some game, boys."

Ned scanned the snow-covered terrain from a knobby mound, the .22 at his side. Only a few scrub trees and scraggly brush emerged out of the white blanket of snow. There was nary a trace of life anywhere. "Let's go a little farther, Tom."

Tom stopped and drew in his lower lip, as if to say, "This is far enough."

"Look, Tom, it's up to us to help get some meat." The cold invaded Ned's body as a great gust of wind roused up swirls of dry snow. "We got to keep movin'. Just a little bit more."

Tom shivered. "Ned, I can't feel my toes."

"You go on in, then. I'll stand watch."

"Come with me, Ned. Your face is kinda blue."

Ned heard the crunching of boots in the snow. Their grandfather, wearing his coarse overcoat, was limping toward them.

"This leg gets worse every year." William rubbed his thigh. "Damn Apache lance. Go home and warm up, boys. I'll stand guard for a while. There's onion broth on the stove."

"I'll stay with you, Grandpa," Ned said. He brought the rifle up from his side.

"No, boy. Hand me the rifle. You and Tom head in."

Ned started to say something, but his grandfather's iron gaze stopped him. Dropping his head, he mumbled to Tom, "Let's go."

Inside the farmhouse, the wood stove and the hot broth combined to warm Ned outside and inside. He couldn't remember a better feeling. How good the house felt, and how cold it was out there. Two shots rang out. Tom jumped up from his chair. "Grandpa musta got something."

From the oak tree behind the barn, Tom waved for Ned to hurry.

Ned caught up with his cousin. In the distance, they could see the faint figure of a man.

"Grandpa, we're comin'." they hollered.

William, his face beet red and sweat beading on his forehead, gasped for air as steam rose from the warm carcass of an enormous mule deer. "Never expected to get anything," he said. "I didn't even bring a knife to quarter him. We'll have to try to drag him back."

William went to the rear of the animal. "You both grab the front legs, and I'll get the rear."

They grunted and strained, but could not move the deer.

"That sky's up to no good," William said as snow began to fall. "Let's cover it with snow."

All three began scooping the light, airy snow over the deer.

Ned started to speak, but felt like there was a tight cord running down from his throat to a knot in his gut. He took a deep breath. "We got to get him back now, or the coyotes and wolves will eat him down to the bone, Grandpa."

William shook his head.

"But the scavengers, Grandpa."

"Not today, boy." William took one last look at the sky, then motioned the boys toward home.

As they made their way over the berm, Ned could only make out the outline of the house through the blanket of snow whipped up by a howling wind. Grandpa's bad leg had stiffened, and he moved in a sideways motion, his good leg leading the way. He would drag the leg, stop, and rest; drag the leg, stop, and rest.

At the bottom of the berm, Ned spoke up. "Grandpa, let me and Tom help you."

William turned and stared at his grandsons. His face was blue gray, and his eyes had the look of a lost dog. "All right boys, each of you get on my side and help me on home."

Ned and Tom each put a shoulder under their grandfather's arm, and they all staggered homeward.

Before they made it to the porch, Ned's mother and Aunt Lorrayne came out into the storm and helped them into the house.

Helen helped William, his face caked with ice, to a chair at the table. "Dad, we're going to get you out of those clothes."

William raised his shoulders, shuddered, and stared vacantly at Helen.

Lorrayne unbuttoned her father's ice-crusted coat and removed his wet boots.

"Oh, Mama," Tom cried, "I'm so cold."

"It'll be okay, dear," Lorrayne said. She helped her father up. "Aunt Helen and I made broth." She placed her arm around William's waist and guided him toward his bed.

"Boys, let's get your clothes off," Helen said. She helped them remove their mackinaws. The boys shivered their way to the table.

It was past sunup the next day, and Ned looked over to the bed at the back of the kitchen. Finally, William stirred. He sat up and gritted his teeth. "Leg's stiff as the damn Apache lance that got me all those years ago."

"Grandpa, what are you gonna do?" Ned said. He went over to his grandfather's side.

William took a bottle from the drawer next to his bed. "Why, lad, I'm gonna drink me some of this good Irish whiskey." He blew the dust off the bottle, smiled at Ned, and said, "It'll ease my pain."

Helen bit her lower lip. "Dad, are you sure?"

"Yes." William took a swig of the whiskey. "I need to stay off this leg for a few days."

Helen rested her gaze on her father's face. "Ned, Tom ... you boys are going to have grow up some."

Ned shielded his eyes from the sun hanging just over the horizon.

Tom, pulling up the rear, hollered, "Ned, we best get back. The sun is gonna dip soon."

"Gollee," Tom muttered. "Just like Grandpa said—Ned's like an old hunting dog that gets half a scent and won't ever quit. Ned!"

Ned plunged forward, determined to find the deer that his grandfather had shot.

"Ned, I'm turning back; you best come."

In the flat gray light, Ned trudged on, ignoring his cousin's warning.

"We're worryin' the folks at home, Ned makin' trouble for us." Tom's voice fell as lifeless as the land around them. "I ain't to be the one called headstrong." Tom stopped. "Ned, I'm turning back, you best come."

"Wait. I see something." Ned plowed through deep snow to the base of a butte, the scene of the kill. A smattering of blood, a shell of bones and ravaged hide, and scattered hooves lay in a depression in the crusted snow.

"Damn wolves," Ned said, leaning over the carcass. "What good are they?"

Never had Ned felt worse than when they came back into the yard that day—not only from the bitter cold, but from the empty sense of failure that gnawed at his stomach. They entered the house stiff and shivering.

Lorrayne wagged her finger at her son. "You two nearly put us in an early grave. I have a good mind to give you a switching, Thomas O'Brien."

"If anybody's to be switched, it's me," Ned said through shivering lips.

"There'll be no corporal punishment in my house, as long as I have a breath to breathe," William said, sitting up in his bed. "Tom, take the .22 into the barn and shoot Maisie. Then you boys strip the hide, quarter her up, and hang the meat on the gangling hooks. Bring in enough for a good meal. Please, boys, not a word."

Ned volunteered to shoot Maisie, but Tom insisted that they follow their grandfather's orders. Tom liked old Maisie well enough, but he showed no qualms about shooting her. She was food, and they needed food.

When the cow fell from the bullet to the head, Ned felt a dull ache down to the bone. Why hadn't he been strong enough to get the deer home?

Outside the barn, Ned looked at the gray sky. It seemed old and used up.

CHAPTER 3

▼

"Do you hear that, Grandpa?" Tom said. He ran out of the barn, and Ned followed close behind. "Dong … Dong …"

As if emerging from the orange sun cresting the horizon, a great sight appeared—a covered wagon, painted red. A great, burly man dressed all in black—seaman's coat, bowler hat, coarse trousers, and heavy, buckled boots—steered two snorting oxen, each with an iron bell around its neck.

The wagon creaked to halt in the yard. Ned noticed the man's scowling eyebrows, dark as charcoal and thick as a sailor's knots. They rose from a red and fleshy nose over great black eyes, arching like the yoke that joined his oxen.

It seemed that the great oxen took notice of him, a mere boy. They shook their heads and snorted, blowing great gobs of mucous from their cavernous nostrils, which seemed big enough to swallow a child. Brass bells tipped their swinging horns, and beaded tassels dangled on the bells. The beads clicked as they swished across the oxen's massive, wrinkled skulls.

Ned wondered if this trio of giants feared anything that rumbled across this great earth.

"Good morning to you, sir." The big man spoke in a thick foreign accent.

"Good morning. I'm William O'Connor, and these are my grandsons, Ned and Tom."

The man tipped his cap, revealing a tangled mass of black hair. "I am Nicholas, and I have something to offer." There was a look of composed satisfaction about him, a look that said he had seen the best and worst life had to offer and had been unaffected by either.

"Well, I'm afraid you come to the wrong place to conduct business," William said as he scratched his chin. "Money is more than a little sparse here."

Nicholas raised his palms. "Money? I say nothing of money." His heavy voice and deliberate tone added a layer of mystery to his already strange appearance.

Tom stood wide-eyed and gaping. "You're not from these parts," he said, "are you, mister?"

"Hah, hah, hah," the stranger burst out. "That is true I am from Ukraine. You hear of it?"

"No." Tom strung out the word.

"Yes, we have," Ned offered. "It's across the Atlantic Ocean, in Asia. We learned about it last year in the geography my mother taught us."

Nicholas leveled his gaze on Ned. "That is good, boy."

"Well, tell me, then," said William, narrowing his eyes, "what type of business do you have in mind?"

"I have wheat kernels I want to grow. Nicholas need land." The big man spread his arms out to his sides.

"Well, I got land, but I don't know if it's suitable for growing wheat. I've tried, but I haven't had much luck."

"This wheat is different. Come from Ukraine. Strong wheat." Nicholas put his thick fist against his chest. "Like Ukrainian."

"What kind is it?" William asked.

"Turkey Red. Good wheat."

"Never heard of it. Course, that don't mean nothin'. Lots of things I never heard of. But I'm always interested in learning new things. What do you have in mind?"

Nicholas stroked his beard. "You let me use your land. I show you how to grow Turkey Red. We split all wheat we grow."

William scratched a tuft of hair in his ear. "Well, sir, I need to save a fair amount of land for corn. What say we set aside twenty acres for wheat?"

Nicholas nodded his massive head. "Is good."

William stuck out his hand. "You got a deal, Nicholas."

The sun peeked over the horizon, and Ned's shadow stretched across the yard. He kept his eyes on Nicholas's wagon camped on a small rise next to the north pasture. His oxen grazed on wild grass, but where was that great, mysterious man? Ned wondered why he'd stopped at their farm. Maybe this man and his team of oxen would change things for the O'Connor clan … or maybe not.

Ned studied the strange sight now dominating their horizon. It seemed as though the earth had opened and this team of oxen and its master had emerged from far away to shake his family awake. To make the O'Connor clan quake, not with fear but with anticipation of change, seemed to be the stranger's mission.

Ned had read the apprehension in the voices and expressions of his mother and aunt. They too seemed taken aback by this giant from some faraway land, yet Aunt Lorrayne spoke for them all when she announced, "He's an omen of something different, of a change for some of us."

Ned hoped so. He wasn't sure why, but he felt this change stirring in his bones. Maybe the great man was some kind of god—a god of wheat, like those old Vikings Mr. Sorenson told yarns about.

Ned saw the canopy of the wagon ruffle, and then the man came out, like a grizzly bear after a long sleep. Nicholas—so different in dress and voice, so strange, a beast of a man who frightened and yet fascinated him.

Hoisting a gangplow from under the canopy like it was a small child, Nicholas hitched it to the yoked oxen and began plowing.

Ned kept his distance as the team turned the flinty soil.

Nicholas stopped and ran a hand through his thick, bristly hair. "Boy afraid of Nicholas or oxen—or both?"

Ned said nothing.

"You want to learn about wheat?"

Ned remained still for a moment, then nodded.

"Come here, boy."

Ned looked at the man and his beasts. They didn't appear to be of this earth. Nicholas, almost as black as the oxen, even looked similar to them: great head, massive shoulders, and dark eyes. He thought of Grandpa's Indian legends of men coming back as animals and wondered whether Nicholas was once a beast of burden. Maybe he had even been a brother to these snorting creatures, which seemed more wild than tame.

Ned reckoned that here stood an unconquerable man, unaffected by the laws of men or even of this great earth.

After hesitating at first, Ned came close—but not too close—to the imposing Ukrainian and his massive oxen.

Nicholas reached into his pocket and brought out a handful of seeds. "This Turkey Red. Open hand."

Ned obeyed, and Nicholas placed the grain in Ned's palm. "Nicholas teach you how to grow Turkey Red. You remember old Nicholas when you good wheat farmer."

Ned rubbed his fingertips over the small, hard seeds. Nicholas spread a hand-ful across the plowed soil. "Spread not too much, not too little." The big man pointed a thick, gnarled finger at the wagon. "Sack of seeds inside. I plow, you plant."

In the long, blue shadows, Ned took it all in—the square field with upturned chunks of soil full of seeds he had sown.

"Hey, boy," Nicholas waved Ned over to the wagon, to which he had hitched the oxen once more.

Ned took one more look at the field and walked to Nicholas.

A grin spread over the big man's face. "You like the wheat, no?" He lowered his eyebrows, and the smile vanished. "Wheat gets in your blood, and no choice but to grow it."

Ned imagined grains of wheat coursing through his veins and how strong they would make him. He saw a farm with a field of wheat behind a barn. He stood tall amongst his wheat, which he knew like one would an old friend. A breath of wind came over a hill beyond the field, and he heard the wheat whispering its secrets to him.

"Come, boy. You go to house before it dark."

Ned didn't respond.

Nicholas loaded the plow onto the wagon and got on board. He motioned for Ned to ride with him.

Ned gave a small shake of his head. "I'll walk alongside."

"Come, boy. I no bite."

"I'll walk on my own."

"Yes … you walk along on this earth and find your place in it. It is good, for the journey will be long and hard, and you must learn to work these things out." Nicholas swept his arms out to his sides. "This earth is my mother and my home. I feel it breathe as my feet walk it, and I hear the wind call to me at night. Its song says, 'More wheat, Nikolai, you are man of wheat. It is why you are here in this time and this place, and one with me.'"

Ned looked beyond the pale moon rising into the last vestiges of the purple sky and thought about his life with wheat.

The family gathered around Nicholas, who stood next to his wagon in the yard.

"Seeding is complete, William." Nicholas looked at Ned, then continued. "In couple weeks, green sprouts will rise. Then it turn brown and go to sleep for winter, like Nicholas. Hah, hah, hah. I leave now and come back when wheat ready for harvest. Boy … Ned, you be ready for harvest with Nicholas?"

Ned stared at the ground. "Where will you go?"

"Nicholas go to mountains, find cave, and sleep like the wheat."

"You gonna sleep all winter?" Tom said.

Nicholas grinned, got onto his wagon, and began to depart. He waved and hollered, "Nicholas come back in spring after good sleep. Hah, hah, hah!"

The wind picked up, and, with it, a familiar odor rose. It reminded Ned of all the manure he had pitched from the pile at the side of the barn into the cart and then spread over the plowed stubble.

This meager land had chiseled a hard, rugged look on young Fallow, now almost thirteen.

Now he stood amongst his wheat; how proud he thought old Nicholas would be of him.

"Take this and stand two paces to my right," Ned said, handing one of two scythes to Tom. "Ain't nothin' but a little work, as Grandpa would say."

"Show me how to cut, Ned."

"See how I hold it, Tom?" Ned started cutting the wheat. The stroke and rhythm returned like no time had passed since he had worked with Nicholas.

Tom began thrashing about like a small twister, and wheat fell every which way.

"Use patience, Tom—like this." Ned slowed down his stroke. "You must use care when cutting wheat."

"You sound like Nicholas, Ned."

"I do? Well, that ain't all bad. Now, we're gonna cut north to south …"

"Hey, Ned, I think I got the hang of this."

"You're doin' good, Tom."

"We're goin' up this field good as any full-grown men, I bet you, Ned," Tom cackled as they came to the end of a row.

Ned kept his head down and continued to cut. "Reckon we are, Tom."

After cutting the wheat, Ned began lacing bundles of it together with straw. Tom wrapped his arms around a shock of wheat and pushed it into the stubble. "Ned, is this right?"

"Like this, Tom." Ned raised a shock and yelled out, "Oomph!" He slammed it into the stubble. "Put four in slot, then add corners."

Tom grabbed another bundle. "Oh yeah, add corners," he said, as if just remembering. "Nicholas said it cures better."

The sun stayed strong in the sky, but Ned spotted clouds forming off in the distance, like an army of darkness.

A rumble of thunder belched out; the rows of shocked wheat, so magnificent and strong, seemed in great peril stacked up against the harrowing sky.

"Hey, Ned, the sky looks bad."

Ned glowered up at the ominous clouds, which were now a sickly green and coming fast from the west. A jagged bolt of lightning lit up the sky, which slit open to release a thunderous torrent of rain.

Ned hollered, "Let's get to the root cellar."

Ned reached for the box of matches that rested next to a lantern on a dirt shelf. "It's lit, Tom. Close the door." Ned sat on a barrel in the far corner, wishing he could dig a hole and bury himself. There were thunderous explosions, and bursts of hail riddled the wood-plank door.

Then, it was over. "Tom, take a look."

Tom creaked open the door and peeked out. Drab light dulled the room. "Ned, there ain't nothing left." Tom climbed out.

Ned's body went numb. He stood, blew out the lantern, and dragged himself up the steps.

Standing among the destroyed crop, Ned fixed his eyes on the monstrous gray clouds laughing in the sky. "Let's save what we can." His heart hadn't ached this bad since his father died. Tom began crying, and Ned put his hand on his cousin's shoulder.

"It ain't fair, Ned. It ain't fair."

"Ain't nothing in this life fair."

PART 2

CHAPTER 4

▼

From the earth and sky comes all that will break and make a man ...

A gusty wind swept across the yard, rousting sagebrush around. It was hard to believe, but it was 1891. Ned had spent all of his nineteen years in Ketchum, on this land of empty promises. What had it given him? Nothing. But it had taken plenty in return—his father, his uncle, and, now, his beloved grandfather.

And, two days ago, his mother and Aunt Lorrayne had sold the land and scraggly livestock and departed for Boston and Great Aunt Edith.

"So long, Tom. You take care of yourself." Ned looked at his little cousin, who wasn't so little anymore. Both of them were the size of men—big men.

Tom leaned on the barn door. "Well, now you got your chance," he said, squinting at the sun peeking over the distant hills.

Ned put the last of his supplies behind the cantle of his mount. "And you get yours."

"Yup." Tom picked at a splinter in the barn door. "Things sure are gonna be different. Me joining a cattle drive, and you becoming a full-time sodbuster."

Ned tied his supplies down with a sailor's knot, which reminded him of his grandfather. "Well, after Grandpa died, there wasn't much reason for any of us to stay." The roan stirred as he tightened the cinch. "Easy, boy." Ned looked over toward the old oak tree on the berm past the barn. It was where their granddad had been buried. "That man gave us and this land everything he had."

Tom took William's corncob pipe out of his pocket and turned toward the empty house. "Lotta memories here, Ned. I'm gonna hold onto this as a keepsake. Whenever things get tough, I'm gonna pull it out and remember what he went through for us."

Ned felt his throat tighten as he thought of his granddad. Those twinkling light eyes, the unconquerable spirit, and the decency of the man made Ned wish for one last evening to listen to one more of his tales. One more day to say thank you—and maybe even how much he loved him.

Soon, it would be as if they never even lived here. Would the struggle and loss be forgotten? Never, for Ned Fallow. "Well, little cousin … you take care."

Ned extended his hand. Tom grabbed it, then hugged Ned. "Ned, we'll cross paths again."

Ned took a deep breath, unaware of it until he exhaled. He moved out, turned, and waved one last time to Tom and Ketchum.

Ned cantered the roan through a patch of buffalo grass. A gust of wind ruffled the back of his shirt and swooshed down into the plain. He pulled tight on his campaign hat, an old memento from his grandfather's days scouting for the army.

Ned raised his free hand over his eyes and squinted toward a distant hill. This land seemed different, from the long-stemmed grasses to the yellow and purple flowers to the fields of prairie clover. This land had the feel of life to it.

From the top of the bluff, he spotted a trail through a patch of pigweed, leading to a small town. Thin gray lines led out of the town, cutting into the prairie checkered with farms.

"Ain't it somethin'." Ned caught the reverence in his voice. *And rightly so,* he thought. The great sweep of land seemed to go on forever until it met the big sky that draped the earth like a blue shawl. Never had he seen such land—land touched by the hand of God.

A tight grip on the reins, his brogans in stirrups tight against the horse's flank, he switchbacked across and down the steep hill.

At the outskirts of town, the train depot came into sight. It was a modest two-story clapboard structure with a gray slate roof. He rode straight ahead, toward a bulky, gambrel-roofed structure with bold red letters over double doors: Grange Hall, Midland, Kansas.

From the Grange Hall, Ned turned left into the town. He passed a collection of mostly one- and two-story wood-framed buildings lining the rutted dirt road. He saw eyes following him and heard the voices of the townsfolk, who stopped and gawked at the young stranger. An old-timer croaked, "He's a biggun."

Halfway up the street, Ned dismounted at a limestone structure with wooden cornices. The Midland Savings and Trust had a regal stability about it that seemed to diminish the more uneven nearby buildings.

Inside, a teller shuffled papers as two men in overalls waited.

The manager, a thin man with tired eyes and a well-trimmed mustache, introduced himself. Ned took a seat in a corner office.

The manager put down some papers and ran his thumb and forefinger over his mustache. "Robert Fallow ... would he be your father?"

"My uncle."

"Did you know your uncle, Mr. Fallow?"

"Never met him."

Ten minutes later, Ned left the bank with a deed to 160 acres and $175 in a thick envelope.

Outside the bank, a heavy-set man in bib overalls approached Ned. His shoulders swayed like a great, rollicking vessel.

"You must be the fella from Texas who's taking over the Lowry place. I'm your neighbor, Bill Etheridge." A smile creased his open, friendly face.

"I'm Ned Fallow."

"Well, now, if you need anythin', give me a holler. Storm come through a while back and hit your place pretty hard. Soon after that, the Lowrys packed up and headed back east. They were the second set of tenants who didn't make a go of it there. Folks around here help each other, but this is no life for the faint-hearted."

Ned noticed the older man appraising him through grinning eyes, as though he were studying a prize steer come to auction. "Keep that in mind." Ned stole a glance up the street.

"You can pick up supplies across the street." Etheridge pointed to a building with a glass storefront and Grove's General Store printed in green lettering above the entrance. "Owning one's property gives a body more desire to see it through, I reckon."

Etheridge smiled and raised his upper lip, revealing a gap between his front teeth. "I got plenty of tools. Come by anytime, and I'll lend you what you need."

"'Preciate it." Ned looked back to the route out of town.

"Whereabouts in Texas you from?"

"Ketchum." Ned heard the impatience rise in his voice.

"Your folks still there?"

"My father's been dead a long time; mother moved to Boston."

"Left it all behind, I gather."

"Yup." Ned glanced toward his pocket and the deed, checking to ensure that he still had it close. A pause settled between him and the big man, whose smile had begun to fade.

"Well, I see you're anxious to make way."

After visiting Grove's store, Ned walked his horse south, with a sack of canned goods and supplies strapped across the saddle.

At a fork in the road, he saw a farm to his right. The fields had square-cut corners, and cottonwood-rail fencing ran along the perimeter. Ned figured it to be Etheridge's place.

Up from the fork, Ned came to the periphery of his hodgepodge farmland. Buffalo grass, bluestem, and wild rye were scattered about, and small groves of trees were speckled amongst the dormant plots—cottonwood, box elder, oak, ash, and walnut.

Along the western edge, a winding creek wound north to south. It was thickly lined with trees—mostly catalpa, with an occasional hackberry and mulberry. A hedgerow of Osage orange trees formed an imposing windbreak on the northern perimeter. To the east sat a bluff. The land lay low and stretched flat. A stone foundation and a few boards and beams were all that remained of a farmhouse with a yard of dirt and tumbleweed. Some house wares and weatherworn furniture lay strewn about. A short distance from the house was a barn that had seen better days.

A bolt of lightning crackled across the sky, and sheets of rain soon followed. Ned led the horse into the barn, where he stepped around puddles of water fed by the leaky second floor. A few farm implements and a hayrack sat in one corner, and some tools hung on a side wall. Along the back wall, a harness and bridle lay on the floor, inside a bin for storing grain.

The rain stopped, and Ned picked his way to a patch of land full of sod and pigweed. It sure hadn't seen a plow or a harrow for a good while.

He grabbed a stick and dug into the sod. He pulled out a cluster of weeds, and black soil clung to the roots. He rubbed the dirt in his hands and felt a firm, moist texture that was entirely new to him. He brought his hands to his nose and smelled the earth. No wonder the weeds didn't want to leave it.

Ned imagined his granddad standing here with him. "Ned, this land has been fallow for more than a while; it's got substance. Good soil will nurture more than just a man's pocketbook." Ned wished that his granddad could have had the chance to work land like this—to nourish and care for soil that would have eased his burden.

He imagined himself and William O'Connor in a long field of wheat rising from a sun-drenched field. Never had he seen his grandfather smile so wide and his eyes so bright. "Lord's finally looked down upon us, Ned. Yessir, he surely has."

C H A P T E R   5

▼

Bill Etheridge usually didn't mind milking a cow, but, this morning, he grumbled to himself. "Not one bit friendly when we met, and just yesterday turned down my second offer to—"

"Goodness sakes, Bill Etheridge, are you talking to yourself?" His wife's voice startled him. Looking up, he saw Mildred Etheridge standing at the chicken loft along the far wall, holding a twig basket.

"Ned Fallow not only turned down my offer to help, but was downright snooty about it." Etheridge shook his head, rose from his stool, and placed the bucket of milk on the ground near the door. He turned to his wife and said, "Mildred, I fought drought, renegade Injuns, and every other thing the Good Lord could bring down on us, and, somehow, we made it. Took a long time, but I got one of the best farms in these parts. But I needed the help of my neighbors."

Mildred dug into the straw bed and took out a large brown egg. "I haven't met him yet." She inspected the egg and placed it in her basket. "But Henrietta Grove tells me he's one fine-looking young man."

Etheridge walked over to the back corner and opened the corncrib. "First time I met him, he kept eyeing the route out of town and then gave me a look that said, 'I ain't got all day to talk.'" He took out four ears and put them in his wife's basket. "That ain't gonna sit right with some folks. Ain't even come by to say howdy. The boy's not a natural man, no he is not. Loner, pure and simple." He closed the crib latch, walked over to some tools hanging along the wall, and straightened them.

"He might just be shy, Bill. Did you ever think of that?"

"I know the difference between shy and rude."

A thin smile creased Mildred's face. "The chickens have given us their eggs for the day." Mildred tapped the basket with a finger. "The cow has given us her milk, and now it's my turn to get breakfast ready. Don't forget the milk when you come in." She turned and left the barn.

Etheridge sunk a pitchfork into a pile of straw and tossed it into a stall. He thought he heard something and turned. There stood Ned Fallow. Etheridge patted the cow on the rump. "Hello, neighbor."

"Mornin'."

Etheridge gathered a grain tub. "Tool box been sittin' over there," he said, motioning his chin toward a corner, "for the last two weeks, with your name on it."

Ned stared down and scuffed the dirt floor with his boots. "I appreciate it."

Etheridge stepped into the yard and fanned the feed for the clucking chickens that scurried around the stranger.

Ned shifted his shoulders. "I appreciate you lending me tools."

"Been here over twenty-five years now. Goodness, it don't seem possible." Etheridge looked toward his house. "Come on in and meet the wife over a glass of buttermilk."

"I'd best be going."

"It'd just take a minute, Ned. Then I'll gather up those tools you need." Etheridge started toward the house and waved for Ned to follow.

"We've been through it all," Mildred Etheridge said as she sat across the kitchen table from Ned. Twisters, drought, blizzards—you name it. I imagine I'm not telling you anything new. Like Bill told me earlier, you look like a person who isn't afraid of work. You look like you've seen your share of hard times, too."

Ned nodded, swallowed down the rest of his buttermilk, and stood. "I best head back."

Etheridge rested his elbows on his kitchen table. "You'll be needin' help fellin' some of that timber on your property. You're gonna need it to rebuild what the Good Lord took down." Etheridge took a gulp of his buttermilk and wiped his mouth with the back of his hand. "I know just the men to help us."

"Here, now, don't forget this." Mildred handed Ned a loaf of bread.

"Thank you, ma'am." Ned shifted his gaze toward the door.

Etheridge stood. "Now, let's gather that box of tools in the barn."

Outside the front door, Etheridge watched his neighbor stride off. He had the look and way about him of a young man with a purpose, a focus, and drive. *But to go it all by yourself—that's no life,* he thought.

Etheridge thought about his only child, the son he and the missus had lost at childbirth. How he wanted to pass on his wisdom and share this life of wheat and earth.

Bill snapped out of his reverie and watched Ned disappear around the bend.

Morning thunder rumbled in a blackening sky.

CHAPTER 6

▼

The fallen timber lay spread across the land as though a twister had come through. It bothered Ned—he needed to stack the great logs, but they were too heavy. He needed help again.

Ned heard the heavy sound of horses' hooves plodding on the road, and he spotted Etheridge driving a lead wagon, with two in the rear.

"Hey there, Ned." Etheridge's voice flowed like water over smooth stone.

Ned wondered if Etheridge ever had a bad day. "Howdy," he said as he admired the strong, sturdy wagons that halted at the downed timbers.

"Ned, this is Vern Swensen and Dan O'Hurley. They got farms north of town."

"Mornin'," Ned said.

Swensen, a big-boned, rangy man of about forty, tipped his wide-brimmed hat.

O'Hurley scratched his dark stubble of beard, and a plug of tobacco swelled his cheek. "Glad to meet you there, lad."

Ned noticed a vein standing out on the big Irishman's thick neck. This reminded Ned of his grandfather's description of Ned's great-grandfather—"a great, dark beast of a man, but with a gentle soul."

Etheridge waved the men over to the timbers.

"On three, men," Dan O'Hurley said from the rear of a long timber. The others stood an equal distance apart, with Ned in front. They hoisted the big log up and short-stepped their way over to the wagon.

O'Hurley hollered, "Ready, men." The log thumped loudly onto the wagon floor. "Ned, you have the look of a worker," O'Hurley said, leaning on the side of the wagon to catch his breath. "Bill, I bet he lasts a while longer than Lowry."

Etheridge smiled at Ned. "I believe he might. Plus, he owns this property, Dan."

Ned noticed Vern Swensen cutting some branches off a timber and looking up on occasion.

"I did my share of tenant farming in the old country," O'Hurley said, wiping his brow with a bandana. "We should all be grateful to own such land." O'Hurley nodded at Etheridge and then turned a keen eye on Ned. "Should be grateful for having good neighbors, too."

Ned tightened the rope over the timbers that were piled to the top of the wagon's sideboards. He was about to board Vern Swensen's wagon when he heard a short, whooping yell. O'Hurley grabbed a hatchet from his wagon and flung it into the grass two feet from where he stood.

"Lord have mercy, what you got there, Dan?" Etheridge asked.

O'Hurley raised up a headless rattler three feet in length. It had six rattles and a button. "Ha!" O'Hurley said, tossing the dead serpent into the grass. "That'll teach it to mess with an Irishman."

Etheridge grabbed a bandanna from his overalls, grinned, and wiped the perspiration from his broad face. "Ned, Remus Hungerford's sawmill lies northeast of town, along the river. We'll get you there."

Ned climbed up beside Swensen, and off they went, the rumbling wagon easing the silence between the two men. He had figured that he would be more comfortable with the taciturn Swede than O'Hurley, whose boisterous, lecturing manner could wear on a person. Grandpa O'Connor had made no excuse for his Irish brethren. "The only place you'll find a quiet Irishman is in church, and even there, it's a struggle," William O'Connor had said now and again.

Ned had never ridden in such a strong wagon. Its iron straps creaked and groaned some, but Swensen's rig seemed almost to welcome the bumps.

Over a rise, they came to a river lined with cottonwood trees. Ned noted the exposed roots of many of the trees, and saw that others had lost their anchors to the swelling rapids, and now floated along the shoreline.

Around a bend, Ned spotted a churning waterwheel connected to a low circular limestone building with an enormous windmill attached. It reminded him of the picture of a lighthouse in his grandfather's album.

The three wagons came to a halt in a row at the yawning doors to the mill. A stocky man dressed in overalls came out and nodded at Etheridge, who raised a hand and said, "Howdy, Remus."

Remus Hungerford looked over the wagons brimming with timbers. "See you didn't waste any space on 'em." He walked over and ran his hand over a log. "Well, let's get 'em drug in here."

After the timbers had been stacked inside the mill, Ned handed Hungerford a list of cuts and materials he wanted.

The millwright took a pencil off his ear and wrote out some figures on a scrap sheet of lumber. "That'll be $34.75, including yellow pine board for roof and floors."

Ned took a deep breath.

"Can do half down and half on credit," Hungerford said.

Ned dug into his pocket and handed the money in full to the millwright.

Remus Hungerford wiped the sweat and sawdust off his forehead. "Got my men coming tomorrow. Come back day after, and I'll have it ready."

"Ain't no way you can cut it now, Remus? Save us a lot of time," Etheridge asked easily, a grin spreading across his face.

Remus folded his arms across his chest and sized up Etheridge and the others. "Well … if you all willin' to help, I reckon we can get it done quick-like."

They reached Ned's place before dusk and stacked the lumber near the old foundation.

The men got on their wagons and Dan O'Hurley leveled his gaze on Ned, the Irishman's dark face a shadow in the dusky light. "Glad to have helped you today, lad."

Ned felt the appraisal of the older men. "Thank you … thank you," he said, looking at the ground, then at Bill Etheridge.

Etheridge's smile couldn't hide his fatigue.

Ned paused for a moment. "Sorry, I don't even have a cup of coffee to offer you."

Etheridge gave his chin a scratch. "Well, there's always next time."

CHAPTER 7

▼

Mr. Edward A. Tharrington liked what he saw below—his store humming with bustling employees and customers. He slid open the plate-glass window and took in the smells of heavy burlap bags of seed, bins of grain, and the ever-present whiff of lime. His gaze shifted to a loft where workers opened crates and delivered supplies to the first floor in grid baskets attached to a wire pulley system strung from the rafters.

The double-wide doors to the entrance opened, and a young man he had never seen before came in and walked down an aisle packed with shiny new mauls, picks, and other hand tools.

Tharrington pulled his gold watch out of his vest pocket and checked the time. He then went down the staircase to the main floor and the aisle where the newcomer was looking over tools.

Tharrington removed his wire-rimmed glasses and breathed on the lenses. "I suspect you've used one of those before." He polished the lenses with a white handkerchief.

The man nodded and placed the tool back on the rack.

A figure hurried toward Tharrington.

The grating voice was sandpaper rough. "My order arrive yet?"

Tharrington put his glasses back on. "Pete Lomax, I'll be with you when I finish here."

Pete Lomax straightened rudely, with his hands on his hips and his elbows cocked. There was a dark and sinister air about this stump-hard man. A coarse tangle of coal black hair lashed over a primitive forehead. "This how you treat good-paying customers?"

"Good-paying?" Tharrington leveled his sternest gaze on Lomax. "Don't interrupt me again until I finish talking with this man."

Tharrington turned back to the young man. "Tharrington is my name, and I am the Mercantile's proprietor."

"Ned Fallow, here. I hear from Bill Etheridge you might need some carpentry work around here."

"Might be the case." Tharrington stroked his chin and took in the man before him.

"I can handle a hammer."

"Am I gonna get any damn service around here?" Lomax rubbed the stubble on his chin as his slit eyes darted from Tharrington to Ned and back to Tharrington.

Tharrington glanced at Lomax out of the corner of his eye, then turned his attention back to Ned. "So Bill tells me."

"You won't ever regret hiring me." Ned narrowed his gaze on the merchant.

Tharrington could almost feel heat coming from those eyes. "I give a sheet each day listing work to be done. Long as it meets my standards, I stay out of the way. We could work out a swap arrangement for tools and equipment you need."

"You got some interesting-looking tools." Ned took the last trenching spade off the wall, unaware that Lomax had been reaching for it.

Lomax growled. "Hey, I was gonna buy that." He raised his upper lip like an aggressive dog.

Ned shot a cold stare at Lomax, then turned to Tharrington.

Lomax grabbed the rear of Ned's collar and tugged hard.

"Pete, stop it," Tharrington ordered.

Ned pivoted around and, with the spade in his left hand, grabbed Lomax by the front of his shirt with his right and lifted the foul man off his feet. Tightening his grip, Ned pulled him in close. "You done barked up the wrong tree, mister."

Lomax's eyes widened and his mouth hung open, revealing two very crooked front teeth.

Tharrington put his hand on Ned's arm. "Let him down."

Ned released his grip.

Lomax fell backwards and gathered himself.

Ned looked down as if to say, "Anything else?"

Tharrington raised his voice. "Pete Lomax, I don't ever want that type of conduct again."

Lomax glanced at Tharrington, then back at Ned. He raised up his shoulders and leaned forward. "I got a long memory … boy." Lomax turned and walked away.

Tharrington shook his head and said, out of the side of his mouth, "Ned, you need to be careful with him."

"Yeah?" Ned's eyes stayed keenly fixed on Lomax until he turned the corner of the aisle and was out of sight. "How's that?"

"Pete Lomax was the main suspect in the burning of a man's wheat crop a few years back, over something as trivial as this. He is a very bad man."

CHAPTER 8

▼

The dry, withering sky mustered up a slight breeze as Ned snapped off a kernel of wheat and rubbed it in his hands.

He flicked away the seed. It was time.

Along the western perimeter, he cut two swathes, tied the bundles with a lace of straw, and stacked ten per shock, with butt ends plumped down hard into the standing wheat stubble. Ned thought of old Nicholas's words: "Wheat gets in your blood, and that is all. No choice but to grow it." And grow it he would.

At the edge of the field, Ned took off his straw hat and swatted at the persistent blackflies. Neither those flying marauders nor anything else would get in his way. Today was his day, come what may. He grabbed the dipper from an oak bucket of water and took a long, thirsty swallow of water. He placed the dipper back, took a deep breath, wiped his forehead with a sweat-sopped denim sleeve, and took in his land.

Weeks often passed without him seeing another person. He rose before dawn and retired well after sunset. And now, he could see the results of his labor in thirty acres of wheat that swept across his land as though God had taken a brush and painted it plush gold. The heads of wheat, standing tall and proud in a gentle breeze, seemed to meld right into the blue sky.

Ned turned and admired a patch of corn he was growing for feed. Farther up, his garden sprouted onions, cabbage, beans, beets, okra, green tomatoes, carrots, and plenty of potatoes.

Bill Etheridge had offered to help his young neighbor with his wheat crop. "I can handle it," Ned had said. He, Ned Fallow, was not some tenant farmer from back east, who would pack up and run at the first sign of trouble—he *owned* this land.

Yes, it was hard—damn hard—but he would see it through, and then some.

Ned knew that after he had tied the last bundle in the last shock of wheat, he would have to let it cure. He thought of Nicholas's words: "Must always be as patient with wheat as with this life we live." Yes, patient with the wheat—but the other part, Ned did not dwell on.

So Ned fussed and worried while his wheat cured. He took apart the hayrack and rebuilt it, and tended to his garden and livestock, but his wheat never left his mind.

At last, the time arrived, and he hitched up the hayrack and drove it to the wheat field. He pitched the shocks on, and then drove a load back to the yard. He placed the wheat on a stretch of burlap and thought of Nicholas teaching him and Tom how to thresh wheat with a willow flail. The great Ukrainian had bellowed, "Hah, hah, hah!" as he separated the wheat from the straw.

Six days later, the threshing complete, Ned felt a swell of pride at the bags and bags of grain filling his barn. He had done it. He had worked his land and grown his wheat. Here, piled high, sat the end result. Oh, what a day tomorrow would be. He would haul his bounty to the Mercantile and reap the rewards of his labor.

"Mr. Fallow," Mr. Tharrington said in greeting.

"Swap you this wheat and another wagon of it for a No. 8 cast-iron stove and a twenty-five-dollar credit." Ned pointed to the back of the wagon.

Tharrington opened a burlap bag and grabbed a handful of grain. He took off his wire-rimmed glasses and inspected it closely. He looked up at Ned, his tiny eyes seeming to approve of more than just the grain. "Deal," he said.

"Swap a bushel each of potatoes, carrots, and corn for a pickax and a mattock."

"Another bushel of potatoes," Tharrington said. His clipped tone revealed his New England roots.

"Deal," Ned said. He thought about the slow, slow trip over. "Need a grain wagon."

"Build me a storage barn, and I'll swap you a spanking new wagon."

"What size barn?"

"Twenty by thirty."

Ned paused for a moment. "Need a buckboard, also."

"Need it done by March."

"You can count on me."

Tharrington paused for a moment. "I believe I can, Ned Fallow."

CHAPTER 9

▼

Shorty Swanson, holding a basket of canned goods, stepped up on a stool. He placed a can of beans on the top shelf, reached for another, and stopped. He peeked around the corner to see whether his boss was around. Shorty reached into his vest, snuck a quick swig from a flask, and quickly stashed the liquor as Hank Grove came out of the storage room to check on the cream separator.

Saturday morning was a busy time at Grove's General Store. After twelve years in business, Hank Grove had the look of a storeowner. His gray hair was trimmed close at the sides and complemented the gray blue eyes set into his once-lean face, which was now starting to fill. A work apron clung tightly against a small pot-belly, its pouches full of brad nails, tacks, and such.

Hank pulled a sharp pencil off his ear and wrote up a sale. He shifted his gaze past the aisles bulging up to the ceiling with racks of flour, canned goods, and the like, to the back wall, where oak-plank shelves held stovepipes, buckets, funnels, and other utensils. A good merchant always kept an eye on his entire store, and Shorty had to admit that Hank Grove was a good merchant.

The front door jingled open, and a customer entered. He joined a group of men, all dressed in flannel shirts and overalls, standing in an alcove around a pot-bellied stove. They spoke in hushed tones. "Lookin' like it might rain." "Can't go wrong with Turkey Red." The men stood near—but not *too* near—the manne-quins in long dresses with mutton-leg sleeves and high, frilly collars that filled the storefront window by the alcove.

Shorty continued to stack shelves and, keeping an eye peeled for Hank, snuck a sip when he could. To Hank's right, along the counter filled with glass bowls of chocolates, rock candy, gumdrops, and other sweets, a small boy, held by his mother, reached into a bowl for a gum ball. He plopped it into his mouth, and his cheek swelled. "It's yummy, Mama," he said.

The smell of leather, nails, and dry goods just out of their boxes filled the room and mingled with the taps, thumps, and clicks of footsteps on the creaky planked floor—these were the sounds and aromas of good business.

Hank finished with a customer and hollered into the storage room behind the counter. "Bo, help Shorty get them shelves stocked."

Bo Fielder pushed a cart full of cans and dry goods out of the storage room. "H-hank said I should help you stock, S-Shorty."

The front door jingled open.

"Damn, S-Shorty that there's a big man. Who is h-he?" Bo stared at the stranger like an awed child.

"Ned Fallow. Owns the old Lowry place." Shorty shook his head in disgust. "But you'd never know, the way he keeps to hisself. Thinks he's better than the rest of us."

Shorty approached Ned at the counter. "Excuse me there, Ned, but you need any help working on your place?" Shorty jerked a thumb over his shoulder. "Bo and I could use some extra work on Sundays."

Ned looked down at Swanson with a cold blue gaze. "Dollar a day."

"Tomorrow's Sunday. What time you want us there?"

"Sunrise."

A stinging burst of late-March air greeted Shorty on the empty street outside Grove's Store. Already, he regretted his offer to Ned Fallow the day before.

"Hey, Bo. You up?"

A window on the second floor opened. "That you, Shorty?"

Shorty shivered. "Who the hell else you think it is?"

Bo leaned out the window. "I got to sweep up before I can go."

"Let me in. It's cold out here."

"I'll be r-right there, Shorty."

Shorty waited, but Bo failed to appear. Shorty held his arms together and bobbed up and down on his toes. Once again, he found himself waiting on simple-minded Bo Fielder. Shorty had half a mind to leave and abandon the whole enterprise, when he heard the door creak open.

Shorty knocked on Ned's door and hoped it wouldn't be answered. He noticed Bo breathing hard, and so was he. The long walk against a stiff breeze in bone-chilling air had tempted Shorty to turn back.

Ned barked from the barn. "You're late. Come over here and grab some tools."

Ned handed Shorty a mattock and hoe, and Bo a broadaxe.

"Wood on the side of the house needs to be split and stacked, the garden needs hoeing and to be spread with manure from that pile next to the barn."

Bo and Shorty looked at the pile of wood; it must have held four cords of stumps and huge branches. Shorty saw the garden, which looked enormous to him. He wanted a drink real bad. Whatever had he got himself into? Half-drunk the day before, he had never thought that Fallow would take him up.

Shorty trudged into the garden and started to break up the clumped, crusty earth. Up and back he went, working the mattock into the soil.

It wasn't even noon yet when Shorty flexed his cramping hands. His entire body felt like a block of ice. He hadn't worked this hard in years. His dry mouth craved the corn whiskey that was stashed in his dresser. He saw Ned approaching, looking none too happy.

"Swanson, what the hell kinda slipshod work is this?" Fallow pointed to a clumpy upturned section.

Freezing in his tracks, Shorty dropped his mattock. "What time you givin' us lunch?"

"Lunch? Ain't no lunch."

Feeling a twitch coming on, Shorty put his hand to his cheek and said, "You 'spect us to work all day and not get fed?"

"'Spect you to feed yourself. I want this garden done proper, or no pay."

Son of a bitch, Shorty thought to himself as he picked up his mattock.

From the woodpile, Bo hollered, "Hey, Ned, I'm a-gettin' there."

Ned walked over to Bo. "It's good what you done, Bo, but you need to work quicker." He'd figured out that Bo was probably slow-witted.

Bo grinned. "Sure enough, Ned."

Fallow returned to a stretch of thirty acres with tiny green leaves of winter wheat that would soon head out. Every row ran straight and true, and every corner of the field was square. Shorty had noticed that the house and barn that had been a shambles before Fallow took over were now solid, well-built structures. Try as he might, Shorty couldn't deny the competence of the arrogant man who had turned this dilapidated property into something of value. The thought came clear in Shorty's mind that Ned Fallow had only just begun.

Shorty sunk the pitchfork into the manure cart and spread the fertilizer into the broken-up soil. He couldn't remember *ever* being so tired. Grabbing the rake, he worked over the last corner of the garden.

"Hey, S-Shorty, you 'bout done?"

Shorty ran his fingers across his parched lips. "Yeah, Bo."

"That's a good piece of work you did, Shorty."

Shorty looked over the well-tilled patch, feeling no pride in work done for the likes of Fallow. "Let's get our money and go," he said, motioning Bo to the barn.

"We're done and wanna git back before dark," Shorty said to Fallow, who was spreading straw in a stall.

"Money sittin' on the barrel at the door," Ned said, keeping his back to them.

"'Preciate the j-job there, Ned," Bo said.

Ned continued to work, and the two stood there for a moment before realizing there would be no response. Shorty and Bo turned and headed home.

Dead tired and cold from head to toe, Shorty looked over his shoulder when Fallow's place was no longer visible. "That son of a bitch thinks he's God's gift to farming. Someday, somebody gonna knock him down a peg or two. Sure hope I'm there to watch it."

Bo looked straight ahead. His bottom lip drooped, and his eyes were wide with shock.

Shorty started in again. "He thinks he's so tough; he ain't so tough. He ain't the only man who ever built himself a farm." When Midland came into view, Shorty fell quiet the rest of the way, dismissing his cold, hungry body. The thought of whiskey took precedence.

CHAPTER 10

▼

From the bluff, Ned took in his three years of work—the new windmill he had bartered for with Mr. Tharrington, the well between the house and creek, the root cellar near the house, and the cottonwood rail fence along the southern boundary.

A gusty north wind swooped down; overhead, a flock of Canadian geese flew into it and honked its displeasure. As the cacophony faded into the red-streaked horizon, Ned heard the tapping of a woodpecker in the Osage orange trees along the north border. Good luck banging on *that* twisted stuff. *Yes*, Ned thought, *old Bill Etheridge had been right about it being tough*. Ned admired the Osage orange. Many thought it a scrub tree useful only for windbreaks, but they reminded Ned of Midland—hard, resilient, and stubborn to the heartwood core. Yes, three years had passed, and now Ned could see the fruits of his labor.

From a distance, the barn looked like a neat red box, all shiny and new. He had practically rebuilt it board by board. This reminded Ned of some lumber and supplies he needed to pick up in town. He descended from the bluff and headed toward the barn.

"*Señor*, need *trabajar*."

Ned stopped and turned to see two men standing in ragged, baggy clothes. Each wore a poncho and had a bedroll strapped on his back. Ned made a shoveling motion. "You want work?"

"*Sí, señor,*" said the stockier and older of the two, who looked at Ned with eyes lined red. "We work."

"I pay you one dollar a day, plus meals."

"*Bueno,*" said the older one. His friend stared at the ground.

"Hard work, long hours." Ned said.

The man straightened his slouched shoulders and said, "*Sí*, we work *bueno*."

Ned pointed to himself. "My name is Ned. What is your name?"

"César."

Ned pointed to the younger man. A bronzed face with high cheekbones looked up. He stood taller and was leaner than the sturdy César.

"Tino," the young man said.

"You Mexicans?"

César's eyes searched Ned's face. "*Sí*. We come from Colorado, work for railroad. But no more work."

"Colorado. That's a far piece to come. You walk?"

"*Sí*. No work in Colorado. Need work."

"Come with me," Ned said.

Ned took César and Tino into the room off the front door. "You can sleep here."

They placed their tattered bedrolls on the floor.

Ned motioned for the men to follow him. "Have a seat," he said, pointing to the table, "I'll rustle up some food."

The Mexicans sat dead-still with their hands folded on their laps while Ned served a lunch of hardtack biscuits, beef jerky, and a bowl of raw vegetables.

"Dig in, amigos."

The men swallowed the food in great, rapid gulps.

César wiped his plate clean with the last of his biscuit. "*Gracias*. We work now," he said.

"All right then, follow me."

Ned handed both men hoes, then pointed to a patch of land next to the garden. "That's my potato patch."

César straightened his stance, and his timid look turned resolute. "We go," he said.

And go they did, working side by side, up one row and back down another. They reminded Ned of himself and Tom back in Ketchum.

At dusk, Ned returned to the patch. The soil had been chopped into fine bits, and straight rows shaped into crowns rose two inches above ground level.

"That's good. Come on in, and we'll have some dinner."

The Mexicans paused, and then continued to work.

Ned got a hoe and joined them.

Ned hollered, "Whoa," and pulled tight on the reins of the plow, bringing the Belgian horse to a stop. He went around to the front of the animal and tightened the cheek strap. He then looked over to the barn where César and Tino were cleaning the stalls, laying fresh straw, and collecting eggs from the hen loft. *Nothing they're not willing to try*, Ned thought as he returned to the horse's rear and secured the harness straps over his shoulder. And they didn't seem to have any interest in going into town or the need for other folks. They had been working for two months now, and they worked with purpose and drive. Ned had noticed, however, that in the last few days, they had started moping a bit in the evenings after chores. He wondered whether they were getting a little stale, never leaving the place.

As the sun began to set behind a low bank of clouds, Ned thought that it had been a good day of plowing. He looked over the rows and rows of earth churned up black.

Leading the horse into the barn, he spotted Tino emptying a pail into the garden.

Ned suspected what was in it. For two days prior, Tino had pointed to bats nesting in the barn louvers and had said that he wanted to add guano to the soil.

Ned took the horse to its stall, finding fresh straw in place and a bucket of crushed oats and corn waiting. "Sweet feed for you tonight, big fella," Ned said, stroking the horse's mane.

After feeding the Belgian, Ned walked over to the garden.

He waited until Tino came to the end of a row. "Amigo, start putting some molasses in the Belgian's bucket of oats and corn."

"*Sí*, Mr. Ned." Tino smiled, and his gleaming teeth highlighted his handsome, brown face. He tapped the hoe on the ground. "Guano *bueno*, Mr. Ned."

"*Bueno*, amigo. Tomorrow, we go to buy some supplies."

Tino spread the bat dung into the soil and looked up at Ned, his eyes quick and alive. "*Bueno*, Mr. Ned, *bueno*."

Ned banged open the front door. "Let's get 'er goin', amigos." Ned stood for a second on the porch, buttoning the top button of his placket work shirt. In the yard, Tino and César hitched the team to the wagon.

Up a ways, they neared a bridge crossing over a hollow, on the other side of which Ned saw a wagon approaching. He recognized the driver by his wild thicket of black hair.

Pete Lomax shielded his eyes with his hand, stood up, and lashed his team hard, heading hell-bent for the bridge.

Ned leaned forward, slackened the reins and hollered, "Yah, yah!" to his horses. They lurched forward, then bolted toward the bridge.

César turned to his boss. "*Señor* Ned?"

Ned clenched his jaw and urged his team on. "Yah!"

The sound of horses snorting and gasping clashed with the jangling creaks and groans of the wagon.

"You want a race, Lomax? I'll give you a race." Ned leaned forward, his every sense alert as the wagon thundered toward the bridge. The other team was farther away, but closing hard. Lomax lashed his team. His eyes burned like hot coals.

"Mr. Ned!" César screamed. "This *loco!*"

The hooves of Ned's team pounded onto the bridge floor, and cracking sounds shot through the floorboards.

César yelled, *"No es bueno*, Mr. Ned, *no es bueno!"*

As Ned's team came off the bridge, he could see the mucous flying out of the nostrils of the approaching team.

Just when they seemed seconds apart, and the thought flashed in Ned's mind what thousands of pounds of horseflesh colliding would sound like, Lomax veered off hard, coming so close that Ned could see his horses' eyes—big white globes lined red with fear.

Ned looked back as Lomax pulled hard on the reins, stopping his team right at the edge of the gully. "Good manners are hard-learned by some," he said in a flat, cold voice.

With his fist raised over his head, Pete Lomax bellowed, "Damn you, Fallow. I'll get even if it's the last thing I do. I've got a long memory."

Inside the Mercantile, Ned spotted Etheridge and Mr. Tharrington going over an inventory sheet at the front counter.

Etheridge walked over to Ned. "Hey there, Ned. See you got the new hands out and about."

Etheridge grinned at Tino and César. "Old Ned working you too hard?"

"No, *señor*," César said.

"Say, Ned, why don't you come over for supper tomorrow night? My sister-in-law and her daughter are in town from Topeka. Bet you wouldn't mind a little home cooking."

"No thanks."

"Now, come on Ned, what's it gonna hurt you to have a good meal and a little company?"

Ned shifted his gaze over to a gangplow stationed in the middle of the store. "First off, I don't want to leave my men alone."

Etheridge scratched his chin and shifted his eyes to the Mexicans. "Why, I hadn't thought …"

He turned to César and Tino. "Dinner, my *casa, mañana.*"

Tino stood stone-faced. César shrugged and looked at Ned.

Ned said, "Don't think so."

Etheridge turned back to Ned. "Now, come on, Ned. Mildred wants you to come."

Ned looked at his men, and their eyes questioned him with a trace of anticipation. He figured that they would appreciate a chance to eat a good home-cooked meal made with a woman's touch. Ned turned back to Etheridge. "What time you want us?"

As Ned steered the buckboard into the Etheridges' yard, he peeked over at César and Tino, both of whom had the wide-eyed jitters of children about to open their first Christmas presents.

César whispered to Tino, *"Casa hermosa,"* as he admired the long, ranch-style house with exposed log rafters. Flowers sat in a vase on the front porch, and a welcome sign carved in wood hung over the big oak front door.

As they walked up the limestone steps, César seemed almost in a trance as he studied the intricate detail work on the milled railing. White paint only improved its appearance.

Ned knocked on the front door, and a tall blond girl of around nineteen greeted them.

"How do you do? I'm Stephanie Smith, Mrs. Etheridge's niece."

"Hello, Ned Fallow here … This is César and Tino."

"Please come in."

To the left of the foyer, a braided rug covered most of the pine floor of a large parlor. A fieldstone fireplace anchored the wall opposite the porch window, under which a large sofa rested. A comfortable-looking cushioned armchair was adjacent to the near corner of the sofa. To the left of the big room was a large kitchen area with a brick fireplace against a far wall. A hallway at the rear of the living room led to a dining room off the kitchen, to the right of the foyer was a large bedroom, and straight back from the foyer were two more bedrooms. Etheridge and two women came from the kitchen.

"Welcome." Etheridge said. "Come right in and make yourself at home. I see you fellas have met Stephanie. This is my wife Mildred and her sister Florence Smith."

The two older women nodded and forced smiles through tight lips at César and Tino, who both lowered their gazes to the floor.

Ned felt like leaving right then, but he held his ground.

Florence Smith extended a slender hand with long, delicate fingers to Ned. "How nice to make your acquaintance, Ned. Bill has told us what a splendid job you've done on your farm."

Ned straightened and said, "How do you do?" He tilted his head toward the tall, striking woman.

"Supper is ready," Mrs. Etheridge said. "Ned, please come to the dining room. I've set up a separate table for your men in the kitchen."

Ned felt his insides stiffen. "They eat at the same table as me, or we're leaving."

Ned saw César and Tino look longingly into the kitchen and a table brimming with food.

César grabbed the sleeve of Ned's shirt. "*Es bueno*, Mr. Ned."

"No *bueno*, César."

Ned glared at Etheridge and motioned his men toward the door.

"Wait, Ned." Etheridge raised his palms. "We thought they'd be more comfortable eating separately. We'll make room at the big table." Etheridge leveled his gaze on his wife and sister-in-law. "Won't we, ladies?"

Ned sat at one end of the dining room table and Bill sat at the other. The three women sat across from César and Tino. The table was piled high with platters of venison, sweet potato, string beans in a butter sauce, thick and crusty white bread, a large crock of churned butter, and an apple and cherry pie for dessert. The entire room was full of the wonderful aromas of good food.

Bill motioned to Ned. "Ned, would you say grace?"

The thought of Sunday dinner in Ketchum, with his grandfather saying grace, rose strong in Ned's mind. He placed his clasped hands on the table. "'Bless us, oh Lord, and these thy gifts which we are about to receive from thy bounty, through Christ, our Lord. Amen.'"

"Thank you, Ned." Bill looked at César and Tino and said. "Fellas, please dig in and start passing platters."

César looked over at Ned, his eyes unsure.

Ned pointed to César's plate. "Go ahead, César."

Very carefully, César sunk the serving fork into the venison and placed a piece on his plate. He then looked at Ned who motioned for him to pass it to Tino.

After everyone's plate were filled, Mrs. Etheridge said, "Everyone, please begin."

And with that, it was as if a tight chain had been broken as everyone seemed to relax and enjoy the splendid meal.

As the wagon turned onto the road from Etheridge's house, Ned looked over at César and Tino.

They smiled at Ned, their eyes shining proudly. César said, *"Gracias,* Mr. Ned, *gracias."*

"You're welcome, amigo … you're welcome."

CHAPTER 11

▼

"Had good rainfall, amigos." Ned removed his straw hat and wiped his brow as he squinted at the sun that ruled the sky, shining its benevolence over his field of wheat.

"Amigos … this is a scythe." Ned swung his scythe at the standing wheat. "See how I do it?"

Tino and César nodded and swung their blades in a smooth motion, but Ned didn't like the way they struck the stalks, and he stopped them.

"You did this before?"

"A little," César said.

"Like this." Ned stopped just before striking the wheat. "See where the blade is? Not so high."

By noon, César and Tino were cutting wheat like experienced threshermen, with Ned encouraging them. *"Bueno, amigos, bueno."*

Cutting north to south, two arms' lengths apart, they moved up and down the field. The Mexicans seemed to feed off of Ned's working fury.

Ned anchored a shock into the stubble. To his left, César and Tino stacked the wheat. As he moved toward another shock, Ned made out a buggy on the periphery of the field. Shielding his eyes, he walked over and recognized the driver as Doc Auld.

"My goodness, Ned, you done some kinda work around here." Doc said, peering at the shocked wheat. He then turned toward the barn and admired its new roof and fresh coat of paint, and then looked at the east field. "See you're growing corn." Doc rubbed a tired eye with a finger.

"Crop rotation. Agricultural journal says it keeps the soil from stagnating. Plus, it's good feed."

Doc pulled his meerschaum pipe out of his coat pocket and banged it on the side of his buggy. "Stagnation is an interesting concept. I reckon it applies to folks, also." Doc dipped the pipe into a tobacco pouch and raised a thick, gray eyebrow toward Ned.

Ned felt the appraisal of the older man and turned toward the Mexicans in the wheat field.

Doc scratched a match and held it lit for a moment. "Will you look at that garden." He put the match to the bowl and drew until a small white puff came from it. "I've never seen healthier-looking plants." Doc scratched a two-day growth of stubble on his neck, making Ned wonder if he had been out in the country making rounds for the last couple of days—sleeping in spare rooms and trading his services for livestock and such.

"Ain't nothing but a little work, as my Grandpa used to say," Ned said. He removed his hat and knocked dust away from his shirt and pants.

Doc anchored his pipe stem in his cheek and kept an inquisitive eye on Ned. "What type of man was your grandfather, Ned?"

"The best. He did it all in his life. Worked on whaling schooners as a boy; scouted for the army. This old, used-up campaign hat ..." Ned stuck his finger through a hole in the brim, "... was his from those days. He helped raise my cousin and me after our fathers passed. A great man in his own right." Ned felt a catch in his throat; looking up at Doc, he noticed the fatigue that now washed over the older man's face. Ned figured that he had been rattling across the prairie looking after folks for more years than he cared to remember.

Doc straightened the lapels on his wrinkled coat, as if he realized that he, too, was being appraised. "This country was good breeding ground for great men. Not many left like your grandfather."

Ned raised his hand over his head. "Amigos. Keep them shocks straight." Ned and Doc watched the Mexicans scurry about, lining up the rows of wheat. "What brings you out this way, Doc?"

"Just took a gander at Vern Swensen's workhorse, and thought I'd come by and see how you're farin'. Haven't seen much of you in town." Doc's gray eyes narrowed.

"Workin' sunup to sundown, and then some." Ned cocked his head toward the Mexicans.

Doc dangled the reins in his hands and said, "Told Vern Swensen that his big bay needed a rest. Been working it too hard. Let it go to pasture for a few days, and then bring it back to work."

Ned turned and faced Doc. "Old Vern, now *he's* a worker. Can't fault a man for that."

Doc Auld bit down on his pipe, and said, "Stagnation … that's an interesting word." He nodded as if to say that there was no point continuing. "Ned, you take care."

Ned watched Doc's buggy until it had turned the corner at the south fork. He gritted his teeth and looked back to the wheat field, its shocks lined straight and true. "Ain't nothin' but a little work," he said under his breath.

CHAPTER 12

▼

"Ned Fallow's got a hell of a nerve." Shorty Swanson opened the creaky front door, swept dirt out onto the boardwalk, and slammed the door shut. "Hirin' them wetbacks, when there's good men right here in Midland."

Shorty noticed Bo shaking down the stove's grate and its load of ashes and casting a nervous glance at him.

Doc Auld struck a match on the stove and lit his pipe. "Well, now, Shorty," he said as he lowered his gaze and drew on his pipe, "you and Bo know what a taskmaster Ned Fallow is. Perhaps those Mexicans will tire of him and take off in the middle of the night." Doc raised a quizzical eye toward Shorty.

Bill Etheridge leaned forward on an empty nail keg. "I don't know, Doc. Ned told me he's plum happy with those two. Says they're the first fellas who can keep up with him. Bet he wants to help make their lives a little better."

Shorty began sweeping up loose ashes around the stove. "Yeah, well, Lomax and them says them Mexicans will steal Fallow and this town blind, and maybe even do worse."

Hank spoke up. "Lomax been spreading rumors, Shorty? Be like him to declare a crime wave in the territory."

Doc pointed his pipe toward Shorty, "Man's got a right to hire whoever he damn well pleases." He turned his gaze to the other men. "Lomax and them others need to remember this is a free country."

Shorty opened the stove door and dumped the loose ashes in. He started to respond to Doc, but caught Hank's sharp gaze. It was the "go find something to do" look. Shorty closed the door and headed to the storage room.

As the day went on, business dwindled to only an elderly woman wandering around looking at fabrics. Hank left to run some errands, and Shorty started sneaking sips out of his flask as he stocked the candy jars.

Bo stood behind the counter. "S-Shorty, Hank ain't gonna be pleased if he s-smells liquor on your breath."

"Can't you ever just mind you own damn business, Bo?"

The front doorbell jingled, and in strode Ned with the two Mexicans.

"Hey, Ned, I h-hear them new workers are b-better 'n me and S-Shorty," Bo said, shifting his weight from one foot to the other as Ned leveled his gaze down on him.

"They do more than I've seen from the labor around here." Ned pointed toward the back shelf.

Bo placed a package of jerky on the counter. "They drinkers?"

"No, and what's it to you, Fielder?" Ned placed his cash on the counter.

"Shorty has his reasons, N-Ned, that's all."

Shorty fumbled with a full jar of candy, nearly dropping it. "Bo, pipe down!"

Bo deliberately counted the change, placing one coin after another on the counter.

Ned breathed heavily with impatience. "You just count your blessings, Bo, that you haven't lived the life of them two." Ned jerked his thumb over his shoulder toward the two Mexicans standing at the door.

Shorty placed the jar on the counter. "You think you've had it tough, Fallow? Crawl inside my skin for a day—just one day. There'll be a ghost rattling inside your head that'll make your skin crawl. Take a look—a *good* look." Shorty wiped the saliva from his chin and put his hand to his twitching cheek.

Ned backed away from the counter, and his narrow gaze softened. Shoving the change into his pocket, he turned and walked out with his two workers in tow.

Shorty saw Bo sneaking a peek at him.

"What you lookin' at, Bo? Huh? What you lookin' at? Why you got to run on so with Fallow?"

Shorty sighed, then walked to the back room with his little shoulders slouched forward.

"Goddamn Fallow acts like this town owes him a living," Shorty said, banging the claw of a hammer against the ribbing of a crate. "Ain't right them Mexicans are here." Shorty heard his own voice screech into his ear and fell silent. He looked, out of habit, to see if anybody had heard him. In the safety of the storage room, Shorty took a deep swallow, finishing off his flask.

Bo came into the room. "Shorty, I d-didn't mean to speak out for you."

Shorty placed the hammer on the crate. "Them Mexicans are a threat to workin' folks like us, Bo."

Shorty noticed Bo's mouth hanging open as if he had just been told a revelation. "Next thing, there'll be a whole trainload of 'em comin' in, and where'll that leave you and me, Bo? You tell me. Where's that leave us?"

"You think so, S-Shorty? They don't seem like bad fellas."

"Why'd Fallow have to take them on? That man's always goin' against the grain." Shorty heard the wariness in his voice as he sunk the hammer claw into another box.

But, deep down, Shorty wished that he could *be* Ned Fallow—tall, strong, and handsome, too. Ned Fallow was everything Shorty wasn't, and would never be. And if Shorty was never going to be Ned Fallow, then he could hate him for it.

Damn you, Ned Fallow, damn you.

CHAPTER 13

▼

From the perimeter of the north field, Ned took a breath and detected the first scent of autumn. He turned and watched the Mexicans loading his hayrack. The shocks of spring wheat glowed gold.

"Always work with folks who value the labor as much as you, Ned, and you'll be rewarded with more than just a good crop," Grandpa O'Connor had said, more than a few times. Now, Ned understood what he had meant. Day after day, he had pushed these two men, rising before dawn and retiring after sunset. And they responded with a vigor and eagerness that surprised and gladdened him. No longer timid, César and Tino were strong and long-enduring.

A grainy image rose in Ned's mind of Ketchum and working shoulder to shoulder with his cousin. Now, he and his amigos were a team—kindred spirits, surrendering themselves to an ethic of blood and sweat.

Ned joined the men along the north edge of the field and took the reins of the hayrack while they loaded the shocks of wheat.

Tino, who had been reaching for a bundle of wheat, let out a scream and grabbed his left arm.

"Mr. Ned, *la culebra.*" César sunk the tines of his pitchfork behind the head of a rattler, killing it.

Tino, down on one knee, gripped his left forearm with his right hand and stared at two puncture wounds. His fear was palpable.

Ned inspected the wound, then tore a bandana in half and applied a tourniquet above and below the wound. He picked up Tino and carried him to the house and his bed.

"César, boil water—*el agua, pronto.*" Ned pointed to the stove.

César grabbed a pot and ran to the well. He returned and got the water heating on the stove.

Ned took out his pocketknife, lit a match, and ran the flame over the blade. "Amigo, hold Tino."

Ned slit open the bite marks, and Tino screamed, "Ahh, it hurt."

"The worst is over, Tino," Ned said before sucking blood from the wound.

"César, watch Tino." Ned went to the stove and steeped a washcloth in the boiling water. After letting it cool for a few minutes on a plate, he placed the cloth on the wound.

"Tino, you must stay still."

"*Sí*, Mr. Ned," Tino's long lashes flickered over glassy eyes as his bronze face turned ashen. "Oh, Mr. Ned, I no feel good," he said before losing consciousness.

Ned went to cupboard, got a out a pencil and scrap of paper, and took them to the table. "César, go to Grove's and find out where Dr. Auld is. Here, I'll write you a note. Ride one of the horses, pronto."

Ned watched from the window as César took off, riding bareback at a full gallop.

Shorty looked up from inspecting a rifle with Pete Lomax to see a horseman come to an abrupt stop, dismount, and scramble up the boardwalk. It was one of Fallow's Mexicans.

"*Señor*, help." The man extended the note over the counter to Shorty.

"You good-for-nothing Mexican," Shorty barked. "Get out of this store."

"Please, *señor*, I am César. I work for Mr. Ned."

Lomax took a long knife out of its sheath. "I believe this hombre's trying to rob this here store, Swanson." He placed the knife under César's throat as a crooked-toothed grin spread across his face.

"Wait a minute, Lomax, no!" Shorty reached for Lomax's arm holding the knife.

Lomax thwarted Shorty with his free hand and raised the knife up, forcing the man to raise his chin. "Swanson, you stay out of this. The only good Mexican is a dead one." Lomax brought his dark, stubbly face close to the frightened César's.

"*Señor*, please, no."

Lomax's black eyes gleamed with evil. "I think I'll just carve my initials on this here hombre."

Shorty chopped Lomax across the arm, knocking the knife to the ground. César turned and made a run for it. Lomax brought the knife to his ear and let it fly. As the Mexican reached for the door, the knife whistled past him and split the doorframe.

César jerked open the front door. Its bells were still jangling as he scrambled onto his horse. He reined around, slapped the horse's flank, and screamed, *"Pronto!"*

The animal quivered underneath him, then exploded out with powerful strides.

Ned waited on the front porch, searching the south fork for Doc Auld's clattering buggy. Finally, he saw César round the bend at a gallop and head toward the house.

"What happened?"

"No es bueno, Mr. Ned."

"César, what happened?"

"Señor Shorty and hombre." César pointed to his mouth and ran his finger across his teeth. "Hombre, *los dientes no bueno."*

"Lomax." Ned spat out the name. "Wait here, and don't let him move if he wakes." Ned got on the lathered horse and took off hell-bent for town.

Ned dismounted in front of Grove's before the horse had come to a complete halt. He stomped into the store and saw Etheridge and Dan O'Hurley at the counter and Swanson behind it. Shorty looked like he was expecting Ned's arrival.

Ned stormed up, grabbed Shorty by the shirt, and pulled him over the counter and in close. "If he dies, I'm gonna whup you and Lomax from here to next Sunday." Ned dropped Shorty in a heap.

Shorty gathered himself up, his face flushed red and his cheek twitching.

"Bill, where's Doc Auld? One of my men's got a snakebite."

"I saw him this morning. Said he was making rounds and be back by this afternoon."

"Can you find him and get him to my place quick? I got a man in bad shape."

"Sure thing. Dan, you take the west side of town. I'll take the east. We'll get him to you, Ned."

Ned stared at Shorty. "Little man, if he comes in here, you best get him to my farm. You understand?"

Shorty stared at the floor and nodded.

The afternoon shadows spread across the yard, stopping at the porch where Ned paced back and forth, looking again and again for the doctor. All Ned could get out of César was, "Bad hombre, Mr. Ned, bad hombre." Ned figured that Lomax had been the culprit.

Had Ned been too hard on Swanson at Grove's earlier? Had he been a bit abrupt in his opinion of Shorty—and of Bo Fielder for that matter? Ned had heard from Etheridge the story of Shorty's difficult childhood. But life was hard for everyone. It was no excuse for being a shiftless drunk. Or was it? The thought left Ned's mind as he saw a buckboard approach.

Doc sat next to the patient and examined his puffy red wound. He felt Tino's feverish forehead and examined his eyes and throat. "Get me some water."

Ned filled a cup from the water jug at the sink and brought it over to Doc.

Doc removed a vial from his medicine bag and got two white pills down Tino's throat. "Who administered to the wound?"

"I did," Ned said.

Doc leveled an approving gaze on Ned, then said, "We'll know by tomorrow. Meantime, give him two of these quinine pills every four hours, and keep a damp compress on his forehead. I'll be back in the morning."

Ned paced the porch and searched through the early-morning fog for the doctor. He looked into the house, where César sat watch over Tino. It had been a sleepless night for Ned and César.

"César, you stay with Tino, and I'll take care of the chores in the barn."

César looked up, his eyes dim. "*Sí*, Mr. Ned."

As the sun peeked through the dissipating morning mist, Doc Auld rode up in his buggy.

Doc pulled up in the yard next to Ned, who was spreading feed to the chickens. "How's the patient?"

"He slept through the night and woke up groggy before sunrise."

"Let's take a look."

After a cursory examination, Doc got up. "He'll make it. Just don't let him work for the next couple of days."

"*Gracias*, César" César said, nodding his respect to Doc.

"Any problems, come get me." Doc gave Ned a half-salute and departed.

After Doc left, Tino slept for most of the day and through the night. Doc's medicine had begun to work, for the following morning, Tino was up and sitting at the table with César. Ned felt relieved.

"Tino, no work for you today." Ned spooned oatmeal into three bowls, then placed them on the table.

"Mr. Ned, we talk," César said.

Ned took a tin pan of biscuits out of the oven and placed them in a bowl. He sensed that something big was coming. "Yes, César?" Ned took his seat.

"Tino and I go." There was surrender in his voice.

Ned looked at César's stony expression, then Tino's. "What say you work till we get the wheat harvested? I'd like you to come back next year."

César looked up at Ned with hollow eyes, "*Muchas gracias,* Mr. Ned. Maybe next year, we come."

Ned looked into those aching brown eyes and, for the first time, realized that there were people on this earth who had suffered much more than he knew, or could even imagine.

The morning of their departure, red-pink clouds scraped the haunting blue horizon as if trying to find safe harbor from the omnipresent blueness. The gathering chill signaled the oncoming winter that waited impatiently around the corner. The threshing of the wheat coincided with a clear sign from Mother Nature, providing a clear sense that this chapter of these three men's lives was ending.

When the last tool had been returned to the barn, Ned said, "Like you to come on inside. I got something for you."

"Here's something extra for a job well done." Ned leaned over the table and handed each man a five-dollar bill. He then pointed to the corner, where two brand-new bedrolls lay, one on top of the other. "Figured they might come in handy on the journey back. Where are you going?"

"Mexico." César said.

Ned looked at Tino, then rested his gaze on César.

César cleared his throat. "Maybe we come." His eyes told Ned otherwise.

Ned watched them disappear into the land whence they had come, and he realized that he knew little more about them than he did when they had first arrived. The only sign of their stay was the spotless barn brimming with healthy livestock, a root cellar stuffed with vegetables, and the largest and best wheat crop he had ever grown.

Later that morning, Ned saddled the roan and rode into town to pick up a few items.

Departing the smithy, Ned noticed Bill Etheridge ambling up the boardwalk.

Etheridge grinned and hollered, "Neighbor." Dressed in overalls with his denim shirtsleeves rolled up above the elbow, he looked every bit the farmer. "Good news. Dan O'Hurley got hitched last week. A grand wedding it was. Mildred's still talking about it."

Ned nodded at Etheridge and felt his jaw tighten.

"Dan lost a wife back in Ireland. Never thought I'd see this day."

"Good for Dan."

After some small talk about the weather and Ned's need to stop by for a meal, Etheridge departed. Ned now thought that coming to town hadn't been such a good idea, after all.

Riding out of town, Ned looked back from the top of a rise. Midland seemed tiny against the great sweep of prairie and farmland. He felt the greatness of the land—land that could swallow him up. And who would care that he was gone?

Ned wondered whether he would ever give up a part of himself to another.

He turned and headed toward home. For the first time in what seemed an eternity, Ned Fallow felt loneliness.

CHAPTER 14

▼

Ned placed a bucket on its side in the creek. "I reckon I'd best get some rain soon," he said aloud as the water trickled in. He lugged the half-full bucket back to the house and drained it into a washbasin on the porch.

After splashing his face, he walked out to his crop of Turkey Red. The shafts of the stunted, thirsty plants drooped in defeat.

It was nine months since the Mexicans had left, and Ned had seen hardly a drop of rain in that time. Or another person, save for during a few trips to buy supplies, and Bill Etheridge coming by.

Ned took a handful of dry soil and looked up at the stark, barren sky. "Rain. I need rain."

He felt something crawling in his hand. "Chinch bugs," he croaked. He saw more of the little black devils scurrying up a plant stem. "Damn," he whispered. "Damn."

He tried every trick he could think of to kill the deadly pest. He mixed a pint of vinegar with a bucket of water and sprinkled it at the base of the wheat plants. He spread dry flour along the furrows in hopes of offering another source of food to the voracious insects. But nothing seemed to halt them—with the lack of rain, Ned wondered if it even mattered.

Day after day and week after week, no rain fell. Standing in the wheat field with scythe in hand, Ned shielded his eyes from the sun sinking over the catalpa trees. The big leaves on the trees hung like brown, wrinkled victims awaiting their final sentence.

Taking a deep breath, he began to scythe the damaged stalks. "Cut. Cut. Cut this useless stuff. For what?" He swung the scythe in furious strokes, and dead wheat and dust flew all around him.

After completing two rows, he stopped at the back swath. Dropping his scythe, he fell to his knees and looked up. Small, puffy clouds seemed to lollygag like taunting children. Ned Fallow had taken this Kansas sky and soil for granted, and now both had turned on him.

Ned remembered the day in Ketchum when he had lost his first crop and the monstrous gray clouds seeming to laugh at his lot. "Ain't nothin' in this life fair."

Ned grabbed his scythe and stood up again, feeling betrayed. "What the hell? Just cuttin' it for straw. Straw. I'm a damn wheat farmer, not some yahoo cuttin' straw."

By dusk, Ned had piled the stalks into windrows in the field. He retreated to the barn and brushed down the Belgian. He stroked the big horse's flank. "Tough year, big fella. Tough year."

Doc Auld had told Ned of wheat farmers he had seen go crazy over the years. "Work and only work is just not good for a man, Ned. And if you combine it with a failed crop or two, well … I've seen more than a few good men go stark raving mad. Yes, sir, now *that* is a fact."

"I ain't gonna let it get to me. No, I am *not*. Whatever comes, comes." Ned pushed the brush up and down the horse's side. Up and down, up and down. Harder and harder he pressed the brush against the animal's flank. The horse turned its head and snorted. Ned stopped himself. "Sorry there, big fella."

He held a kerosene lamp outside the barn, and the moonlight cast his shadow on the barn wall. It seemed so natural now—just Ned, and his silhouette his only companion. Stopping halfway to the house, he looked up at the sky awash with stars. He had known the feeling of abject failure in Ketchum, but that hadn't been his alone. He had never before felt it here, on this land that the angels had smiled on.

"Ketchum … now *there* was a struggle. These people, they don't know. Lived on broth many a winter. I can do it again." Ned heard his voice pierce the night, and it startled him.

Picking his way to the house, he thought about his supplies on hand, and of going to Grove's Store. "What day is tomorrow? Saturday? I'll go to Grove's and pick up a few items," he said to the twinkling stars.

Ned went right to his bed, too tired and low to think about food, or even washing himself, and he fell fast asleep.

Hank Grove peered out the glass storefront and saw a familiar sight—a barren sky with nary a cloud to be seen. He straightened up, as if to say, "I'm ready for whatever may come." The drought had been difficult on everybody in Midland, including Hank.

His store depended on good wheat crops to provide the money to allow folks to spend. He had already stopped credit to a few, bruising the feelings of some old friends. But he couldn't live off other folks' debt.

Since the drought, business had slowed to a crawl, even on Saturdays.

He had noticed some of his customers walking and talking differently, especially the young ones. They hadn't been through something like this before. Their movements and gestures said to the observant eye, "Whatever will I do?"

Hank saw a buckboard heading up the deserted street, its broad-shouldered driver's hard-edged countenance not only still in place, but even more so. It seemed that the drought had brought out a new level of toughness in Ned Fallow, reminding Hank of a mountain man he had once known—a loner, through and through. The tougher the going, the deeper down that man dug for the wherewithal to see it through.

Quiet and a bit aloof, yes, but Ned paid his bills on time, and a merchant couldn't ask for much more from a customer.

Ned entered the store and scoured the room with a hard-glinting gaze, his taut, strong body pulled bob-wire tight.

"Can I help you find something, Ned?" Hank asked.

Ned stayed anchored near the front door. "Just lookin'."

"I'll be in the back," Hank pointed to the storage room, "if you need any help."

Ned looked off, as though his mind was elsewhere.

"Ned, I'll g-get you what you n-need, when you're ready," Bo said from an aisle near the front door, where Ned remained stationed.

"Hey, Fallow, you 'bout ready to throw in the towel?" Shorty's scratchy voice carried over the shelves from a back corner.

As Hank came out of the storage room to shush Shorty, he heard the door creak open and saw Ned Fallow departing. He could imagine the red streak rising up his neck.

CHAPTER   15

▼

Ned hollered, "Sooey. Sooey."

The middling sow, searching for feed in a splotch of snow, seemed to pay little heed. Hammer in hand, Ned moved toward the pig, which scurried away, squealing. He cornered it between the pigpen and the barn.

The mallet struck the pig between the eyes. The animal stood stunned for a moment, then fell in a heap.

After butchering the pig in the yard, Ned wrapped the sections in wet burlap and loaded up the buckboard.

Riding past the south fork, Ned looked over to Etheridge's puny wheat seedlings, and thought of how badly snow was needed for cover.

The flat, endless land was bare, save for a few patches of snow from last night's dusting. The vastness of this land that stretched on and on was something he couldn't put a name to, but it had held him from the first time he saw it to this day. The greatness and breadth of it had made him think that he had never really seen the world before he came here. But this great world of earth and wheat needed moisture, or that barren, unsheltering sky would take them all, one by one.

Ned hitched his wagon in front of the Mercantile. Out of habit, he checked the sky and noticed dull gray clouds coming in from the west. He hoped they contained some moisture.

He spotted Mr. Tharrington and Etheridge approaching as he pulled the burlap off the back of the wagon.

Bill Etheridge tipped his straw hat back. "See you gonna do some good eating this winter, Ned," Etheridge said, nodding. "Now, that's some good-lookin' pig meat you got there."

Ned caught an extra inflection in Etheridge's voice. It was as though he were trying to lift the spirits around him.

"Reckon so," Ned replied.

Tharrington lowered his wired-rimmed glasses. "Fine job of butchering." His eyes searched Ned's face. "I see you didn't waste anything."

Etheridge chipped in. "Why, Mr. Tharrington, I don't think there's anything Ned can't do around a farm."

Tharrington's gaze remained on Ned. "Yes, I do believe there isn't anything Mr. Fallow couldn't do, if he set his mind to it."

Ned felt trapped by the stares of the irrepressible Etheridge and the austere merchant. One set of eyes was hopeful and friendly, the other narrow and gleaning—one admiring him for what he could be, the other for what he was. "Where do I take it?"

"Pull over to the smokehouse." Tharrington drew back a step and pointed toward a small brick building. "Wilson," Tharrington spoke to a man—in overalls and a floppy, wide-brimmed hat—who had been hovering about. "Gather up some logs and start a fire, then get this man's order together."

"Yessir, Mr. Tharrington." Wilson nodded, his face marked with a look that blended servitude with a desire to please. He turned from his boss to Ned. "Good-lookin' pork, yessir, good-lookin' pork."

Tharrington folded his arms across his chest and turned a cold eye toward Wilson, who stood for a moment before shambling off.

Tharrington turned to Ned. "I'll be in the store." He nodded at Etheridge and walked away.

Etheridge's eyes followed Wilson toward a pile of green hickory logs. "Been a tough year, Ned. How you fixed for vegetables?"

"Not good, but I've gone without greens before. Reckon I can do again."

"Well ... I'll be heading out. And Ned ... don't be such a stranger."

Inside the Mercantile, Ned spotted Tharrington on the second floor, megaphone in hand, like a ringmaster surveying the big show. Ned had heard from Etheridge that Tharrington had no family or friends.

"Rumor has it," Etheridge had said, "that he was once engaged, but she ran off with another fella, and he came out all this way with a sister who died within a year." Even from a distance, Ned could see the sadness that draped the small, stooped, sepulchral figure in the black suit. "A little old man with a pot of gold and no one to share it with." According to Etheridge, that's what folks in town believed. Ned admired Tharrington's business acumen, but the other part, he didn't dwell on, especially in the midst of a god-awful drought.

"Not sure I'll have any work for you this winter, Ned."

"Figured as much."

"That storage barn you built me …" Tharrington put the megaphone to his mouth, and shouted, "Wilson. Wilson, get that debris swept up and square away that grain." He pointed to an aisle where a bag of grain had split and its contents were seeping out onto the floor. "Now, where was I? Oh, yes … that storage barn is solid as the day you finished it." He turned to Ned, and his sharp gaze slackened.

"That's good," Ned replied.

A clerk came over to Tharrington with an inventory sheet. Tharrington removed his glasses and ran a bony finger across one line, then the next. His face, its momentary soft guise gone, had a hard-glinting businessman look that told Ned that the social visit was over.

Ned decided to inspect the storage barn while he waited for his order.

Along the storage barn's back wall, great wooden shelves rose over ten feet high. They were crammed with hand tools, harnesses, saddles, and such. Stacks of bricks and bags of mortar were piled in a corner.

Memories of working nights with kerosene lamps in cold, cold weather came back to him. Ned eyed the precise bird's-mouth cuts he had made in the joists.

He stood very still, and a sense of accomplishment came over him. His eyes ran from the corbel brace to the anchor beam to the rafters where a lone sparrow rested. "Going it alone, huh, little fella?" Ned said.

Wilson put the last sack of feed on Ned's wagon. "Mr. Fallow, meat should be ready in a couple of days." The aroma of the smoking pork seeped out of the smokehouse eaves into the cold air. "Ain't nothing like good pork, no sir, there surely ain't."

Ned nodded at Wilson and drove off.

Past the south fork, Ned avoided looking at the north field wheat, which was losing its anchor to the earth. He kept his eyes on his house, which rested straight and true.

The air seemed stale inside the barn, not from the scent of the livestock, but more from the mood that clung to the air like some overstaying houseguest. The animals weren't as lively as usual—it was as if they, too, knew about the consequences of the drought.

Ned took the feed bag off of the Belgian, "We'll make it there, big fella." He stroked the horse's neck, thinking about Ketchum and hardship.

Ned put the horse into its stall and headed back to the house. At the front door, he found a bushel basket chock full of vegetables. *I don't need Etheridge's damn charity,* was his first thought. But still, he sorted through the basket and found carrots, red potatoes, sweet potatoes, and string beans. He brought it into the house and placed it on the table. Then he got out a pencil and paper and wrote, "Thank you, Ned Fallow."

He then pushed the front door open.

As he neared Etheridge's house, Ned heard a big, mellow voice coming from the barn. "Hey there, neighbor."

Ned felt trapped. He turned and walked to the barn door. "Thank you for the bushel."

Etheridge hung a pitchfork on the wall. "Why, think nothing of it, Ned. Like I always say, people around here help each other out."

"Well, thank you again. I best head home." Ned turned to leave.

"Ned, why not take a load off and come in for some buttermilk and cookies? Mildred just made them." Etheridge motioned toward the house.

"I think not."

"A man living only inside himself with no room for others just isn't a whole man."

Ned felt his jaw tighten. "Look, Bill, I'm not in any mood for milk and cookies. Nor small talk, neither."

Etheridge fiddled with a harness draped over a sawhorse. "Lord have mercy, Ned Fallow. Didn't you ever think that sitting with your neighbors and sharing small talk might just ease the burden a bit?"

"Only thing I think about," Ned blurted out, "the *only* thing, is rain." Ned raised his hand and began to walk away.

"Ned, don't be such a stranger."

Man just won't quit, Ned thought as he nodded goodbye and turned away.

CHAPTER 16

▼

Ned knew something was wrong. The handwriting on the envelope wasn't his mother's, but the postage stamp was from Boston.

November 27, 1897

Dear Ned,

Your mother passed away last night. She had been fighting an infection in her lungs and it got the best of her. You should know our time together in Massachusetts had been comfortable, but I must confess we both missed you and Tom so much. Her last words were to make sure I wrote you and let you know how much she loved you.

With love,

Aunt Lorrayne

Ned dropped the letter from his hands. His mother had been dead for nearly two months, and he didn't even know it. Ned dropped to his knees on the kitchen floor, folded his hands together, and rested them against his chest. His eyes welled up, and then the tears flowed down his cheeks.

He went outside and sat on a bucket. The morning light cast low, slanting shadows across the yard. The cold air stung his face, but he didn't mind—he needed some physical suffering to go along with the agony inside his head.

His mother, Helen Fallow, was no longer a part of this life of his. She was now just a memory—a memory of a good woman who loved him with patience and kindness, with never a harsh word. Lord knows, Ned had given her cause.

Ned had chores to do, but, for once, he didn't feel like doing them. Here he was, sitting on a bucket in the yard—just like William O'Connor had done most mornings, looking toward the far-off hills that shone blue in the early light of dawn. William's empty corncob pipe would make his cheek bulge as he pondered things. Now, it was Ned's time to ponder the loss of a good woman and mother who had shown so much love each and every day to a son who gave back little in return.

The drought had brought out in him a deeper appreciation for his mother, grandfather, and aunt, and all they had endured for him and Tom, and with nary a complaint. They were righteous people with a good spirit. "We'll see it through somehow, Ned. Don't you worry none," William O'Connor would say. Those words had been so reassuring to young Ned. And, somehow, they *did* make it through.

Ned pictured his mother and father together. Her eyes were no longer worried, but shining bright as she rested her head on Jim Fallow's shoulder and waved goodbye to her son.

Ned saw a buggy coming around the bend and stood up to wait for it.
"My meat ready so soon, Wilson?"
"No, but Mr. Tharrington says he'd like a word with you about a job."
"I'll saddle up a horse and be right in."

Tharrington set down an inventory clipboard on a shelf and lowered his wire-rimmed glasses down the bridge of his nose. He motioned for Ned and Wilson to come over. "Ned, I've been thinking about building a new smokehouse, but it could be awful hard work in the winter."

Ned noticed how Wilson stood near, but not too near, Tharrington. "I can handle it." Ned pointed toward machinery on display in the center of the store. "That one-horse plow." Ned took a hoe off the wall. "One of these, two garden spades, and ... a fifty-dollar credit."

"Twenty-five dollars cash, and you got a deal."

"Done."

Tharrington picked up his clipboard and began counting tools. "The bricks are stacked at the site, right near the old smoker." He paused to scribble down some figures. "Concrete and mortar are in the barn. Now, you know you got to keep the mortar protected from the cold." Tharrington turned a sharp eye toward Wilson. "Why aren't these shovels hanging straight?" Tharrington pointed to a row of shovels against the wall.

Wilson placed the blade of a shovel between two pegs. He stood back, looked at the straight shovel, and sidestepped on to the next one.

Ned turned to Tharrington and said, "I'll mix it with hot water. You got plenty of firewood?"

Tharrington nodded at Ned while keeping an eye on Wilson.

"And I'll cover the work with burlap to protect it."

Wilson hung the last shovel, stepped back to his place near Tharrington, and said, "Could get some kinda cold out there, Ned."

Tharrington's busy gaze inspected the now-straightened shovels. "Wilson, something tells me Mr. Fallow here has seen worse." Tharrington removed his glasses, rubbed his left eye while the right stayed vigilant on his store, and then reversed the procedure.

"I'll start tomorrow." Ned heard the spirit rise in his voice.

Wilson drew in his chin. "You gonna work on *Christmas*?"

"Good a time as any."

There was no one to greet Ned at the Mercantile on Christmas morning. There was nothing there but a hard job for a hard man.

He unlocked the door to the supply barn and found the hundred-pound bags of concrete and mortar piled in a corner.

At the site of the new smoker, string lines indicated the perimeter of the building. "Build it like the one I already have," had been Tharrington's instructions. The hard surface around the eight-by-eight border fought against excavation by Ned's pick.

Dusk came early, draping the land in dullness. Ned got lanterns from the storage barn and placed them on the perimeter of the trench. Inside the existing smoker, he started a fire in the red-brick fireplace. He took an iron kettle from the storage barn, placed it on a grid over the crackling fire, and filled it from a barrel of water in a corner.

Ned dipped a pan into the kettle of warm water and mixed concrete in a wheelbarrow until it had a pasty consistency.

The sun peeked over the stark eastern horizon, giving promise of a good day to work. Ned hoisted a bag of mortar over his shoulder and headed for the storage barn.

Returning to the worksite, he found Wilson walking around the site, peeping under the burlap. "Ain't humanly possible, what you done here."

Ned gave his shoulders a small shrug, then picked up a trowel and scraped mortar off a hoe.

Wilson shuffled over to Ned as Tharrington drove up in a one-horse buggy.

Tharrington nodded at Ned, got out of the buggy, and removed the burlap cover from one section to find the footers lying straight and true. A thin, catlike smile spread over his small, pale face. "Ned Fallow, you are an interesting fellow." He then turned and walked into the Mercantile.

Wilson scratched his cheek. "Ned, you plannin' on sleepin' anytime soon?"

"Might as well. Gotta let it cure."

Two days later, Ned moved bags of mortar into the smoker and started heating water. Outside, a light snow fell from a gray morning sky. He mixed two wheelbarrows of mortar, then removed the burlap cover from a section of the footing and began spreading the pasty mortar and placing bricks.

He now had a routine and rhythm to his work: he would first mix and place the mortar, then lay the bricks, and finally point the mortar between the bricks. The warmth provided by the smoker made the job more tolerable. The smoker also doubled as a comfortable sleeping quarters.

When the job was finished, Tharrington placed the crisp bills in Ned's palm. "Here's your twenty-five dollars. Tools and plow are in the back." Tharrington stroked his chin. "I've seen some things in this life," he said as his flinty gaze softened, "but not what you did out there."

Ned scratched his unshaven face, "I'll pick up the plow and tools in a few days." Ned rubbed his eyes and wondered whether they looked as bloodshot as they felt.

Outside, Ned saddled his horse and overheard Wilson talking to another worker around the corner at the new smoker.

"That man ain't human, that's all there is to it, and here's the proof. Top-notch work, to boot, and done in just two weeks."

Ned mounted the roan and said to Wilson in passing, "Ain't nothing but a little work."

CHAPTER 17

▼

Ned pulled up to Grove's General Store and read the sign on the front door. "Closed for the 4th. See you at the Grange Hall."

He blurted, "God Almighty."

Ned heard a hacking cough behind him. He turned and saw Shorty Swanson staggering toward him, his eyes lined red. Ned figured that Shorty had been "under the weather" for the last couple of days and imagined that Hank Grove had given him an ultimatum—something along the lines of, "Them shelves better be stocked proper when I open up on the fifth."

As Shorty approached the door, he reminded Ned of a sad, lonely dog.

"Swanson, I—"

"Figure it out Fallow—this store or any store ain't open on the Fourth of July." Shorty straightened himself and tucked his shirt down tight.

Ned stared at Shorty, who stared back with a resolution he had to acknowledge. He slackened the reins and started to move out.

"Some folks I might let in to buy goods on credit," said Shorty. "But not you, Mr. High and Mighty."

Ned heard the door slam, turned, and saw the blinds close shut.

Pip-squeak drunk, Ned thought as he turned his wagon around and moved out.

Ned's wagon passed the Grange Hall. Inside, red, white, and blue festoons hung from the oak rafters, but they didn't seem to sparkle or shimmer as in years past. Bill Etheridge straightened the pictures of American patriots like George Washington and Abe Lincoln that hung on the wood-planked walls. Their faces seemed more austere than ever. Two kegs of beer sat in a big basin of ice in a corner nook, both almost full.

The three-piece musical group, including Doc Auld on the fiddle, had been playing rollicking, joyful music, but folks just sat.

Nothing much mattered in Midland, Kansas, on this Fourth of July other than the gripping drought. The spring harvest had failed, and late summer's was shaping up no better. Bill peeked outside the Grange Hall window to see a buckboard clattering up Main Street.

Bill Etheridge sat with a group of men clustered around the beer kegs. They all held cups of lukewarm beer. A voice wafted across the hall, then died under its own weight. "Seen drought before, but ..."

Dan O'Hurley put a plug of tobacco between his cheek and gum and said, "Say, Doc, I hear old Vern Swensen's mind strayed a bit last week."

Doc Auld put down his fiddle and tightened his bolo tie. "If I can keep him rested, he should be all right."

Hank Grove removed his glasses and polished their lenses on his shirtsleeve. "Heard he's thinkin' of sellin' his place." Hank put his glasses back on. "Larry Stude sold his place for less than he paid, and he's moving back to Illinois. Says this land is cursed."

Doc shook his head clucked his tongue. "I don't believe Vern's in serious shape. The heat got to him—he'll be all right."

"Drought's bad enough, but worryin' about money and feedin' a family ..." Dan O'Hurley caught himself and looked off.

"It's bad, all right," Doc said. "It's gonna separate the wheat from the chaff. Mother Nature's way of doing things." Doc grabbed his pipe from the pocket of his black vest.

"Bill, heard anything out of Fallow?" O'Hurley asked, more just making conversation than expressing genuine concern.

"Not lately. Last time, he seemed more distant than ever. I fear for him."

"Why do you bother, Bill?" O'Hurley shifted his shoulders and spat tobacco juice into a spittoon.

"He's gonna be all right someday. Takes some men longer to sort things out. A fella with all his qualities just can't stay hollow forever." Bill looked at Doc for affirmation.

Doc scratched behind his ear and jutted out his jaw. "Ain't anything for sure in this life, Bill. The man's lived in these parts for over seven years now, and he's harder to figure than when he arrived."

Etheridge looked up from his recital sheet. "I'll stop by later today and see how the cistern he's building is coming."

Rounding the bend, Bill Etheridge saw a tall, lean figure hoeing in a small plot. *That man,* he thought, *would rather die in the field than surrender.*

Etheridge hollered, "Whoa." and pulled back on the buggy reins.

Ned looked up at Etheridge as if trying to make out who it was.

"Whew," Etheridge said, pulling a blue bandanna from his overalls and wiping his brow. "Gonna be another hot one, Ned. Say, your garden doesn't look any better than ours—more dust than soil."

Ned straightened up and looked at Etheridge with shipwrecked eyes. "Reckon you got enough stashed away to ride it out."

Bill caught the tone of resentment. "I paid my dues on this land, Ned."

Ned leaned on the hoe, seemingly lost in a dark shadow of gloom. His gauntness seemed to border on hunger. "I intend to see this through on my own, come what may."

Etheridge dangled the reins in his hands. "I'll be glad when this drought ends, so folks'll start smiling again." Bill sensed something beyond Ned's normal terseness—something had wound around him tight and gotten hold of him.

"That'd be good, but I'll take on whatever comes." Ned clenched his teeth, squinted, and looked far off into the distance.

Bill pointed to a wooden structure on the side of a bluff. "Looks like you finished your cistern. Thought I'd take a look at it."

Ned seemed to focus, and his body straightened. "Squeeze over, and we'll ride up the backside."

At the top of the bluff, Etheridge looked down in disbelief at a large hole with a mortared limestone base. Wooden chutes connected the cistern to a sluice in the field below. Etheridge examined the skilled carpentry work as he walked around the limestone cistern.

"Where'd you get the material?"

"Wood scraps from the sawmill, and the limestone from credit at the Mercantile."

"How's it work?"

Ned got out of the buggy and quick-stepped down the hill. "Right here," he said as he opened and closed handles on the side of the sluice.

"I'll have to bring Doc Auld by to take a gander at this."

Ned got to the top, caught his breath, and then said, "Damn thing's a waste of work so far."

"When the rain comes, you'll be glad you did it."

Ned got into the buggy. "'When is a big word."

Etheridge drove down the backslope and headed toward the yard. "Ned, I have no doubt you'll see this through and be a better man for it. Why, Mildred and I are so pleased with the way you turned this place around."

The buggy stopped in front of the barn, and Ned climbed down into a swirl of dust kicked up by the hooves and wheels. "Hangin' on is more like it."

"Mildred and I had thought long ago of buying this place for our children. But it wasn't to be, and … well, it just gladdened us so when you got it." The mare lurched forward. "Whoa." Bill commanded, drawing back the reins. "It's a dream come true, seein' a young man fixin' this place up so." Bill knew that he was making Ned feel uncomfortable, "You'd make any man proud to call you his son, the way you've endured."

Ned narrowed his eyes, and the far-off look returned. "I ain't your son."

Bill felt the spirit die in his throat at this rebuke. "No, but … well," he said, hearing the heaviness in his voice, "you take care, Ned." Bill clucked at the mare and began to drive off, but he pulled up short.

"Why don't you come by the house for supper? Wife's making pot roast, oatmeal cakes, and apple pie for dessert."

"Thank you, no."

"Yes, well …" Bill knew he couldn't hide the smile of resignation he felt at being turned down. "We'll set a place for you, in case you change your mind."

Ned watched the buggy rattle down the south fork until it turned toward Etheridge's place. He didn't know what had made him lash out so at his neighbor, and he could hear his grandfather's scolding voice: "We're all in this together, Ned. A man who doesn't appreciate a good neighbor is no neighbor at all."

Ned looked at the sky and whispered, "Rain."

CHAPTER 18

▼

Ned tied the roan to the post at the train depot and spotted Bill Etheridge and a group of men huddled in a circle in front of the Grange Hall. Their gregarious voices and excited laughter filled the street, and Ned noticed even Vern Swensen breaking out in a guffaw. Something had piqued the interest of this placid community.

Spirits had picked up since old man winter had swept through—snow and more snow had broken the drought—but this gathering was something different.

"Hey there, neighbor." Etheridge waved to Ned and broke from the men.

"Mornin'," Ned said.

"Thought you'd like to know about the goings-on."

"How's that?"

"We've contracted a fella who owns one of them newfangled steam-powered threshing machines. Supposed to do the work of twenty men. The fella's name is Jim Cotton, and he's giving a demonstration at the Grange right now. Might be worth your while."

"Let's go."

Forty men or more clustered around the great threshing machine, which looked and sounded like a small locomotive.

A man wearing a checkered flannel shirt and overalls stood up from the driver's seat and hollered over the rumbling, hissing engine that spewed puffs of smoke from its stack. "Howdy, folks. My name is Jim Cotton, and I'm about to give a demonstration." Cotton motioned to two men, who began feeding bunches of wheat headfirst into the feeder of the separator. The separated grain was elevated out the side into a grain wagon, and the straw was shot out of a blower in the rear to the ground.

Cotton cut the engine, and an animated crescendo rose out of the throng. He cupped his hands over his mouth. "I can thresh a thousand bushels a day and save you time and money. I'll be signing up anybody interested inside the Grange."

"That there was somethin' else." Etheridge said, to no one in particular. "That machine's gonna change things 'round here."

"I hear you, Bill," Dan O'Hurley said.

"Well, I figure you need at least sixty acres to make it worth your while." Etheridge clucked his tongue. "What do you think, Ned?"

"I think I'm goin' in there and sign up."

Leaving the Grange, Ned spotted Etheridge in his wagon.

"See you didn't hesitate to sign up, Ned." Etheridge's face flushed red, and his eyes seemed ready to pop. "You plannin' on doing the rest yourself?" Etheridge paused as though trying to calm himself. "That's a lot of work, even for you."

"You got someone in mind?"

"Bo Fielder asked me to see if anyone needed a hand for a couple of days during harvest. I'd be glad to bring him by."

"Bo?"

"Ned, he's a bit slow, but, being cramped up in Grove's all day, he misses the earth and soil … I know you can understand that."

Ned nodded. "All right."

Ned sunk the pitchfork into the manure and spread it in the garden. He thought about the excitement—and a bit of fear—in some faces at the threshing demonstration last week. It could change a whole lot of things in Midland, and change had a way of scaring some folks.

Ned began working the hoe, churning up the soil and chopping it down. He worked the hoe harder and harder down one row and back up as he pictured the threshing crew in his field of acres upon acres of shocked wheat ready for threshing.

At the end of a row, Ned heard a voice in the distance.

"Ned! Ned!"

Ned turned and saw Etheridge and Bo in a buckboard in front of the barn. He paused for a second, then walked over to the wagon.

"My goodness, Ned, you were working like a daggone tornado." Etheridge said through a wide smile. "Bo here is good with livestock—sorta like you with wheat."

Ned motioned to Bo. "Been a while … let me show you around."

Bo got off the buckboard and nodded his thanks to Bill.

"Now, Ned, you need anything, just give me a holler." Etheridge slackened the reins and drove off.

It started as a hum coming from the south. "Bo, hear that?" Ned asked as he inspected an egg, then placed it back into the straw loft.

Bo leaned on his pitchfork. "What is it, N-Ned?"

From the yard, Ned squinted toward the south fork as the sound grew into a low rumble. Then came a long whistle blast, shattering the quiet of morning.

Bo came from the barn. "She's a-comin', Ned."

Ned kept straining to see something.

"Not a cloud in the sky, Ned. We couldn't have a better day to thresh."

Then something black rounded the bend, glinting proudly in the early sunlight. Ned thought about the spring day Nicholas had returned to Ketchum in his great covered wagon, and how Tom had run like the wind to greet the great Ukrainian. Ned remembered how he used to think that wheat coursed through Nicholas's veins, and he couldn't help breaking a smile.

Bo caught the smile and grinned at Ned. "It sure is something. The whistle let out another long blast. "Ain't it, Ned?"

"We gonna thresh us some wheat, yessir, we're gonna. Reminds me of when old Nicholas came out of the mountains like something out of one of Mr. Sorenson's stories."

"Nicholas?"

"From back home." The threshing machine chugged toward them, and never had Ned seen a prettier sight. "I'll tell you about him during evening chores. Let's get to threshing."

The caravan rumbled into the yard, and Bo let out a long whistle. "What are all those differ-er-ent wagons for, Ned?"

"He's got two hayracks … nine, ten … an eleven-man crew, and a cook shack pulling up the rear."

"What are the goggles and handkerchiefs for?"

"You'll see."

Jim Cotton idled the engine to a low rumble. "We'll start at the low end of the field. Looks to be a good day to thrash."

Cotton lined up the caravan in the middle of the east field. His crew then unhitched the separator with the feeder facing into the wind and leveled it by shoveling dirt here and there beneath the wheels. It was just like Ned had read in his agricultural manuals. This crew knew what they were doing.

Meantime, Cotton pulled the engine around in a circle to face the separator. The crew connected the engine and thresher with a long belt, Cotton pulled on the steam whistle, and they were ready to go.

Ned and Bo stood on the periphery of the field, watching the bindlestiffs feed bundles of wheat into the separator that then delivered the grain into the grain wagon. The men all wore the goggles and handkerchiefs around their faces to protect them from the dust flying all about.

"Ain't gonna stand for that." Ned stalked over and waved to the operator to hold up. "You tell them bindlestiffs to quit horsing around and place my wheat proper into the feeder. I ain't paying to have my grain lost in a straw blower." Ned glared at the nervous, stocky man, who had a hint of gray around the temples of his close-cropped hair. Not a soul moved.

Ned bellowed, "Understand?" He only knew what he had read in his manuals about threshing machines, but he knew when good grain was being wasted.

"Yessir, Mr. Fallow." The operator glanced furtively at Cotton, then motioned to the crew. Ned glared at the bindlestiffs, none of whom appeared to be over twenty-one. They hurriedly placed the bundles into the feeder headfirst and correctly spaced.

A grin spread over Cotton's face as he nodded at Ned, as if to say, "Them boys needed to hear that."

Ned pointed Bo toward the water kegs wrapped in burlap. "Make sure they stay filled."

Bo hustled over.

Ned spotted Doc Auld and Bill Etheridge approaching in Doc's buggy. Walking over to them, he felt his spirit rising like the sun that on this day seemed to own the timid sky.

Jim Cotton gave three long toots of the whistle. The cook had set up a long folding table and chairs right in the stubble.

The ravenous crew gobbled up plates upon plates of fried chicken, steamed potatoes, salad, and biscuits, and washed them down with pitchers of lemonade. Ned's appetite had been squashed by the excitement stirring in his gut.

"Jim, that machine is something else, I tell you—something else," Etheridge said. He held a drumstick in one hand and swatted flies with the other.

"Yeah, we're gonna make a good day's run, that's for sure. Next year, I'm gonna buy a binder."

"Damned if that won't cut the workload." Etheridge wiped his mouth with his sleeve.

"Can't stop progress, no sir, you surely can't," Doc said. He looked past the group at the table, as though searching for the old days.

"Until they make a machine to control the weather, farming ain't ever gonna be easy," Cotton said between quick swallows.

"No, farming ain't ever gonna be easy, that's for sure. Well, Doc, we best be movin' on." Etheridge pushed away from the table.

Cotton swatted his cap at the blackflies descending on the food scraps. "Yeah, we best get back to work and give these pests something to think about."

As Cotton's crew lined up his caravan for departure in the yard, Ned could hardly believe the mountainous stacks of straw in the threshed field, or the bushels and bushels of grain safely stored in the grain bin.

Ned pulled a wad of bills out of his pocket and said, "What's the damage, Jim?"

Jim Cotton said, "You wanna' wait until you sell your wheat? That's how I normally do it."

"Rather pay now."

A smile spread across the thresherman's rugged face—a face that had the West written all over it. "I sure ain't gonna complain about that." Jim Cotton scratched his sandy hair, and his eyes brightened. "Let me write out a bill for you."

"Remember, I'll need you for fall harvest."

Cotton handed the invoice to Ned. "Don't you worry, I'll be back to thrash for you."

CHAPTER 19

▼

Outside the smithy, Ned put a mended wagon wheel on the back of the buck-board and headed out of town.

He pulled back on the reins, and the team slowed. The wagon rose up and then back down over a patch of ruts in the road. He one-handed the reins and swatted at the blackflies buzzing around him in the hot, sticky air.

A breeze picked up, and, off in the distance, Ned saw *it* coming. He slackened the reins and shouted, "Yoo!" The team lunged forward, knocking Ned back into his seat.

Pulling up in front of the barn, Ned felt the frightening stillness in the air. Enemies from the sky gathered in the form of sickly green clouds. It was a sky he had seen before—a deadly sky. Losing his crop in Ketchum jangled in his mind.

Ned took the team inside the barn and unhitched and stalled them. As he secured the barn doors, he heard a bolt of lightning strike nearby. Turning, he saw a splintered catalpa tree crash into the creek. A small plume of smoke rose from the remains.

Ned ran for the root cellar, covering his ears against the booming thunder.

Safely inside, Ned thought of Tom's prophetic words and his reply when Ned had lost his first crop.

"It ain't fair, Ned."

"Ain't nothing in this life fair."

Finally, the rain subsided, and there was silence. Thank goodness he had got-ten his winter wheat harvested—but was anything left of his spring wheat? He emerged above ground.

The western sky glowed shiny and new, with nary a cloud. Other than a few broken stems, his crop was okay. He took a deep breath and exhaled. "Thank you … thank you."

After inspecting the house and barn and seeing that they were fine, Ned climbed to the rise from which he could see Etheridge's place. A huge twister, spitting out of a motley yellow green cloud, spun away toward the northeast. Halfway down the rise, Ned slipped on the wet surface and fell head over heels to the bottom. He got up muddy from head to toe and ran toward his neighbor's place.

Ned bent over in Etheridge's yard, gasping for air. Straightening, he saw that the roof of the house was nowhere to be seen, and a wall of the barn lay smashed into kindling. The crop of spring wheat looked as though someone or something had roared through with violence in mind. Some plants lay about with their roots pulled from the ground, and the others were bent and drooping.

The door to the root cellar creaked open, and Etheridge emerged.

Mrs. Etheridge came out and stopped dead still, her hands covering her mouth. "Oh, dear Lord, Bill, whatever will we do?" She fell onto her knees, as if praying.

Etheridge, his face as tight as dried beef, assessed the damage. "It'll be all right, Mildred, dear." Bill went toward his wife. "It's just some wheat, a roof, and a wall—nothing that can't be fixed." He bent over, took her hand, and said, "As long as we got each other, my dear, we're going to be just fine. Now, come on up."

Ned said, "Bill, you and I can take some measurements and make a list of what we need. I'll run it over to Hungerford's, then I'll go to town and get folks here first thing in the morning. Fella once told me that we help each other out around here."

Etheridge turned to Ned, and his eyes widened, as though recognizing him for the first time. His face had soon adopted its usual friendly expression, save a trace of concern. He smiled softly at Ned. "Thank you, neighbor."

Approaching Etheridge's place with toolbox in hand, Ned heard banging hammers and the busy voices of working folk interrupting the quiet of daybreak. Coming round the bend, he spotted nearly twenty men already clearing off the damaged material from the barn and house.

In the yard, some women plucked chickens, while others entered the house with brooms, pots and pans, and plates and bowls piled high with food. They moved about with a purposeful righteousness, and were in and out of the house like worker bees.

Inside the barn, Shorty Swanson helped load broken timbers onto a buckboard. "Surprised I beat you here, Fallow?"

Ned grabbed a hammer and began pulling out damaged wallboards. "I don't spend much time in dwellin' on your movements, Swanson."

Shorty left the group of men loading the wagon and walked over to Ned. "I was born and bred in Midland. Person needs help, I'm there. No questions asked."

Ned noticed that Shorty's normally droopy eyes seemed wide and confident. "Swanson, why don't you quit yammering," he said as he yanked a plank from the broken wall to the ground, "and work?" Ned leveled his gaze on Shorty.

"I was in this town before you, Fallow, and I'll be in this town after you done packed up and left." Shorty thrust out his jaw in spite and went into the yard, where two big wagons of lumber were rumbling in.

Shorty motioned to Bo. "Come on, let's give them a hand."

The first wagon creaked to a halt, and the big workhorses snorted their displeasure at pulling such a heavy load.

"H-hey, Remus." Bo looked up at the driver's seat.

"Bo. Shorty." Remus got off the wagon and plopped his hand down on a thick, rough-cut beam that ran the length of the wagon and hung a good three feet over the back. "This lumber is heavy. Gonna need some help gettin' it off."

"Us three can handle it, Remus," Shorty said.

"Hey, N-Ned, can you give us a h-hand?" Bo waved to Ned, who was hauling a large broken section of a stall to a rubble pile in the yard.

Ned dropped the debris into the pile, where it made a great thudding sound. "Sure."

Shorty grabbed his cheek to quell a twitch. "Dammit, Bo, we can handle this."

Remus scratched under his neck. "Shorty, we ain't got time for none of your nonsense today. Ned, you and Shorty grab the back end, and Bo and I will get up on the wagon and get the other."

Shorty said, "Fallow, I'm gonna get under and wrap my fingers around the top; then we can raise 'er up."

Ned hunched his shoulder under the great timber and put his hand on top. He then stood straight up, lifting his end up. Shorty hung on with his feet dangling off the ground.

Ned looked over his back and said, "Be right easier, Swanson, if I didn't have to carry you along."

Shorty dropped to the ground and looked around to see a group of snickering men pointing at him. He scrambled onto the wagon to help Bo and Remus ease the timber off as Ned moved forward. When they got to the wagon's edge, the three jumped off and lifted it from the bottom. "Head over toward them saw-horses, Ned." Remus hollered.

Ned placed his end on top of a sawhorse, grabbed the other sawhorse, and placed it under where Shorty and the other men stood.

"N-Ned, you some k-kinda strong," Bo said.

Remus gave his head a shake, "That's what I like to call country strong."

Shorty's face flushed red. His confident swagger had been destroyed by one great raising of Ned Fallow's shoulders.

Ned gathered shards of glass inside the barn and placed them in a bucket. He had meant to embarrass Swanson, but he now felt guilty about the men making fun of him. The little man tried to hide it, but Ned saw defeat in his sad, hound dog eyes. He knew that Swanson had just been feeling his oats when he had sassed Ned in the morning, trying to impress the other men. Ned should have let him have his bit of sunshine. He thought of William O'Connor's old saying: "Every dog needs a bone once in a while to let him know he's still a dog."

Around noon, Ned heard a bell ringing from the front porch. Everyone stopped working and went over to long, planked tables under an elm tree by the house. They were brimming with fried chicken, potatoes, biscuits, fried green tomatoes, succotash, and apple and cherry pies.

Sitting at the end of a table, Ned bit into a juicy drumstick. The women hovered around, keeping the jugs of lemonade full and the platters brimming with food. He figured that they had arrived before sunrise, and he imagined them in the yard in their aprons, cutting off chicken heads and dressing the birds, their voices quiet, as though they didn't want to disturb the darkness. Others would have been on the porch washing vegetables in basins, and others in the kitchen kneading dough and tending to pots of food boiling on the stove.

At dusk, Ned and a few other men tied down the last of the damaged stalks and stacked them in the field. Over at the barn, the new wall was now complete, and the house was as good as new. Their voices grew quieter and their footsteps more measured as a happy weariness overcame the helpers.

On the porch, Etheridge and his wife held hands. They watched the men pack up tool boxes and the women load pots and pans onto wagons. Bill motioned for the people to gather. "Could everyone come on over? First off, I expect to see everybody tomorrow at the Fourth of July dance at the Grange, 'cause I'll be supplying the refreshments." A great cheer rose from the men. "Secondly, the wife and I appreciate all your help. I must have the best neighbors any man could ever ask for." He put his arm around his wife's shoulder, and their heads touched.

He's got something special with that woman, Ned thought.

CHAPTER 20

▼

Lily Thomason sat in the sunroom, reading. She leaned forward in the high-backed chair and poured tea into a porcelain teacup stationed on a polished mahogany table.

She heard the iron gate in the front yard clang shut and saw her father coming up the front walk.

She went to the front door and opened it. "Welcome home, Father."

A smile came over Vernon Thomason's long, fleshy face that was crowned by a great, bald head. "Hello, Lily. What more could a father ask for than to have his beautiful daughter greet him after three days on the road?" Vernon placed his briefcase down on the marble floor of the foyer and kissed his daughter. "Where is your mother?"

Just then, a door opened on the second floor and Sarah Thomason came up to the railing. "Vernon, you're early." She walked down the sweeping staircase and kissed her husband on the cheek.

Lily motioned toward the sunroom. "I have tea."

"Splendid," Lily's mother said as she primped her hair. "Vernon, you can tell us about your trip."

Lily poured tea into two cups, placed them on saucers, and handed one each to her parents.

"Vernon, you must tell us how the Groves are doing," Sarah said.

Vernon placed his tea on the table, and his large, bulging eyes seemed ready to pop from their sockets. "How could I forget. I have some news for you, Lily."

Sarah turned a sharp eye on her husband. "What possible news could Hank and Henrietta have from a place like Midland?"

"They need a schoolteacher."

"Really?—"

"What?" Sarah cut in. "Lily did *not* spend four years at the University to teach a bunch of hayseeds and country rubes."

"Mother, please let me speak for myself."

"What is there—"

"Sarah, let the girl talk."

"Why should I sit around Abilene waiting for an opening? It might be a good adventure to spend time in Midland."

Sarah leveled her gaze on her daughter, sat back, and crossed her arms across her chest. "And what do you think Ted will have to say about all this?"

Lily sat in the hanging rocker on the porch, waiting for Ted Riggins. Before long, he appeared around the hedgerow and came up the brick sidewalk. He wore a light gray suit and notch-collared vest. He was of medium size, with wavy golden hair and those pale blue eyes that had drawn Lily in from the first. He had a soft, delicate face, with a nip of pink in the cheeks. He looked every bit the up-and-coming businessman.

Ted had a confident air that some of Lily's friends from the Literary Society found a bit much. They had never said as much, but she could see it in the quick glances they shot at Lily after one of Ted's sharp defenses of the railroads or one of his railings against the Populist Party as a threat to free enterprise. "If the farmers and Populists in this state don't like the freight rates, let them build their own railroad." Ted had said more than once.

Although his opinions sometimes gave Lily pause, she tried to concentrate on the gentleman who opened doors, drew back dinner chairs, and made such witty conversation with her parents. "A young man like Ted Riggins doesn't come around every day, dear," Lily's mother had said after the first time she met him. Yes, Ted Riggins was her mother's ideal son-in-law.

Lily waved to Riggins as he opened the front gate. She had decided to just come out tell him her plans. She had thought Ted Riggins a reasonable person, but ...

"Lily," Riggins said as his confident smile faded, "whatever would make you want to leave Abilene and waste your time teaching those yokels?"

"Those *yokels* are the ones who grow the crops that allow people like you to make a comfortable living without ever getting your hands dirty."

Riggins took her hand. "So now I'm to understand that you think less of me because I work for a bank and not behind a plow?" He put his other hand on her shoulder. "Listen to reason, Lily. we have a social standing in this town. It doesn't look good for my future wife to be traipsing off to some hick town to teach ignorant farmhands."

Lily pulled her hand away. "I'm a teacher, Ted, and that means a great deal to me."

"I don't like it, Lily."

Lily looked out the train window, and Midland, Kansas, came into view. It seemed a tiny little nothing of a place—a fragile collection of two-story clapboard buildings in the middle of a lonesome prairie. For miles, she had seen nothing but monotonous stretches of wheat fields and grassland. All the farms had seemed alike—a white A-frame house, a red barn, and a whirling windmill. Already, she was feeling homesick for Abilene and its music hall, the new library filled with a variety of fascinating books, and the Literary Society. As the engine groaned and hissed to a stop, Lily started to have doubts about the wisdom of this adventure. Two thoughts kept these doubts from growing—she was away from her mother's scrutiny, and, dare she think it, away from Ted Riggins's sharp words and unpleasant attitude regarding her choice.

The conductor assisted Lily down the steps into a light mist of steam rising from the train's undercarriage.

Lily heard a woman's voice chirp, "Lily. Lily, dear."

Lily waved to Hank and Henrietta Grove, who approached her. "Hello. Thank you so much for taking me in on such short notice."

"Why, anything for the daughter of our dearest friends in Abilene. My goodness, haven't you grown into a beautiful young woman." Henrietta opened her arms and hugged Lily.

Hank said, "Hello, Lily." He then gave her a welcoming hug.

"I hope this isn't too much of an imposition."

"Not at all, dear." Mrs. Grove smiled. "Now, let's get you home, and we can have a nice chat in the parlor."

Lily sat between the couple as their wagon eased up the town's main street. There was a coziness to this place—geraniums and pansies in window boxes, neatly trimmed buildings that all seemed freshly painted, and smiling faces on the street. "Hello, Hank and Henrietta," a heavy-set, middle-aged man in bib overalls hollered from the boardwalk. He tipped his straw hat to Lily and offered a gap-toothed smile. *What a friendly face,* Lily thought.

The wagon creaked along, and there were more waves and hollers from people. This was a welcome change from Abilene, where most people were strangers to one another.

Henrietta Grove placed the tray on the table and sat next to Lily on the loveseat. Hank sat in an easy chair in the corner, a folded newspaper in his lap.

Henrietta poured out the tea. "I miss having tea with your mother back in Abilene. We always considered ourselves kindred spirits. Do you take cream, Lily?"

"Nothing in my tea, thank you."

Hank started to open the paper and paused. "Is this your first teaching job, Lily?"

Lily nodded her thanks as Henrietta handed her a teacup. "Yes. Tomorrow, I meet with the superintendent at the school and review my curriculum. Later in the week, I'll pick up my textbooks."

Henrietta placed her hand on Lily's. "I have a grand idea. Hank, you've been wanting help on Saturdays at the store."

Hank looked up from his newspaper, and a hint of a smile cracked the corner of his mouth. "Lily, if you'd like to earn some extra money, I could use the help."

"That would be wonderful. And it would give me a real chance to meet people."

Hank leaned back in his chair. "Sure won't hurt business any to have a pretty girl working behind the counter."

Henrietta rattled her cup on its saucer. "Hank Grove! You're going to embarrass the girl."

Lily smiled to herself and thought that maybe Midland, Kansas, might not be so bad after all.

PART 3

CHAPTER 21

▼

In the resurrection or destruction of a man's soul, one usually finds a woman's touch ...

As a brisk wind swirled across the train-depot platform, Ned passed a woman with the hood of a cloak tight over her head. He stopped at the far end, near the grain elevator. Down the tracks, a puff of white smoke wafted over a stand of oak trees, followed by the faint sound of a train whistle.

Ned heard footsteps on the wooden platform and turned to see the woman now standing near him. She removed the cloak from her head, revealing honey-colored hair that complemented a golden face highlighted by high cheek-bones. She had the air of a well-to-do country girl.

Ned nodded a hello.

A polite smile creased her lips.

As the train clattered and groaned to a stop, a conductor came off a passenger car and walked toward Ned and the young woman. His rumpled blue uniform, gray hair draping over his collar, protruding belly lapping his white shirt over his belt buckle, and old, worn brown shoes hinted more than a little at veteran rail-road man. He looked at Ned, then the woman, and tipped his hat. "Mike O'Shaughnessy, at your service. May I help you, miss?"

"Yes, I'm Lily Thomason. I'm here to pick up readers for the Midland school."

"You must be the new schoolmarm. I'll be right with you." The conductor turned to Ned. "Give me a minute to help this lady."

Mike O'Shaughnessy opened the boxcar door, grabbed a small ladder from inside, attached it to the catwalk, and climbed inside.

After struggling to get two crates to the edge of the boxcar, he returned from the rear of the car and handed a package to Ned. "There you go, Ned Fallow—more journals."

Ned took his package and began to walk away.

"Say, Ned. Would you mind giving Miss …"

"Thomason. Lily Thomason."

"… Miss Thomason a hand getting these boxes to the school?"

"All right." Ned walked up to the boxcar door and hoisted one crate after the other from chest level down to the platform.

O'Shaughnessy let out a long whistle. "Picks them up like they were nothing."

The crates of books thumped down as Ned placed them in the back of the wagon. He took his package from Lily and placed it beside them.

"Thank you so much, Mr. Fallow," Lily said as they got on the buckboard. "I don't know what I was thinking, coming to pick up these books on foot."

Ned nodded, slackened the reins, and steered the wagon toward the schoolhouse at the edge of town.

Passing through town, Lily saw a man come out of the blacksmith's shop staring daggers at Mr. Fallow, with eyes as black as coal. There was an aura of evil about this dark, foul-looking man.

Ned Fallow shot a hard, cold glare at the man, then turned back to the road.

The beady eyes then fixed on Lily, and a lecherous, crooked smile emerged, revealing snarled, crooked teeth. A hollow chill shot through her.

At the edge of town, Lily looked over her shoulder and saw that the man was gone. Her curiosity was overruled by her good manners, and she said, "I couldn't help overhearing about your journals. What type are they?"

"Wheat."

"Yes, I've learned wheat is king in these parts."

Ned pulled up beside an old chestnut tree at the school, and fallen nuts crunched under the wagon wheels. He looked past Lily toward the school. "Where you want 'em?"

"Excuse me, Mr. Fallow, but where did you learn your manners?"

Lily jumped off the wagon, walked to the front door of the school, and opened it. "If you would be so kind," Lily pointed to a room in the back, "as to put the crates in the back, you can be on your way."

The clacking of Mrs. Grove's darning needles greeted Lily as she entered the parlor. Sitting in her easy chair, the landlady peered over her glasses and rested the needles on the calico pattern in her lap. "Lily, dear, did you manage to get the books to school all right?"

"Why, yes. A man named Ned Fallow helped me out."

Mrs. Grove's eyebrows arched up. "Ned Fallow? That's one fine-looking young man."

Feeling a slight flush rise in her cheeks, Lily looked down for a second, then rose to meet Henrietta's gaze.

Mrs. Grove continued, "Fine looking, he surely is, but Hank tells me he's as hard as any man he ever met. Got one interest—growing wheat. I don't ever recall seeing him at a social event in all the years he's lived in Midland. When he comes into the store, he picks up his order and leaves. Never so much as a howdy-do." A thin smile crossed her face.

"I'm looking forward so much to working Saturdays at the store," Lily said.

Mrs. Grove removed her glasses and rubbed under her eye with her index finger. "How nice, dear."

Business at Grove's slowed to a trickle as the afternoon pushed on. In the morning, Lily had met Bo Fielder and Shorty Swanson, who blushed like a schoolboy when she shook his hand and said, "So nice to meet you, Shorty."

"My pleasure, Miss Lily." Shorty raised his hand to his cheek to quell a twitch. "You need help with anything—anything at all—you let me know."

Hank looked up from placing brad nails in his apron. "All right, Shorty, let's get to work. Now, Lily ..." Hank brought out a thick leather book from under the counter, "... let me show you how I keep my books."

With that, Lily started work at Grove's General Store. She rang up sales to smiling, friendly faces. "We're looking forward to you teaching the children," said one mother, her hands on the heads of two tow-headed boys.

"You must come by for dinner after you've settled in," said another.

"You need any help fixin' up the school, give me a holler," said the gap-toothed gentleman who had waved hello on her first day in town. "Bill Etheridge, here. Just call me Bill."

As Lily looked over the now-quiet store, she thought that although the people in Abilene were well mannered, for the most part, the warmth and genuine kindness of the citizens of Midland, Kansas, was something new.

Hank Grove came out of the storage room holding a bookkeeping journal. "Lily, can you check my figures and watch things for a while? I got some errands to run." Hank placed the journal on the counter.

"Why, certainly, Mr. Grove."

Hank walked to the front door, stopped, and turned back toward Lily. "Oh, if Ned Fallow comes by to pick up his order, it's along the back wall in the storage room. Also, give him his bill for the month."

She smiled. "All right."

Late that afternoon, Lily, alone in the store, saw Ned pulling up in his buckboard.

The door opened, and there he stood, almost filling the doorway. Ned walked toward the counter. "I have an order to pick up."

"I need to add up your bill. Would you like a cup of coffee?"

"How 'bout I get the order, and you total the bill."

"How about you drink the coffee while I add the bill, and then I can show you where your order is?"

Ned shook his head and rubbed the back of his neck. "Never thought I'd wish for Swanson to wait on me."

Lily pointed to the potbellied stove and began to total Ned's bill.

Ned muttered something under his breath and retreated to the stove.

Lily tapped the pencil point on the paper for emphasis. "Here's your bill, Mr. Fallow."

Ned took a last swallow of his coffee, returned to the counter, and paid Lily.

Placing the change in his hand, she noticed that it was as rough as sandpaper. She thought of how different it was from Ted Riggins's soft, pink palm.

"Thank you, Mr. Fallow." Lily forced a smile at Ned, who dismissed it and headed for the storage room.

Lily wanted to say something to this impudent wheat farmer, but she decided to be the bigger person. She went to the back and watched as he began hauling out his order.

Ned tossed the last sack onto the wagon and got on board.

As the clatter of the departing wagon grew fainter, Lily went to the window. At the edge of town, past the Grange Hall, Ned Fallow steered right and headed toward a thin, gray horizon where a hint of sunlight lingered.

CHAPTER 22

▼

Union Pacific Mixed Train #544 clickety-clacked along at a good pace. The steam engine's loud whistle stirred Ned from a light sleep as the train pulled into a small town much like Midland.

He looked out the window and saw thistles on the side of a berm, tenuously hanging on until the snow melted into the earth and the sun sat high and strong in the sky. Although Kansans considered it a hostile invader, a part of Ned had always admired the thistle's tough durability and resilience to drought—it was like an iron weed.

The drought had reinforced the need to make money. "Company needs a strong fella over the winter to make some special deliveries to Abilene," Mike O'Shaughnessy had said to Ned. *The part-time work will help,* he thought as the train rounded the bend, bringing the Abilene skyline into view.

The town looked like a collection of miniature buildings under the great blue horizon, which seemed to stretch on and on. It didn't look like a city, but a made-up place that had popped up from the earth. So fragile and tiny, it seemed as though the sky might swallow it up in a great gust of wind.

As the train pulled in to the Union Pacific station, Ned took in the long, three-story brick depot with six chimneys and two rows of long Victorian windows framed by arched wooden shutters. A tin overhang supported by posts jutted out from the first floor. There was grace, charm, and beauty to this structure.

Ned and Mike O'Shaughnessy handed their baggage to a porter and walked to the rear of the train. Ned opened a boxcar door, placed his hands on the floor, and lifted himself into the car.

O'Shaughnessy watched from the platform as Ned began bringing crates and boxes of various sizes to the door.

After hitching his belt up over his ample stomach, O'Shaughnessy pulled the stogie from his mouth and flicked ashes away from his uniform. "When you lifted those crates for the schoolmarm, I said to myself, 'Now, *there's* a fella who's got a grip.'"

Ned jumped off the car.

O'Shaughnessy took off his dark blue conductor hat and gave his head a thoughtful scratch. After a short drag on his cigar, he turned a probing eye toward Ned. "That girl sure is a pretty thing. She still teaching in Midland?"

"Yes." Ned spotted a large dray with four draft horses at the side of the depot.

O'Shaughnessy flicked more ashes from his coat and straightened himself. "What's she like?"

"Snooty." Ned began moving the boxes from the car over to the wagon.

O'Shaughnessy ambled over to the wagon as Ned kept hoisting the crates from the boxcar up against his chest, short-stepping his way over to the wagon, dropping them, and pushing them to the wagon's rear. He quickened his pace, trying to avoid the railroad man's incessant chatter.

O'Shaughnessy followed Ned back to the car, to the last and biggest crate. Ned wrapped his arms around it and eased it off the boxcar. Straining, he turned and moved toward the wagon with O'Shaughnessy pulling up his rear. "Big, handsome man like you and her would make a fine-looking couple."

Ned leaned back and dropped the crate onto the wagon with a heavy thud. "You gonna rankle me or let me work?"

"Easy there, big fella."

"Mike, she's engaged."

O'Shaughnessy waved his hand, as though he had just figured something out. "That's the load. Get on, and I'll drive it over to the storage garage."

Ned began to relax as he listened to the rhythm of the clopping horses' hooves and felt the wagon rocking over the bumps of the dirt road. He thought back to his stopping by every Saturday at Grove's, and always searching for her. Yes, he had to admit that Lily Thomason was pretty. As a matter of fact, after leaving Grove's, that golden face would stay stuck in his head the whole ride home, and then some. Also, come Fridays, he found himself already thinking about his trip into town and seeing her smiling face behind the counter. Not only was Lily Thomason easy on the eyes, she had a natural way about her in dealing with folks. Ned couldn't be sure, but he thought he had seen her stealing glances at him as he loitered at Grove's front door. But what was the use? She was spoken for.

Ned joined O'Shaughnessy in the dining room of the Sycamore Hotel. Like the rest of the hotel, it had the warm charm of stained wood and tasteful furnishings. Heavy voices, soft feminine laughs, and the clinking of glasses resonated in the plush room. The confluence of sounds came in waves, each like a separate crescendo rising up before fading into the high ceiling. From his seat, Ned gazed up and admired the intricate arrangement of beams, each stained a deep russet and edged with fluted cornices. His gaze ran past the reception desk to a double-wide stairway with hand-carved balusters leading to a cantilevered balcony. The place had the smell of sizzling steaks cooked in freshly churned butter and spices mixing with good leather and fine upholstery. The Sycamore was a very fine hotel.

Their waiter, an older man dressed in jacket and bow tie, introduced himself as Sims. He was short, with thinning, close-cropped hair that rested on a square head, and he had round, deep-set eyes. Ned wondered if Sims was his first or last name. The waiter spoke with an accent Ned figured to be British.

After taking their order, Sims turned his attention one table over, to a noisy group of young men dressed in expensive suits. One of the men jabbed his index finger on the table. "Sims, see here. When I order a bottle of cognac, I expect brandy snifters, not *these*." The man raised a shot glass to Sims's face.

"Forgive me, Mr. Riggins, but we are short at the moment." Sims bowed to the man.

The man waved Sims off. "Little man, I am growing tired of your excuses every time I come in here."

In a raised voice, Ned said, "I'd say the *real* little man was the tenderfoot being waited on." He glared at the Riggins.

Riggins stood, seeming to ignore Ned's remark. "Gentlemen, excuse me while I adjourn to more hospitable quarters." He looked sharply at Ned and ran his gaze over Ned's worsted jacket and plaid shirt. He squinted, as if to say, "Who let the likes of *you* in here?" He dropped his cloth napkin onto the table and walked away.

O'Shaughnessy pushed back from his empty plate and stoked a cigar. "That was a fine meal, and all compliments of the Union Pacific." He raised his head and blew a ring of smoke. "Love this country. Where else could a Mick like me get waited on all proper and such by an Englishman? Come on over to the backroom bar, lad, and join me in tippin' a few."

Ned looked up from his plate, which was empty save for the bone of his steak. "Backroom bar?"

"Aye … Terrible thing, lad, Kansas being a dry state. One has to know the hidden nooks where a man can indulge in a libation."

"All right. Show me the way."

Ned enjoyed the comfort of the backroom bar with its grand wooden beams running across the ceiling and the stained glass behind the bar, where bottles of whiskey were arrayed in tiers. His grandfather would have loved this place. He felt a hint of shame come over him—it had been so long since he had thought of his family.

O'Shaughnessy ordered another round and paid the bartender. "One more, lad, and then we'd best call it a night. We got an early train to load in the mornin'."

O'Shaughnessy took two long swallows, draining his beer.

"You head on up. I'll be a little longer." Ned took a sip on his beer.

"Good evening to you, Ned." O'Shaughnessy pulled his belt back up and over his stomach, and he left the bar.

On his way out a little later, Ned passed a painted mural in the lobby. It was a grand painting of a threshing crew. A mellow sun anchored in a rich blue sky provided a backdrop to the separator and threshermen in the golden field of wheat.

"It can touch a person's soul." Sims looked up at Ned with big, inquisitive eyes.

"That it can."

A frown furrowed over the little Englishman's forehead. "Retiring for the evening?"

"Thought I'd take a walk and maybe find a little place to have a beer."

"Yes, I see. Well, it is Friday night, so I might suggest you try the backroom at Emerson's Tool and Die. Now, it's a bit frayed around the edges …" Sims raised his shoulders as if to say that it would do, "… but I think you might find it interesting."

"Would you join me?" Ned put out his hand. "Ned Fallow here."

"Sims here. It would be my pleasure."

Ned and Sims walked two blocks and turned right at a tannery onto a cobblestone street lined with warehouses.

At the end of the street sat a two-story brick building. Around the corner, at the back of the building, a set of steps led to an entranceway. The wrought-iron hinges of the vertically planked door creaked as the two men entered a small vestibule with a batten door on the other side. Sims knocked, and a peephole opened. "Yeah?"

"Sims from the Sycamore."

Inside, an empty brick fireplace with a raised hearth sat at the far wall, and a round bar with stools anchored the middle of the room. A few shadowy forms sat at tables in an alcove to Ned's and Sims's left. They took a seat at the bar, where a bartender with a rag over his shoulder chatted with two men.

"What'll it be, there?" The bartender had graying hair, whiskey-burned cheeks, and a crooked nose. Ned caught a flicker of wilderness hidden in his tired eyes and guessed that he had been a formidable man in his day. His thick neck and shoulders seemed to verify Ned's appraisal.

"Beer."

"Cognac."

Sims took his glass from the bartender and raised it to Ned. "Cheers."

Just as Ned clinked Sims's glass, a commotion came from a table in the alcove. A shrill woman's voice shouted, "I ought to just tell them about you! Yes, that's just what I should do."

The bartender leaned on the bar. "Get all types in here."

Ned took a swallow and nodded.

"Take them lovebirds back there."

The bartender pointed a thick, gnarled finger toward the shadowy figures of a woman and man talking in hushed tones. The man stood up, and Ned recognized him as Sims's rude customer from earlier in the evening. The man placed his hand under the woman's chin, and she pushed it away. The man stumbled toward the bar.

Ned noticed a smooth, soft hand drumming the bar top while the other motioned for two drinks. They were delicate hands, like a woman's. The tailored sleeve of his suit and his white cuffs suggested to Ned a young businessman who had never done a day's labor in his life.

A soft hand pointed to Sims's drink. "I see they let the hired help in this place—and he's drinking cognac from a brandy snifter, no less."

Ned stood, grabbed the man's fancy lapel, and pulled him in close. The weak body offered little resistance.

Sims put a hand on Ned's arm. "It's all right, Ned."

Ned released his grip. The man backed off a step, his eyes on Ned. He looked as if he were going to speak, but seemed to think better of it. He took his drinks from the bartender and returned to his seat.

Sims motioned for two more drinks. "That chap is very well connected in Abilene. Family is in the banking business."

Ned nodded his thanks to the bartender and took his beer. "That doesn't give him the right to treat you like that."

"Sad thing …" Sims stared into his cognac. "He's marrying a wonderful girl—a schoolteacher on assignment in the hinterlands, whose family I have waited on for years. They don't realize what type of person he is."

Ned put his mug carefully on the bar and turned to Sims. "Her name wouldn't be Lily Thomason, would it?"

The train's whistle blast stirred Ned from a light sleep. Outside, he could see the familiar sight of Midland's grain elevator in the distance. The sliding door opened, and O'Shaughnessy entered the car. "Ned, detectives got a couple of wetbacks they found in a boxcar. Say they work for you."

Ned sat up. "César and Tino?"

Ned and O'Shaughnessy entered the boxcar, where two small men sat on the floor, handcuffed back-to-back. Their heads, two tangles of matted black hair, jolted up. "Mr. Ned!" César's dark eyes looked like those of a trapped animal. Those eyes full of fear and anguish told Ned all he needed to know about what their lives had been like since they left. Their ragged clothes hung loosely on their gaunt bodies. They looked to have aged threefold.

"Amigos." Ned nodded at O'Shaughnessy. "That's them."

Ned poured two cups of water from a pitcher on the kitchen table and motioned for the men to sit. "How about some grub?"

"*Sí.*" César's eyes, lined red, smiled meekly at Ned.

Ned reckoned that he was seeing real hunger.

"Go ahead, have a seat. I'll get something rustled up." Ned knocked the ashes through the grate of the cast-iron stove and lit it. He sank two big spoons into the lard barrel and placed the fat in two skillets on the stovetop. He then went to a small storage shed at the side of the house and cut off a slab of the smoked pork ribs that hung from a horizontal board.

As one pan crackled and sizzled with bits of pork fat, Ned sliced potatoes and onions and put them in the other pan, adding salt and pepper. He lowered the heat and covered both pans. While the food cooked, he sliced up tomatoes, carrots, cabbage, and green peppers, and filled two bowls with them.

As César and Tino chomped and chewed on the raw vegetables, an image of his grandfather's stories of the Irish Famine came to Ned's mind.

Ned placed the contents of the two skillets into a bowl and mixed them together. The heat and aroma of the pork drew César and Tino's hungry eyes toward Ned, who ladled the food onto the two skillets that had been used for cooking.

Ned brought a crusty loaf of bread to the table. Greedy brown fingers with dirt packed under the nails tore off chunks, which they used to clean the grease and gristle from the pans, until only bones, picked clean, remained.

"*Muy bien, gracias,*" César said in a thin, tired voice.

"You two go to the well and wash up, and I'll set up some blankets for you." Ned pointed to their old room off the front door.

Tino struggled to keep his eyes from blinking shut as his head nodded off to the side. "We work, Mr. Ned," he said, raising his sleepy eyelids.

"Work tomorrow. Now, go." Ned handed Tino a bar of lye soap and a bowl.

That evening, Ned sat on the porch and thought about his lot in life. It seemed pretty good when stacked up against what his two amigos endured every day.

He took a deep breath and scanned the western horizon. The waxing moon was in the first quarter, and the sky was awash with stars. Just then, a meteor blazed low across the sky. The wheat field shone in an iridescent glow of gold, red, and yellow. In an instant, the shooting star was gone.

Ned fell fast asleep and dreamed about his granddad's tales of Indian legends. He saw himself and Tom sitting on the porch, Indian-style, while William sat in his rocker.

"Watch now how the coyote does things." William pointed to a scraggly coyote watching a prairie-dog hole. "He doesn't just run to the bait hellity-larrup. No, sir, he sits back and figures. 'Let's think it over, first.'"

Tom and William then faded from the dream, and Ned sat alone on the porch. Their absence felt like losing a chunk of his heart.

Over on the horizon, the coyote waited patiently.

CHAPTER 23

▼

"Nothing like a pretty girl ..." Pete Lomax shifted his slit eyes from Lily to Hank Grove, "... to keep me a-comin' in every Saturday."

Hank placed his hands on the counter. "What can I get you, Pete?"

"Not sure you got what I need." Lomax said through a crooked smile as he tapped his knuckles on the counter. He turned and headed for the door.

Lily watched Lomax cross the street and head down the boardwalk. More than his suggestive words, it was Pete Lomax's sinister eyes that frightened her. Every time he came into the store, those eyes followed her.

The front door opened again, and Bill Etheridge came in. He said hello to Hank, who was putting another log into the potbellied stove, and came to the front counter.

"Good morning, Lily."

Lily, wrapping up a pound of cheese, smiled hello.

"Did the new flannel shirts arrive?"

Lily rang up the cheese order. "Yes ... they're all the way in the back, and down the aisle."

Etheridge turned to go, then stopped. "You know, Mildred loves the piano lessons, and all the folks are raving about your teaching. You're becoming a real asset to Midland."

"That's very kind of you to say." Lily smiled at Etheridge, who then made his way to the back of the store.

As the day wore on, customers came and went. Lily saw Ned Fallow come in and stand off to the side, squinting from the afternoon shadow that slanted through the store's front window.

"Help you get your order, Ned?" Hank asked.

"Not yet. I'm just gonna look around." Ned shifted his gaze toward Hank, and then to the front counter and Lily.

Ned wandered around for a bit, then stepped toward the door.

"Ned, you forgot your order," Hank said, more as a question.

"I'll come back in a bit. Just remembered, I need to check on a harness at the blacksmith's before he closes." Ned looked briefly at Hank, then rested his gaze on Lily.

"Fine and dandy, Ned." Hank adjusted his wire-rimmed glasses on his nose and nodded at Ned.

Lily watched Ned cross the street and mount the boardwalk, where people bustled about, wrapping their coats tight against the chill November air.

North of town, off in the distance, dark and tumultuous clouds gathered. A cold rain was probable.

Lily stood behind the counter and went over the inventory as the last of the customers trickled out. She had seen Ned come in, then leave so suddenly, and it had made her wonder. His presence every Saturday had made it clear that the quiet, stoic man was interested in her—but what a strange way he showed it, with those silent glances.

Ted Riggins and Abilene seemed so removed from her now. One of the older boys at school had started bringing pies to her on Fridays, and now all the kids had their mothers bake cookies or pies for her. Lily felt a close bond with her students and their families.

She enjoyed helping customers fuss over what chocolate to pick, and even the everyday conversation with folks about the weather and such. Plus, she enjoyed giving the piano lessons at the Groves' house. Everything about Midland appealed to her, and going back to Abilene seemed so … well, it was best not dwell on it too much now.

"But, boss, I've made plans." Lily heard Shorty's warbled plea to Hank as the two men came out of the storage room.

"Look, Shorty, Ned will be here in a bit. Then, you can go."

Lily looked up from her bookkeeping. "I don't mind staying a little late." She smiled at Shorty. "I've got to go over the books for last month, anyway."

A grin slashed Shorty's face. "Thank you, Miss Lily. Is it all right with you, boss?"

Hank's eyes crinkled as a small smile crept up in the corners of his mouth. "Why, that's just fine."

Hank and Shorty soon departed, leaving Lily alone in the store.

Lily heard the front door jingle open and looked up. "Just forgot something in the back," Shorty said as he scurried into the back room.

Her eyes followed Shorty into the storage room and back out the front door. Lily returned to her journal, but she sensed a presence in the room.

A tapping noise came from the far end of the counter. Pete Lomax drummed his fingers on the countertop, looking at Lily with a crooked smile. There was a restless, threatening energy about him.

Lily heard herself gasp. It felt as though the air had fled her lungs. "Oh, Mr. Lomax. You gave me a start. I didn't see you come in."

Lomax ambled over toward Lily, his fingers still thumping along the counter-top. He stood at the front counter across from her, his face marked with an animal hunger. "You look to be all alone. Now, a pretty young thing like you shouldn't *ever* be alone."

Fear rose in her throat. Lomax's dark eyes looked like those of a stalking predator. He lunged over the counter, grabbed her shoulders, and kissed her. She tried to squirm away from his stubbly face, but his grip was ironclad. She felt his coarse tongue penetrating her mouth, and his breath smelled of alcohol and strong tobacco.

"Now, we gonna get acquainted proper." Lomax wrapped his arms around Lily and lifted her over the counter. She hit him behind his shoulders as he brought her in tight, jabbing his tongue down her throat, causing her to gag.

"Stop! Stop!" Lily coughed out. She grew faint as she felt her feet being lifted off the ground. Lomax brought her down on the floor. He raised up her dress and started pulling off her undergarment. Lily tried to scream, but nothing came out.

The grunting Lomax had the undergarment down to her knees, and his hand started up her leg.

The front door opened. From the corner of her eye, Lily saw Ned Fallow, under a full head of steam, striding toward them.

Lomax rolled off, and Lily scrambled away.

Lomax turned, and Ned grazed him with a kick to the head. Ned kicked again, but Lomax caught his foot. Ned went down, with Lomax rolling on top of him. Lomax raised his fist, but Ned blocked it with his forearm and pushed Lomax back.

Ned got to his feet, and Lomax butted him in the stomach. Both tumbled to the floor, swinging wildly.

The thumps of fists hitting flesh and the cracks of their heads ramming horrified Lily.

Ned rolled on top of Lomax, who squirmed away kicking. They scrambled to their feet, and Ned, his eyes red like those of a wild bull, came at Lomax, who swung for all he had. Ned took the onslaught and came in close, engulfing Lomax in a bear hug.

Ned raised Lomax off his feet, leaned back, then stepped forward, banging his adversary into the counter. Candy jars crashed to the floor, and gumdrops and rock candy clattered every which way. Lomax flailed at Ned and even bit into his shoulder, but Ned kept squeezing tighter and tighter, like a great human vise.

Lomax moaned, and he reminded Lily of a squirming rat caught in a trap. Lomax's eyes fell dead, and his head dropped to his side. "Ned, he's unconscious … you can let him go. Lily ran over and grabbed Ned's arm. "Ned, you're killing him!"

Ned released his grip, and Lomax dropped to the floor. When Lomax began to stir, Ned grabbed him by the collar and dragged him toward the door. The heels of Lomax's boots clattered over the small gaps in the hard-planked floor. Ned opened the front door to a gusting rain, grabbed Lomax by the scruff of his neck, and tossed the scoundrel like a sack of dirty laundry into the muddy street.

Lomax rolled over onto his side, his face contorted in pain. He groaned out of the side of his crooked mouth. "I'll get even, Fallow, one way or another." Lomax struggled to his feet, and, with his hand on his back, he struggled over to his buckboard and drove out of town. Ned waited until he was gone, then returned to the store.

Ned came back to the counter. "He's gone."

Lily put her hand to her chest and exhaled. "Thank you, Ned."

"Are you all right?"

"I will be."

Ned leaned forward, his eyes steady. "You need to have the Groves contact the sheriff."

"Well …"

"You can't let that varmint get away with it."

"I'll talk it over with Mr. and Mrs. Grove." Lily could imagine her mother's reaction and the gossip in town, and she knew that she would let it end right here. The thought rose in her mind that she would have to consider leaving Midland.

"He's no good."

"I need to sit down." The room began to spin.

Lily woke up feeling lightheaded. She saw Ned crouching over her. "What happened?"

"You passed out. Here's some water." Ned held the cup under Lily's chin.

Right before her, his turbulent eyes softened, and the tension in his face seemed to diminish. She saw the little boy he must have been so long ago—honest, determined, hardworking, and vulnerable to the whims of Mother Nature. Something—or many things—had hardened that little boy.

She took a sip of water. "That's good. Thank you, Ned." Ned leaned down and kissed Lily so softly that she thought she would faint all over again. She put her arm around his neck and felt his body relax as they held each other. Never had Lily felt so safe.

Lily put her hand on Ned's shoulder. "Can you stay for a while?"

"I'm not going anywhere."

Ned's wagon came to a halt in front of the Groves' house. He placed the reins on the seat. "I'll walk you to the door."

Lily, sitting with her hands folded in her lap, looked down. "That's not necessary."

Ned got out, walked over to Lily, and offered his hand.

She took it. Avoiding his eyes, she stepped down.

At the front door, Ned put his hand on her shoulder, and his eyes glinted.

Lily reached back and placed her hand on the doorknob. "Thank you."

"Wait a minute, Lily." Ned leaned down, and his eyes searched for an answer. "Something happened back there at Grove's. Between you and me."

Lily turned the doorknob. "Again, thank you."

Ned awoke before dawn from a fitful sleep. He figured that Lily would go to church with the Groves this morning, then return home. He needed to see her.

He trudged toward the barn through a low mist that clung to the air. He shoveled out the stalls and laid down new straw. In the yard, he tightened the bolts under the carriage of the buckboard with pliers.

He straightened himself, brushed the dust from his shirt, and squinted at the mist lifting over the eastern bluff. The sun peeked through, promising a warm day for November.

Back in the barn, Ned sharpened a scythe with a stone more out of nervous energy than the scythe being dull. After a few strokes, he hung the scythe back up and realized that he wasn't in the mood for work.

He turned toward the house, and Lily's face rose in his mind. "I want more in this life," he whispered. "Dammit, I want *her*." He hungered to hold her in his arms. He would bring her here and ask her to share this life with him.

As the sun slung toward the western sky, Ned hitched the buckboard and drove out.

Just east of town lay the Groves' house, a white wood-framed structure with a picket fence in front and a great elm tree standing guard in a well-trimmed front yard.

Ned tied his team to a picket, took a deep breath, and went up the cobblestone path to the front door. He tapped the doorknocker, and Mrs. Grove answered the door.

"Sorry to bother you, ma'am. Could I speak to Lily?"

Henrietta Grove's face peered up at Ned with sharp, gray eyes that gave no quarter. "Yes. Come in." She gestured to Ned.

"Thank you, but I'll wait here."

After what seemed a very long time, Lily came to the door and stepped onto the flagstone stoop. She kept one hand on the brass doorknob.

"Hello, Ned." She looked up, and there was distance in her eyes.

Ned felt his heart pounding. "Would you take a ride with me?"

"Ned …" Lily paused and looked past him. "I don't think so."

How dull and flat the tenor of her voice, sounding as if the previous night had never happened.

"I'd like to show you my place."

Lily turned her gaze to him. "Ned, what happened yesterday …" Her eyes, looking into Ned's, reminded him of Indian turquoise stones he had collected as a boy. Strands of her long, brown hair were draped over her shoulder. The smell of her was intoxicating, bringing to mind honeydew plants that his mother had collected in the summertime and kept in a vase on the kitchen windowsill. How could such beauty cause him such pain?

Ned felt his throat tighten. "I don't know much about this sort of thing," he said, reaching for Lily's hand that she kept at her side. "I never felt about anyone the way I feel about you."

"Ned, I'm engaged to be married," she said in a soft but resolute voice.

"That's not good enough. What happened yesterday meant something to both of us. I know that much."

"Ned, I'm going inside now." Lily turned, went in, and closed the door.

"Lily!" Ned pounded on the door with his fist, almost rattling it off it hinges.

The door opened, and Hank stood there, not as the busy-eyed merchant with the sharp pencil on his ear, but as a surrogate parent. "Ned, son, you'd best head on home."

Something inside him had told him to take that chance—to go for the dream of a life with Lily and a passel of their kids laughing and romping through a field of wheat. He had reached for that dream and had come up empty.

Ned turned and walked away.

CHAPTER 24

▼

Ned finished unloading crates from the train car to the wagon stationed alongside the Midland depot. He grabbed his satchel and went around front, wondering whether César would remember to pick him up.

Ned saw Hank Grove come out of his store and make a beeline toward him. "Ned, one of your Mexicans was shot yesterday. Doc is with him at your place."

Ned dropped his bag onto the depot platform and took in Hank Grove's worried face. "Which one is it? How is he?"

"Don't know either. I can have Bo take you home."

"Know who did it?"

"Nobody knows. I wired the sheriff. A deputy marshal will be here in two days."

Pete Lomax's words rose in Ned's mind. "I'll get even, Fallow, one way or another." Past the south fork, Ned spotted Doc Auld's buggy in his yard. A light snow began to fall. The frozen fields of stubble, a lifeless dull brown, seemed to run right into and join with the ash gray sky. All life seemed to have disappeared from the land. Nary a birdsong broke the gloomy stillness.

Ned found Doc in his bedroom tending to Tino, who lay unconscious, his bronze face now a sickly pale. "How's he doin', Doc?"

Doc raised a concerned eye. "I took a bullet out of his back." Doc pointed to a bowl holding the slug. "We'll know in a day or two. Meantime, give him these pills, three times a day." Doc got up, reached into his medical bag, and handed a vial to Ned.

"César, who did this?" Ned saw the fear and pain in his worker's deep-set eyes that screamed, *Why?*

"We work on fence, Mr. Ned, and I hear gun ... and Tino ... he fall. I see no one, Mr. Ned."

"This ain't gonna stand, Doc." Ned clenched his jaw. "I tell you that right now."

Doc rubbed a tired eye and looked up. "Ned ... let the marshal handle this. Don't go flying off half-cocked."

"I got a damn-sure idea who did it, and I aim to settle things up."

"Now, Ned ..." Doc strung his name out. "I need your word that you won't do anything till the marshal comes."

Ned stared at the floor and shook his head in a conciliatory manner. "All right, Doc." He looked up. "But I *am* gonna look around and see what I can find."

A blustery gust swept down and lifted the snow off the ground, creating small whirlwinds of white as Ned searched along the fence near the south fork. Up and down he went, moving further away from the fence with each pass.

Ned straightened and looked across the fork, past the meadow. He figured that the gunman might have left his horse on the other side of the creek. After shooting Tino, he could have run through the cover of the tall grass to the horse and his escape.

He scoured both sides of the creek, raking away the thickening snow with a stick. Down a ways on the south side, he found a horseshoe and noticed a worn area on the back of it. The horse it belonged to would have a deformed hoof.

His first impulse was to ride hell-bent with vengeance to Lomax's place and confront him with the evidence. But he had given his word to Doc Auld. "Don't go flying off half-cocked," kept ringing in his ears.

"How's the patient?"

Ned, who had been collecting eggs from the hen loft, turned and saw Doc Auld in his buggy outside the barn door.

Ned put down his basket and went to the door. "César is giving him broth and that elderberry tea you told me to get. He's doing pretty good, I'd say, for a man shot two days ago."

"Good." Doc stepped off and grabbed his medical bag. "I'll check on him, then come talk to you."

Ned ran a brush down the big Belgian's flank, losing himself in the repetitive motion.

"You gonna rub the hide right off him." Doc stood at the door.

Ned grinned and put the brush down. "How's he doin'?"

"He's doing all right, Ned. Just give him time to heal." Doc reached into his pocket for his pipe.

Ned walked into the yard. "Marshal come yet, Doc?"

Doc Auld scratched a match against the barn door. "He's supposed to be at the Grange Hall some time today. You gonna talk with him?" Doc peered up at Ned and drew on his pipe.

Ned snorted. "I told you I would."

Doc raised an eye toward Ned. "Now, don't go doing anything foolish."

"What's your definition of foolish?"

"Won't do your worker any good, you being sent away and locked up." Doc got into his buggy and pointed his pipe toward Ned. "You're too good a man for that, Ned."

Ned looked out the window of the Grange and saw a horseman approach. The rider dismounted, tightened the flank strap of his saddle, and ran his hand in long, dusty sweeps down his mustard yellow slicker. At the water trough, he scraped dirt off his stovepipe boots.

The man was very tall and lanky, and a black handlebar mustache contrasted with his pale complexion. His hair fell from the cover of a broad-brimmed hat, almost down to his shoulders. He wore a silver-handled Colt .45 on his hip and had the look of a man on salary. A small silver star on his chest flickered in the sunlight.

Bill Etheridge stood next to Ned. "I know you're upset. Let me talk to the marshal first."

Ned kept his eyes on the lawman, who stepped onto the boardwalk. "All right."

"Howdy, marshal," Bill Etheridge said.

"Deputy Marshal A. J. Patterson here. Now, what's this about a shooting?" There was an air of malevolent righteousness about this gangly, forbidding man. His thin lips and long nose reminded one of a bird of prey.

"My neighbor here," Etheridge pointed to Ned, "had a worker, a Mexican fella …"

"Wait a minute. I got drug all the way out here for some Mexican getting shot? Didn't say anything in the report about a Mexican. You the owner of the Mexican that was shot?" Patterson's dark eyes seemed dull and uninterested.

"He works for me. I found a horseshoe near where it happened."

"Don't prove nothing."

"No, but the bullet taken …"

"I hear he's gonna live." Patterson turned to Etheridge. "Where can I get somethin' to eat around here?"

"Why don't you just say it?" Ned stepped toward Patterson. "He's Mexican, so you don't give a damn." The marshal lowered his gaze on Ned, the full authority of the law behind him. "Best be sure-God careful how you choose your words … farm boy."

Etheridge put his hand on Ned's shoulder. "Let's just visit with the marshal here," he gestured toward Patterson, "and bring up some options."

"Ain't no options. Either he's gonna do his job," Ned said, jabbing a finger toward the marshal, "or I'll do it for him."

Patterson raised an eyebrow and leveled a stony glare at Etheridge. "Better settle him down, or he'll be nursing a long stay in a jail cell."

"Now, Marshal, we're all a bit upset around here." Etheridge clasped his hands together. "We're a tight community, and this sort of thing doesn't happen around here." He put his hand back on Ned's shoulder.

"Don't waste your time, Bill. Tino's just a Mexican, and this sorry excuse ain't gonna do a damn thing." Ned brushed Etheridge's hand from his shoulder and stormed out.

Ned galloped out of town, heading east. The clatter of the roan's hooves on the frozen road pierced the dull winter air. *Not fair,* Ned thought. Doc Auld's words of advice faded from his mind.

Ned lay on his stomach on top of a bluff and scouted the farm below. The little shanty and barn with peeling paint, the trash piled at the side of a shed—it all reaffirmed for Ned his opinions about the owner.

Lomax came out of the house, crossed a yard littered with scraggly chickens, and entered the barn.

Ned returned to the thicket where he had tied up his horse, pulled a horseshoe from the saddlebag, and then his .22 out of its scabbard.

At the bottom of the incline, he crept to the rear of the barn. Through a window, Ned spotted Lomax cleaning out a horse stall. Behind Lomax, a rifle leaned against a post.

Ned stood at the front door, his rifle in one hand and the horseshoe in the other, and waited. When Lomax finally turned around, his face dropped, and then anger rose in his eyes. "What you want, Fallow?" He came out of the stall, edging around a big pinto mare that started lurching like a giant rocking horse.

"Got a horse missing a shoe?" Ned stole a peek at the nervous animal, threw the horseshoe on the ground, and raised his rifle.

Lomax looked at the evidence, and then at Ned. "What if I do? It don't prove nothin'." He brought the pitchfork in front of himself.

"I didn't say it did." Ned lowered a gaze on Lomax and walked toward him. "You shot him in the back, didn't you?" Ned put the barrel of the rifle under Lomax's chin.

"You gonna shoot me over a Mexican, Fallow?"

The horse reared up, startling Ned.

Lomax knocked the rifle out of Ned's hands with the pitchfork, and, before Ned could recover, he found himself facing the barrel of his own gun.

Lomax pointed it in Ned's face. "Step outside, real easy. I'm gonna end this, once and for all."

Ned's whole body coiled for action. Everything became sharp and clear—the cold touch of the rifle barrel against his face, the foul smell of Lomax's breath, his crooked, tobacco-stained teeth, the black, scraggly stubble on his face, and how god-awful ugly this poor excuse for a man was.

Ned raised his hands up in surrender. Then, in a flash, he grabbed the rifle by the barrel and wrenched it out of Lomax's grip. Ned saw the foul man's face drop. "You shot my man, didn't you?" Ned raised the rifle at Lomax, then lowered it and threw it behind himself. "Come on, Lomax. Like you said, let's end it, once and for all."

Lomax sprang at Ned, both hands going for the throat. Ned struck Lomax with a right hand to the forehead that would have stopped a team of oxen in its tracks. Lomax stood still for a moment, his eyes blank, before he fell backwards to the ground. He was out cold. Ned picked him up off the ground by the front of his shirt, then tossed the unconscious man back onto the ground, hard. He then picked him up again and wrapped both hands around his throat.

"You gonna kill my step-pa?"

Ned turned and saw a tow-headed boy of no more than seven and a tall, stout woman standing at the door. Her oval face bore the signs of strife and hard work, and her pale eyes, set wide apart, appeared wrought with pain.

"He ain't much, but he's all we got." The woman pursed her lips and looked down.

Ned noticed a dark bruise on her cheek. The anger that had raged inside him now turned to pity. Doc's words whispered to him—"You're too good a man, Ned." He released his grip on Lomax, who dropped to the ground. "I'm taking him into town and having him brought up for attempted murder."

"You ain't gonna get away with this, Fallow. Ain't no lawman in these parts gonna fret over some Mexican trash, 'specially not yours."

Ned had been hearing it ever since Lomax had come to. Midland appeared in the distance. "That pinto you're riding might say different, Lomax. This horseshoe I got matches its rear hoof, and I bet that the slug Doc took out of my man is the same caliber as this here rifle of yours."

"Dammit … Fallow, it's just a Mexican."

Ned spotted the marshal's saddle horse in front of Grove's.

He untied Lomax from his horse, making sure that his hands remained tightly bound with rawhide. "Step off real easy, Lomax."

Ned shoved Lomax inside the front door and saw the marshal sitting at a table, cutting into a steak dinner.

"This is gonna get interesting," Shorty said. "Marshal, looks like you got some work."

Patterson cut into his steak and dipped a big chunk into his gravy. "How's that?" Patterson looked up, saw Ned and Lomax, and stood up.

"Dammit, sodbuster." Patterson pulled his napkin from his shirt and flung it to the table. "I warned you," he said, stalking toward the door.

Hustling toward the front door like a beer keg on wheels, Bill Etheridge said anxiously, "Let's not jump to any conclusions, Marshal."

"What's the meaning of this?" Patterson looked at Ned, who pushed the bound Lomax further into the store.

"He shot my man. I got evidence, and he as much as told me so."

"I did nothing, Marshal. I want this man arrested for assault and anything else you can come up with." Lomax's voice was calm, and his sinister eyes had turned soft and innocent.

Patterson leveled his gaze on Ned. "You better have some sure-fire proof, soddy."

"I got his rifle that matches the slug taken out of my man."

"Plenty of folks got a Winchester around these parts, and that shoe don't prove nothin'. Somebody untie me," Lomax demanded.

Patterson, his long face honing in on Ned, said, "You'd best by God have more than that. There been any sort of history between your man and this man? We're talkin' about a Mexican, right?" Patterson pointed to Shorty. "Get a knife, and untie him."

Ned turned to Shorty. "Swanson, tell the marshal what you know about Lomax and my men."

Shorty took the rawhide off Lomax, whose cunning eyes stayed steady on Shorty.

"What you talkin' about, Fallow?" Shorty said. His eyes stayed on Lomax, as though he were under a spell.

"When my other man came for the Doc, right here in this store. Dammit, Swanson, somethin' went on. Tell the man what you know."

"I've had enough of this small-town feud." Patterson pointed a long, bony finger at Ned. "You're lucky I got more important things to deal with, or *you'd* be the one arrested. This case is closed."

CHAPTER 25

▼

The knot in Lily's stomach tightened as she gathered up a stack of schoolbooks in the empty schoolhouse, put them into a satchel, and left the building.

Inside Grove's Store, she saw Hank Grove stacking shelves behind the counter. Midafternoon was a quiet time, and Lily hoped that this would increase her chances.

"Mr. Grove, I was wondering if I might ask a favor."

"Hello, Lily. What can I do for you?"

Lily cleared her throat. "Could Shorty drive me in the buckboard to deliver some homework and books to a student who has been out sick?"

Hank stuck his head into the storage room. "Shorty, got a job for you."

Shorty brought the wagon around to the front of the store and helped Lily aboard.

He scrambled around to the driver's side and started to climb up.

Lily leaned over in her seat. "Shorty ... would you mind bringing the rifle along?"

Shorty stopped halfway up and looked at Lily with his big saucer eyes. "Rifle? Where we goin'?"

"I have to get some books to Daj—"

"You mean Lomax's stepson? Say no more, Miss Lily."

As the wagon entered Lomax's yard, Lily didn't see a person or other living thing anywhere around. The entire place was a shambles, from the scrubby fields to the rundown house and barn.

Lily scanned the place. "I'm just going to leave these books at the front door, Shorty." Lily had just stepped onto the porch when the door opened and Lomax appeared, freezing her in her tracks.

"Well looky who come a-callin' on me. If it ain't the schoolmarm." Lomax slashed a crooked grin. "Swanson, you head on back to town. I'll take the schoolmarm here back home after we have a proper visit and all."

Shorty jumped off the wagon and came to Lily's side. Lily backed slowly off the porch.

"Why, where you goin', little lady?" Lomax taunted.

"Hey, Lomax, Miss Lily don't need to be talked to like that."

"You sweet on her, Swanson?" Lomax's eyes darted toward Lily, now sitting in the wagon. "Thought you was sweet on Fallow—and spoken for, too. And here you are, traipsing about the country with a no-account like Swanson."

"Shorty, please, let's go." Lily heard the raw, husky urgency in her voice.

Shorty glanced back. "Coming, Miss Lily."

"Why Fallow hired them Mexicans that did nothing but pollute the country, when white men are eager to work …" Lomax fixed his eyes on Lily as though he were enjoying a private joke with her, "… and eager for other things, too."

"Shorty, *please*, let's go!"

Shorty turned to Lily, then back to Lomax, who leaned on the doorjamb with his arms folded across his chest as though he owned everything in his sight. "Say what you want," said Shorty, "Fallow and them Mexicans are a far better sight workers than the likes of you, Lomax." Shorty brought his hand up to his trembling cheek.

"Ha, ha. You best git off my property, you twitching drunk, and take that tramp with you."

Shorty tore into Lomax with both fists. The first grazed his chin, and the second missed entirely.

Lomax grabbed Shorty by the front of his shirt and pushed him off the porch and onto the ground, landing on top of him. "Now you gonna git it, Swanson." Lomax raised his fist.

Lily grabbed the rifle and fired it into the air. Lomax froze.

"Let Shorty go. I don't want to shoot you."

Lomax raised his hands mockingly.

Shorty pushed out from under him, scrambled to his feet, and climbed onto the wagon. He grabbed the reins and lashed the team, and the wagon rattled out of Lomax's yard.

Lomax hollered after them in a heavy, coarse voice. "Schoolmarm. Come back alone next time, so's we can git better acquainted."

CHAPTER 26

▼

César drove the wagon out of town, leaving Ned holding his satchel at the Midland train depot. He looked down the empty tracks for the Abilene train, and then over to Grove's Store. He had avoided the store the last couple of Saturdays. He checked again down the empty tracks, then headed across the street.

Ned stood near the front door and scanned the store. The place bustled with the Saturday-morning crush of customers. Hank rang up sales behind the counter, but there was no Lily in sight. Ned checked every aisle, and still no Lily.

Shorty came out of the storage room pushing a cart of supplies. "She ain't here, Fallow. Gone back home to Abilene."

Ned went to the front counter. "Hank, did Lily leave?"

Hank handed an order to a customer and nodded his thanks. He turned to Ned. "She left two days ago."

Ned heard the whistle blast of the arriving train. "Why?"

Hank beckoned Ned off to the side. "Left in a hurry, like something had spooked her. She'd been acting skittish all week."

Ned looked out the window and saw a plume of smoke from the train rising over the rooftops. "Can you give me her address?"

Hank drew in his chin and exhaled. "Well ..."

"Hank, please."

The Sycamore bustled with men in dark suits and ladies in long, frilly dresses. It looked even grander than usual—as though someone had shined every nook and corner of the place. Ned waited anxiously as O'Shaughnessy checked them in. "Mike, don't count on me for dinner tonight."

"Got a little something on the side, do you, Ned, boy?"

Ned took his key from the clerk and turned to the railroad man. "I'll see you in the morning, Mike."

"You know where to find me." O'Shaughnessy motioned toward the back-room bar. "Take it easy tonight. We have a heavy load tomorrow and the day after." He winked at Ned and ambled off.

Ned waited until Mike had gone, then turned back to the front desk clerk. "Do you know how to get to this address?" Ned handed him a piece of paper.

"Why certainly, sir. You just need to ..."

Ned knocked at the Thomason door and waited. He knocked again—still, nobody answered. Ned knocked harder. He shook his head and walked away.

Lily entered the Sunflower Room at the Sycamore Hotel and took a seat next to Ted Riggins. How she had always loved this private dining room with its richly paneled pine walls and oak floor. It also pleased her that Sims would be serving. *What a gentleman he is,* she thought as he entered the room and stood next to her father, who sat at the head of the long table dressed with white linen and silver cutlery. The ladies at the table wore long dresses with long, tight sleeves that had puffy frills at the shoulders. The men wore short, black coats and white shirts with bolo or hanging ties around stiff, raised collars.

Vernon Thomason said, "Sims, we would like four bottles of your best champagne. We are celebrating, this evening."

"Certainly, sir."

After Sims had filled all sixteen glasses, Mr. Thomason stood and raised his glass. "I would like to make a toast to my daughter and only child, Lily, and her fiancé, Theodore Riggins. They have set their wedding date."

As her father rambled on, Lily's mind drifted back to Midland and all the fine folks who had become her friends. Try as she might, she couldn't get Ned Fallow out of her mind—nor the look on his face when she had spurned him.

Lily saw her mother's eyes beam with joy as she listened to her husband's toast. She saw a look of status and entitlement. It was a look she had seen on no one in Midland.

Lily looked at Ted Riggins. With his wavy, golden hair and sparkling eyes, and with his family background, he was a catch for any girl in Abilene. Lily fought the thought, but she couldn't help herself—Ted's eyes had that same look of entitlement as her mother's.

At the conclusion of the meal, the gentlemen retired to the back bar for cigars and whiskey, and Sims escorted the ladies to the lounge for tea.

After Sims served, the ladies talked in hushed tones, sipping the strong English tea. Lily listened respectfully to the chatter of the women, but her heart wasn't in it. Lily looked up for a second and saw the tall figure of a man walking past the lounge. Her eyes focused. It was Ned Fallow. Lily brought her hand to her mouth as Ned stopped, walked into the parlor, and offered his hand to the sitting Lily. Every woman in the room gaped at this great, rough statue of a man.

Lily stood up and looked at her mother. She had not a clue what to do or say.

Sarah Thomason's face had the look of someone whose orderly life was coming unhinged. "Lily ... is everything all right, dear?"

"My name is Ned Fallow, and I'd like a word with your daughter."

Sarah Thomason rose from her seat. Every eye in the room turned to her. "See here, young man. My daughter is engaged to be married, and—"

Ted Riggins came into the room and put his arm on Lily's shoulder. "I have no idea who you are or what your business is here, but I suggest that you leave. Now."

Ned Fallow leveled a scowling, dark blue glare on Riggins that caused the ladies to gasp in unison. "I'm not leaving until I have a word with Lily."

Lily stepped between her two suitors and raised her hands. "Ned, let's walk outside for a moment." Lily looked at her mother, then at Riggins. "It's fine— just let us talk for a minute." She took Ned by the elbow and walked him out of the room.

Ned and Lily stood in the recessed entryway of the Sycamore. Lily heard a light rain tapping faintly against the door's windowpane. "Ned, I'm getting married this June."

Ned took a deep breath and said, "Only one problem with that. You're marrying the wrong man—a bad man." He put his hands on Lily's shoulders. "I know your life here is full of fancy dinners with rich folks, and such. But you're different than all of *them*."

Lily stepped back. "Ned ... please."

Ned took Lily's hand. "I saw the way you were with folks at Grove's, and I saw your face in that tearoom before you saw me, and there was no happiness in that face. Come back with me, and I'll grow us the best wheat farm in all of Kansas. Build you a house you'd be proud to live in."

With her free hand, Lily removed Ned's hand from hers. "Ned, I'm walking back in there. Please don't follow."

Inside the lobby, she turned to look through the green-tinted window of the entryway and saw the silhouette of Ned Fallow standing sadly alone.

Outside the Sycamore, the light rain continued to fall faintly against the window, but no one was listening

Lily returned to the tea parlor. "Please forgive me." She sat back down in her seat and caught her mother's concerned eye. Lily then raised her cup of cold tea toward her mother and then to Ted and nodded. *All is well.*

Ted came over to Lily and reached for her hand. "I will leave you, now." He leaned over and whispered in her ear. "We don't ever have to talk about this or that *man.*" He straightened and nodded goodbye and left the room.

But something with Ted's reaction didn't sit well with Lily. It wasn't like him to let an instance like this past. She wondered what she didn't know.

Ned put the last crate onto the wagon and rubbed his shoulder.

O'Shaughnessy took a drag on his stogie and spat out a bit of tobacco. "A couple of beers at the Sycamore will ease the pain, Ned."

Ned looked down the long stretch of tracks that seemed run into the long, blue sky. "Maybe later, Mike."

As they entered the Sycamore, Ned saw Sims emerge from the dining room. Ned waved so long to O'Shaughnessy, who shuffled off toward the backroom bar.

Sims approached Ned, and his intelligent eyes searched Ned's face. "I, for one, admired the way you conducted yourself yesterday."

"Bet those old ladies will be talking about *that* for years to come."

Sims's eyes brightened, and, in a conspiratorial voice, he said, "What next?"

"Gonna meet it head-on, Sims. Head-on."

Ned knocked on the front door, and a tall, fleshy man wearing a starched white shirt buttoned to the top and a waistcoat with lapels answered the door. "My name is Ned Fallow, and I have come to see Lily."

Mr. Thomason stood there staring at Ned, his eyes seemingly ready to burst from their sockets. "Yes, Mr. Fallow? And what is it you wish to speak to Lily about?"

"No disrespect, sir, but what I have to say is for Lily alone."

"I'm sorry, Mr. Fallow, but Lily is not seeing anyone at the moment."

"Please, sir, tell her I'm here to see her. I just want to talk with her for a minute."

Vernon Thomason rubbed his chin as he sized up Ned. "Very well, then. Please come in."

Thomason ushered Ned into a small parlor off the foyer. Ned heard muffled voices, then a shriek that Ned took to be that of Mrs. Thomason. "What? He's *here?*"

Lily came into the parlor. "Hello, Ned," she said softly.

"Lily, come back with me to Midland."

"Oh … Ned, please."

Ned figured that the carpet he stood on had come from some foreign land, as possibly had the ornate, high-backed chairs, the set of porcelain teacups on a polished table with thin, fluted legs, and the long, fancy drapes. He ran his gaze out to the marble floor in the foyer and realized everything that Lily would lose if she married him.

Ned tried to hold her hand, but she folded her arms across her chest and looked down to her side. He started to speak, then stopped as he realized the futility of it. "I won't keep you any longer. I'll be in Midland."

Ned saw Lily's parents standing at the other end of the foyer. "Mr. Thomason, I appreciate you letting me talk to Lily. Ma'am." Ned nodded at Mrs. Thomason, who held her hand to her mouth as though she were seeing a ghost. "Good evening," Ned said. He then turned away and walked out the door.

✳   ✳   ✳   ✳

From the French windows, Lily watched Ned walk down the front walk. She remembered the first time she had seen him, at the Midland train depot, and how she had shuddered when he came near. And the Saturday mornings he had come into Grove's and stood around all awkward and unsure, stealing glances at her. And she thought about him holding her in her arms—never had she felt so safe and right.

How righteous and strong he had stood at the Sycamore, when he interrupted the ladies' tea. A true-blue person like Ned Fallow didn't deserve to be treated as she had treated him.

As Ned turned the corner and disappeared from sight, Lily heard the heels of her mother's expensive French shoes click across the marble entryway. Oh, how Lily wished to hear the simple sound of boots thumping on the wooden floor of Grove's Store.

"Lily, dear …" Sarah Thomason's eyelids flitted like a hummingbird's wings. "I hope—I *sincerely* hope—that you're not interested in that roughneck farmer."

"That roughneck farmer, as you put it, once saved me from a terrible situation, Mother."

"Lily, I forbid you to see him again."

"Well, Mother, do you forbid me from becoming like you?"

"You needn't be impertinent."

Mr. Thomason rushed into the room. "Ladies ... ladies, please." He placed his arm around his daughter's shoulders. "Sarah, would you give Lily and me a moment?"

"Vernon, for heaven's sake, talk some sense into your daughter."

"Sarah, if you would leave us ..."

Lily's mother started to speak, then turned and left the room.

"Oh, Daddy, I am so terribly torn."

Mr. Thomason joined his daughter at the window. "Lily, dear, some things are for the best, hard as that may seem. He appears a decent young man ... but *really*, Lily."

Lily sighed and stared at the floor.

Vernon Thomason put his hand gently under his daughter's chin and raised it until their eyes met. "His background and yours are worlds apart." Lily's father placed his hand on her shoulder. "Ted will provide you with the sort of life here in Abilene that you are accustomed to."

Vernon kissed his daughter on the cheek. "I only want what I sincerely believe is best for you." He turned and left the room.

Lily looked out at an old birch tree in the yard. She had climbed it as a girl, but it was now shedding its bark, and its branches drooped down in surrender. Never had she seen a sadder sight.

CHAPTER 27

▼

Hank Grove placed a log in the potbellied stove and closed the firebox door. He turned to the storefront window and shielded his eyes from the flickering morning light above the uneven rooftops. The sun peeked out from behind cumulus clouds and crept eastward through a big, blue sky. Gusts of swirling wind rattled shutters and rippled the puddles in the muddy, rutted street.

Bill Etheridge and Dan O'Hurley came out of the bank and into the street, sidestepping the wet spots. O'Hurley opened the door of the store for Bill and a gust of cold air whooshed in.

Hank raised his hand in greeting. "Well, looky what the cat drug in."

"Calendar says it's April, but it don't feel like it." Dan O'Hurley rubbed his hands close to the warm stove.

Hank poured a steaming cup of coffee and handed it to O'Hurley. "Now, Dan, we've had a good amount of snow and rain this year—you can't have everything."

"Could be a good year," Etheridge said, grabbing a cup from the store owner. "What's new with you, Hank?"

Hank put the coffeepot back on the stovetop. "Just glad things have settled down around here."

Etheridge blew on his coffee and took a sip. "That shooting a few months back did get folks riled up."

O'Hurley straightened himself and reached into his pocket for a plug of tobacco. "Never cared much for Fallow, but I got to admire the way he stood up for his man."

Hank grabbed a whisk broom and a dustpan off a peg and began sweeping up ashes around the stove. "That was a tough pill for Ned to swallow, Lomax strutting out of here free as the wind, gloating at Ned and promising to get even. I'm surprised folks weren't more sympathetic toward Ned."

"Why should we be, boss?" Shorty asked, turning away from the shelves he had been stacking. "Fallow don't give a damn about Midland, so who around here should give a damn about him? Let him and Lomax kill each other."

"Now, hold on, Shorty." Bill Etheridge looked at Bill O'Hurley for support and said, "We don't need to carry on like that."

O'Hurley twisted off a plug of tobacco. "You're a good man, Bill, but when it comes to Fallow, you got a blind spot. There wasn't enough evidence to hold Lomax, anyway." O'Hurley reached for the spittoon resting on the storefront window ledge.

Hank bent down, opened the stove door, and emptied the dustpan. "Most folks were downright angry that somebody would bushwhack that young Mexican, but, like Dan said, there just wasn't enough evidence." He closed the door and straightened up. "It came down to Ned's word against Lomax's."

Hank shifted an eye toward the front counter and saw Shorty sneak a furtive look at him. "The marshal had no interest 'cause it was a Mexican that got shot. No, sir, that just don't sit right with me."

"Bill, how's the fella that got shot doin'?" O'Hurley asked.

Etheridge leaned back in his chair and folded his arms across his chest. "Ned says he's doing all right, except he's having some trouble with his stamina. But Ned ... I don't know. He's got that *I ain't forgotten* look about him, and they're working at some kinda pace. Yessir, all three are working like tornadoes."

"I've never seen a man more wanting to grow wheat than Ned Fallow," said Hank. "Wonder how it's all gonna turn out for him."

CHAPTER 28

▼

The sun crept over the pale horizon, promising another sweltering day. Ned took in the last three days' work and figured that, if they gave it a good push, they would have all the wheat cut before nightfall.

Tino hadn't been himself, and already his cheeks were beet red. "Tino, you need a break from cutting?"

Tino shook his head, but struggled to keep up.

"Come on, we need to get this done today." Ned looked back. "Tell you what. I'll cut, and you shock."

"Mr. Ned, I work like you," Tino pleaded.

"All right, but you need to keep up."

Later in the day, this blast furnace of a wheat field was not for the faint of heart. Ned felt the heat taking hold of him. "Let's go in and eat." He motioned to his exhausted workers and headed for the house, swatting at the relentless black-flies.

Tino sat motionless, his face now drawn and pale. He scratched at a red rash on his neck, then fell to the floor unconscious, his leg twitching out of control.

"Tino! Tino!" Ned bent over him. "César, get some rags and run to the creek." Ned lifted Tino, his leg still twitching, and took him to his bed. César returned, and Ned applied the wet rags to Tino's forehead. He noticed how dry Tino's skin was. Ned looked at Tino's lifeless face and felt his stomach tighten. "César, keep those cloths on him. I'll get Doc Auld."

Ned saddled a horse and took off for town. Passing the south fork, he saw Doc Auld's buggy in front of Bill Etheridge's barn.

He found them inside, looking over Etheridge's mule. "Doc, one of my men's in bad shape."

Doc turned away from the animal. "What's the matter with him?"

"He turned pale and passed out with his leg twitching."

"I'll run up with you, Doc." Etheridge said.

When they got to Ned's bed, Tino's was still unconscious, his face now chalky pale. "Get me a chair." Doc shot a glare at Ned.

César rushed to the kitchen and returned with a chair.

After examining Tino, Doc reached into his bag for a vial of white pills. He opened Tino's mouth and slid a pill down his throat.

Doc paused for a second and seemed to burrow his wizened eyes straight through Ned. "Sunstroke. It's not good." A purple vein pulsed on Doc's forehead. "Ned, look at me. You want to kill yourself growing this damn wheat, that's one thing. But who gave you the right to work this man into this condition?"

Ned looked down, staring at the floor.

"My God, man, what is it with you?"

Ned felt humiliation run down his spine as one of the few men he admired gave it to him with both barrels.

Doc, his eyes afire, tore into Ned. "You couldn't tell that he was in a bad way? Or were you too damn worried about your damn wheat to care about a man who trusted you?"

Ned returned his gaze to the floor as he felt the rush of blood to his cheeks. "I asked him if he was all right, and he said he was—"

"What'd you expect him to say? These men worship the ground you walk on, and to prove it, one of them may die."

The room fell into a stillness so hollow that Ned could hear his heart beating.

Doc shook his head, seemingly to soften his rebuke.

Bill Etheridge stood behind Doc Auld. "Is he gonna be all right, Doc?"

"We should know in a day."

Ned felt the weight of the doctor's glare and harsh words.

After Doc Auld and Etheridge left, Ned and César sat at Tino's side, applying damp cloths to his forehead.

As Ned turned for the house, César came running out, screaming, "Mr. Ned. Come quick." Ned dropped the bucket in the creek and ran into the house, clattering open the front door.

César stood at the bedside. "No breath, Mr. Ned." He began to sob in short, whooping gasps.

Ned put his hand over Tino's mouth and felt no air coming out. Tino was dead.

Ned rode into town and notified Doc Auld of Tino's death. "I'll be right up," Doc Auld said between tight, angry lips. After examining the corpse, Doc said only, "You need to build a casket and get him in the ground today." He then shook his head and walked away.

Ned and César built a box, buried Tino up on the eastern bluff, and put a wooden cross in the ground.

After they had buried Tino, César said, "Mr. Ned, Tino never all good after he shot."

But these words held little consolation, for Tino was dead.

A week had passed since Tino's death and Ned stood on the porch and gazed over the field of stubble and reflected back over the last week. He had slept little since Tino died.

He had passed Doc Auld once in town, and the doctor looked right past him. As much as Doc's advice had stuck in Ned's craw over the years, he respected the older man. And now, the loss of the elder's respect ate away at Ned's insides.

Trying to get back to work had been hard for him and César, but what choice did they have? Plus, Jim Cotton's wife had taken ill, and he had arranged for another crew to come thresh Ned's spring wheat. It seemed that a man hardly had time to mourn a death in this life.

Over at the creek, something didn't look right, and Ned walked over. The water was barely a trickle. His eyes followed the empty bed up toward its source. "Damn…. Lomax," he said under his breath.

He saddled a horse and rode north along the creek. He dismounted at the base of a knoll, in a patch of yellow-speckled wildflowers. He climbed to the top and lay down in the bunch grass. Below lay a dilapidated farmhouse and barn in desperate need of paint. Uneven rows of wheat stubble meandered through a field.

There it was, up the creek: a timber dam diverting water to a trench running to the stubble field. Lomax had owned his land longer, and might have some claim to diverting the water—but to hell with him and any damn laws.

Ned rode home, hitched a wagon, and drove to the Mercantile.

He left the Mercantile with a wooden box and took a roundabout route home, stopping near a stand of oaks and storing the box in the hollow of a tree.

Rounding the bend at the south fork, he saw his remaining worker weeding the garden. He would take care of this business after César had turned in for the night.

Ned peeked into the side room and heard César's gentle snores. He went out the front door, saddled up, and rode out toward the great, yellow moon that shone through the branches of the cottonwood trees.

He crossed the creek and rode along the west bank. He dismounted under the cover of trees and went to the hollow where he had hidden the wooden box. He then walked along the creek until he came to Lomax's blockade.

Ned placed the charge at the base of the log dam, poured in the blasting powder, then covered it with dirt. He lit the fuse, ran for cover, and then ... *KABOOM!*

After tending to the horse in the barn, Ned entered his house.

"Mr. Ned?"

Ned looked into the side room, where César sat up in his bedroll. "Just settling an old score, César."

"*Gracias*, Mr. Ned."

At sunrise, Ned walked over to the creek. Weak rays of morning light filtered through the heart-shaped leaves of a big catalpa tree and onto the gurgling stream. He had his creek back.

After chores in the barn, Ned and César headed back to the house for breakfast. Around the south fork came a horseman at full gallop.

Ned went to the porch and waited.

"Fallow." Pete Lomax leaned on his saddle horn, his black eyes glaring at Ned, then César. "I had a legal right to that water."

"To hell with you and your rights."

"I know you blew up my dam." Lomax spat the words out of a bent sneer.

"I know you shot my man." Ned leveled his gaze on Lomax.

"Like I told you, Fallow, I got a long memory." Lomax turned to César. "Ain't that right, wetback?"

Ned stepped off the porch and said, "We can settle it right here, Lomax. Come off that horse."

"I'll settle things on *my* terms, not yours."

As Lomax rode off, César looked at Ned. "He bad hombre, Mr. Ned. Very bad hombre."

CHAPTER 29

▼

C. R. Voth pulled up in his caravan and seemed not bothered a whit about the struggle ahead. His long, angular face sprouted a beard flecked with gray, adding to his dour, sage expression. "Work at a steady pace. Yah, we have a good run today," he said to Ned.

The caravan consisted of two horse-drawn hayracks, a grain wagon pulled by two blue oxen, and a steam engine, driven by Voth, towing the thresher. The stout young men on the hayracks wore broad-rimmed straw hats, white work-shirts with placket-buttoned fronts, and black vests.

The crew set up in the field, then began loading the wagons from the shocks. They reminded Ned of Nicholas, who had always wanted to pitch the shocks, but didn't have a strong enough partner.

The bundle pitchers used four-tined forks, the tines splayed farther apart than normal. One got on each side of a shock. Spearing it together, they would hoist the entire shock onto the hayrack. The man on the rack had his hands full keeping up with these husky young wunderkinds.

This crew knows what it's doing, Ned thought as he watched them work into the late morning. Just as Ned was beginning to feel comfortable, Voth gave two long toots on his whistle, stopping the work.

"What's the problem?" Ned asked.

"We need lunch. Your wife feed us."

"No wife."

The lanky German stroked his beard. "Have help?" He rested his long, dark fingers on his chin.

"Lent him to a neighbor for the day." Ned wondered what he had been thinking, letting César help Vern Swensen cut his wheat.

"Yah, I know about getting wheat in; but men—my men—work better when food on table and eat good, big meal. You will get wheat when we get fed."

"Give me an hour, and I'll have something. Meantime, I need this wheat threshed."

Voth's forlorn expression grew even more so. He blew the whistle, and the work resumed.

In the kitchen, Ned pulled two large slabs of pork out of the lard barrel. He sliced it up and fried it in two skillets.

He drew a pot of water at the well and placed it on the third burner. When the water boiled, he filled it with potatoes. Steam and smoke filled the stifling room. Ned rushed into the garden, picked cabbage and cucumbers, chopped them, and mixed them with oil. He then diced the pork and mixed it into the salad. He drained the potatoes and added salt and pepper to them. Having no bread or pies, he rode over to Etheridge's place.

"No cook shack, huh?" Etheridge asked as his wife put the food into a basket.

"Do you have anything for them to drink, Ned?" Mrs. Etheridge asked, handing Ned the basket.

"No ... I don't."

"Feeding a group of men is no easy task, Ned." Mrs. Etheridge volunteered a modest smile that said, *Womenfolk have it rough here, too, young man.* "Would you like me to come over and help?"

"Yes, ma'am."

A smile dented the corner of Bill Etheridge's mouth. "I'll run Mildred over in the buckboard."

Mildred Etheridge walked right into the kitchen, and Ned trailed behind. "This is a man's kitchen, all right. Ned, I need a table set up on the porch while I get this food ready. We'll need to serve them in two shifts."

Ned borrowed a bindlestiff from a displeased Voth. "My men have big appetites; need plenty food."

Inside the barn, Ned and his helper hammered together a long table out of scrap lumber. He then went out to the field and motioned to Voth, who cut his engine. "We'll need to serve half the men now and half after."

Voth's forehead tightened, and long crevices furrowed out from the corners of his eyes. "Yah, we need second meal at four."

Ned returned to the kitchen while the first crew carried the table from the barn to the porch.

As he brought out great platters and bowls of steaming food, Ned marveled at the quantities Mrs. Etheridge had prepared.

Mildred Etheridge came out to the porch and looked over the men gobbling down their meal. Her chin drew in a bit, and her eyes let one know who ran this kitchen. "Ned, I need you to run me back home so I can pick up some things."

"I'll hitch up the team." It dawned on him that this was the first time she had had a chance to be a real neighbor to him. He realized how poorly he had done by the fact that he hardly knew this good woman who lived one farm over.

As the wagon rattled around the south fork toward the Etheridge place, Ned glanced over at the person next to him. The creases at the corners of her eyes slanted downward, hinting at buried sadness. She looked back at Ned for a moment, her quiet eyes smiled, and it came clear to him that helping out was something she had always wanted to do. She started to speak, then stopped.

"Were you going to say something, Mrs. Etheridge?"

She primped her hair—she wore it in a bun, its sides flecked with white. "Oh, I was just remembering our first year, when we had a Swedish family, named Sundstrom, come through and cut our wheat. I was just starting to feel better after losing the baby." Her voice caught for a moment as she looked past Ned, as if toward her own past.

"But Bill wouldn't let me feed the crew, so we had the neighbor ladies come in, and we made a hoedown afterwards. Mr. Sundstrom—he was a great story-teller—told old Swedish tales, and Bill read some American speeches with patriotic themes. That's how the get-together at the Grange with the orations started."

Ned remembered Lars Sorenson sitting in his rocking chair after Sunday supper, his eyes filled with magic and his voice as smooth as a calm sea. "We had Swedish neighbors," he said, "and the father could tell a grand story and sing a grand song. He used to say that storytelling and music were magic."

"Yes, Bill says it's a tradition amongst the Swedes—storytelling, that is. Oh, I tell you, Ned, they were a lively group."

Ned stole a glance when he heard the wistful tone in her voice and caught an image of the girl she had been, the young woman Bill Etheridge had found so attractive.

"They taught us their dances, and their little children reminded me of angels, their hair so flaxen in the evening light. Oh, I'm going on and on. Probably boring you to death."

"Not at all. Thank you very much … for today. I'd had a mutiny on my hands if …"

"Oh, I'm glad to do it. It's my way of paying back all the folks who helped me … Bill and me … after we lost the baby."

Ned nodded, and a lump swelled in his throat. He turned toward her and she smiled that friendly Kansas smile. She wore a blue skirt and a white shirt with a sunflower embroidered over her heart. *How appropriate*, Ned thought. "I'm sorry that you …"

"Losing a child at birth and coming up barren … I hope this talk isn't embarrassing you, Ned … that's about the worst thing that can befall a young couple on a farm. But Bill's been so supportive all these years, though I know how he always wanted a son."

Ned pulled up in front of the Etheridge house. Mildred climbed down and marched toward the house, waving for Ned to follow. Inside, they met Bill. "How's it goin' over there?"

Mildred pointed toward the door. "Bill, go to the root cellar and get a bushel of vegetables. Ned, come with me."

It was harvest time, and Ned could see that Mildred Etheridge was running a tight ship, and loving every minute of it. He followed her out to the barn, where they slaughtered and dressed six chickens. "We'll give them fellas a meal they won't soon forget, Ned."

Ned drove Mrs. Etheridge back to his place, then took off for Grove's, where he bought six pounds of bacon, four dozen each of eggs and hardtack biscuits, and three quarts of molasses.

Back at his place, he took all the dirty plates and bowls to the creek, washed them lickety-split, and then hustled to the garden to pick some tomatoes, carrots, potatoes, and radishes.

Ned saw that the grain bin was already half full, and he knew that Voth's crew had things well in hand. One of Voth's men came over to him. "Mr. Voth wants second meal by four."

"He told me, already. That lady in the house is taking care of it." Ned was heading back to the house when he heard Voth's whistle.

Inside the kitchen, everything was clean—the pots were piled in a corner, the stove almost sparkled, and the floor had been swept. On the porch, platters of steaming food awaited the hungry threshermen.

Taking center stage in the middle of the table were platters of fried chicken and bowls of German potato salad, a spicy dish that Mrs. Etheridge had learned from her grandmother, who had been German. "Watch them smile when they taste it," she said to Ned as the first crew sat down.

Voth took his seat at the second seating and pointed toward the potato salad. He filled half his plate with it, then sunk his fork in and took a great mouthful. After ruminating chews and a long swallow that bobbed his prominent Adam's apple, Voth looked up at Mildred Etheridge, his dark eyes gleaming. "Yah, like old country," he said through a thin smile.

Like the first crew, these men ate with good manners, but with a ravenous lust for the food. "Is good chicken," one of the young threshermen said. "Mr. Fallow, you need wife to cook like this all the time," another added. The men all laughed, and Ned grinned and wondered whether Lily could cook.

It had been a long day, and Ned felt the fatigue in the crook of his neck, but the crews had been fed and the kitchen cleaned for the fourth time. Ned carried Mrs. Etheridge's kitchenware to the buckboard, where she waited. He got on board and turned to her. "I can't thank you enough, Mrs. Etheridge."

"Ned, please … call me Mildred." She sat in the wagon, her apron folded square on her lap.

"Thank you, Mildred."

"Bill and I would like it so much if you started coming by for dinner every now and then."

"It'd be a real privilege."

The wagon jerked forward, and Ned noticed the fire dying in Mildred Etheridge's eyes. Her body seemed to slump just a bit, and Ned figured that she must have been plum tuckered out, but still not quite ready to let the moment go. She had done what the good Lord had intended for her to do—she had provided for these men of wheat.

Returning from the Etheridge place, Ned found Voth hooking up the engine to the thresher. The shocks of wheat were gone, and only the stubble remained.

"We thresh 986 bushels. At five cents each, that come to $49.30. Less seven dollars for food, total is $42.30. Is that good?" Voth's eyes had a dark and mysterious quality that reminded Ned of his mentor, Nicholas.

"Fair enough." Ned counted out the money, and Voth and his caravan of big-shouldered youths started heading out. As they left, the young men riding in a hayrack began singing old folk songs in German. Their strong, masculine voices rose up into the late-afternoon air and seemed to embrace it. A breath of wind came from the north, caressing their red-cheeked faces. At the end of one song, they gave a loud cheer, then laughed in unison. It wasn't just any laugh, but one that said, "We are one."

They had worked the wheat like a family, Ned thought as he walked to the south fork and listened. The German threshermen headed into the yellow sun and faded into the great horizon from which they had come.

CHAPTER 30

▼

"Mr. Ned, I need flour, beans …"

"Slow down, César. What's this all about?" Ned pulled a tomato off the vine and placed it in a basket.

César pointed to the chili peppers he had planted last spring. "I make dinner from my country for my last night here."

Ned paused for a moment. "Let's go in the house and make a list. I'll go to Grove's and get what you need."

Steering the wagon into the yard, Ned saw César waiting on the front porch. He reckoned he wasn't going to get much work out of him on this, his last day. César came out and inspected the box of goods in the back of the wagon. "Is good, Mr. Ned," he said. He looked at Ned with big, pleading eyes.

"Yes, you go cook," Ned said. "I'll finish in the garden and barn."

A smile wider than the Rio Grande slashed César's face as he grabbed the box and turned toward the house.

As Ned left the barn, the aroma of the food wafted into his nostrils.

César came onto the porch and waved. "Mr. Ned."

The scent of the hot Mexican food seemed to come from every chink and crevice in the floorboards and batten walls. A huge bowl of a steaming meat dish, a pile of warm tortillas, and a hot plate of cooked vegetables covered the table.

"Mr. Ned? I say …?" César folded his hands together.

"Yes."

César said his blessing in Spanish. The only things Ned made out were his and Tino's names.

After a couple of great swallows of food, Ned said, "César, this is real good food. Real good." He then dug back into the hot, spicy food.

Finally, Ned pushed his empty plate away. "That's more food than I've eaten in a spell."

César looked at Ned with his "please say yes" look.

Ned pushed his chair back from the table and rubbed his stomach. "Yes, César?"

"Mr. Ned, I have something."

"All right."

César scurried outside and returned with a brown bag holding what looked like a bottle.

"What's this?"

"Tequila, Mr. Ned. *Bueno.*"

"What the heck. Let's have some."

César got two glasses and poured a round.

Ned took a sip and felt it warm his insides.

"Is *bueno*, Mr. Ned?"

Ned threw his head back and swallowed. "Phew, that's got a kick to it."

César poured two more drinks. "You *bueno* hombre, Mr. Ned. You *el jefe.*"

Ned picked up his glass. *"El jefe?"*

"You great man, Mr. Ned." A smile pushed up César's reddened cheeks, making Ned think of two scarlet roses on a lonesome brown hill.

Tino's face came clear in Ned's mind. "César, I wish Tino was here. If I'd only known he wasn't …" Ned took another swallow, ran his forefinger across his lips, and continued, "I have to live with his death for the rest of my life."

César stared at his glass and rolled the liquid from one side to the other. He looked up at Ned, his eyes dewy. "Maybe your fault, maybe my fault, maybe Tino's fault." César raised his drink and said, "To Tino."

Ned clinked César's glass. "I want to tell you how much it's meant to work with men like you and Tino. There will always be a place for you here." Ned looked into César's honest, faithful eyes and said, "You come back next spring?"

"You *bueno* hombre, Mr. Ned." Tears streaked down César's cheeks.

Ned wanted to speak, but didn't. He thought of his family at the supper table in Ketchum, all those years ago.

Ned stood in his yard, next to the hitched wagon. "Come on, César, the train isn't gonna wait."

"*Momento*, Mr. Ned." César poked his head out the door.

It won't be the same, Ned thought as he ran his gaze to the northern perimeter, where the long shadows of the Osage trees stretched onto the field of Jerusalem wheat.

To the west, the blood red sun was losing its daily struggle against the horizon. Small bands of clouds circled around it, forming a halo. Two smaller cirrus clouds approached from the southern sky and seemed to dance as they touched the top corona of the sun. Passing over it, they halted for a moment. Inexplicably, one rose up and disappeared, while the other headed back to the comfort of the southern sky. The great star dipped into the horizon, its rays glimmering toward the remaining wayward cloud, as if trying to drag it under. Finally, the sun fell below the horizon, and the lone cloud drifted into the southern sky from whence it came.

As Ned's wagon rounded the south fork, César turned toward the bluff where Tino was buried and raised his hand in farewell.

Bill Etheridge took a gander out Grove's storefront window. "Well, looky there, Doc. Ned's taking that young Mexican to the depot. Good thing he didn't arrive earlier, when Lomax was in town. He's telling everybody who will listen that Ned blew up his dam."

Hank Grove put a carton of canned goods next to a shelf. "Bad blood there. Yessir."

"I'm none too pleased with Ned," Doc said, "but Pete Lomax had no right blocking a man's access to water."

Hank placed a can on the half-empty shelf. "They've been feuding since Ned first got here."

"Well," Etheridge said, scratching his chin, "folks should be thinking about the harvest, not feuds. Ned's got everything ready for cutting and threshing. Says he's gonna use Jim Cotton's new binder to cut his spring wheat."

Doc packed his pipe and watched Ned and César shake hands good-bye. "No good reason that other man's dead." Doc scratched a match on the stove and drew on his pipe.

"Now, Doc, he ain't the first or the last man that's gonna die in a wheat field," Etheridge said.

Doc grimaced and looked out the window.

Hank Grove cleared his throat. "How's the scythe competition coming, Bill?"

"I got eighteen teams registered this year. Hard to believe we can get thirty-six men around these parts to enter, but we do. Gonna be some tough competition. Pete Lomax was talking about his brother-in-law, a big Norwegian from North Dakota, who's coming down. Says he can outwork any man alive."

Hank fanned the dirt out the front door and held it open as Ned walked in.

"Say, Ned, you thinking of registering for the competition this year?" Etheridge asked.

"No." Ned peeked over at Doc, who fidgeted with a checkerboard on the storefront ledge.

"Well, now, it's gonna be a good one this year—plus the hoedown afterward." Etheridge smacked his fist into his meaty palm. "Gonna be the best ever. We got good crops, and good men cutting this fine wheat. Yessir."

"I'll be declining." Ned said.

Doc banged his lit pipe on the lip of the spittoon and put it into his vest pocket. He grabbed his black bag, shot a glance at Ned, and stepped toward the front door. "Got to go to the country," Doc announced to the group. He opened the front door and turned his gaze on Ned. "Why don't you enter this year to honor the man you lost out there?" He looked at the group as if to underscore his challenge and dare them to push it forward, then left.

Hank hung the broom on a nail. "Doc's getting a little crotchety in his old age." Hank opened the door, and Vern Swensen came in. "Vern, have a cup of coffee. Shorty." Hank hollered toward the back room, from which Shorty Swanson emerged. "Get Vern's order together."

Vern pulled up a seat as Etheridge handed him a cup.

Ned watched Doc get onto his buggy and turned to Etheridge. "I take the blame for Tino's death."

Etheridge put a hand on Ned's shoulder. "Ned, we've all paid our dues to live this life." Etheridge turned to the others with open palms. "We're men of wheat—we all have a burden to bear." Etheridge poured a cup of coffee and handed it to Ned. "Ned … have a seat, son."

"I'd better—"

"Ned, your order can wait a bit. Sit a spell." Etheridge handed Ned the coffee, then looked over at Dan O'Hurley, who held a half-carved block of wood in his lap. "When did you lose your hired hand, Dan?"

The big Irishman scratched his dark face with a penknife, "Must have been the winter of '91. Poor devil. I found him clinging to a fencepost not a hundred yards from the house. I still feel bad about it to this day." O'Hurley stared at the wood chips at his feet, then shifted his gaze to Ned.

Ned slunk over to Doc's vacated seat.

Etheridge put a hand on Vern's shoulder and sat next to him.

"Nothing easy about this life we choose for ourselves, wouldn't you say, Vern?"

The taciturn Vern Swensen spoke in a low voice. "I crossed the Atlantic in '66 from Norway." He paused and glanced at his long, labor-worn fingers. "My wife took ill and passed away the eighth day at sea." Vern tapped his chest. "With heart broken, I arrive in New York with little money. Made my way out here on foot. With the help of neighbors, and with more hard work than any man should want, I made something of it. But I'll tell you, Bill ..." Vern paused, his face etched with sadness. "I would not want to do it again."

O'Hurley, the map of Ireland spread across his face, sighed and straightened his great shoulders. "I left my pregnant wife in Ireland in '72. Planned on bringing her over to Boston the next year." The big man's eyes moistened. "Lost them both in childbirth. It was a boy. I decided to disappear into the land, and ended up in Midland. Working the land, remarrying, and having children eased the pain ... but it'll always be there."

O'Hurley looked toward Etheridge, who, after an awkward pause, said, "I've had a good life, 'cept when we lost the baby." Etheridge halted and stared into his hands. "Reckon I'll never forget that day."

Etheridge winced as he looked at the group. "Every man has a burden to bear in this life."

Shorty Swanson had come up and taken a seat next to Etheridge. "I never done nothin' in my life but fail. I got nothin' to brag of. My old man, who turned out to be my stepfather, beat me silly as a kid. If it weren't for the folks in this town, I'd be dead. Guess I need to say thank you." Shorty stood up and nodded once to the group, as if to confirm his words. He then motioned to Vern that his order was ready.

Ned looked at Bill, then over to Hank. "My order ..." Ned said, as softly as if he were in church. "I got a few changes to make."

Ned left Grove's, crossed the street, and headed for the smithy. He found it empty, but saw a chip fire in forge and decided to wait. He needed to pick up some horseshoes—plus, he needed time to mull over the accounts of Etheridge and the others over at Grove's.

He felt ashamed of the way he had thought of Etheridge and the other men. They, too, had suffered greatly in this life. He was not alone when it came to hardship. Ned thought about his rudeness toward Etheridge over the years, and how the older man had never held it against him. He realized that he had some fences to mend.

Ned walked out of the smithy and spotted a woman wearing a bonnet and a gray sack dress, accompanied by a boy. As they neared, he recognized them to be Lomax's wife and stepson.

Mrs. Lomax stopped in front of Ned as if frozen in her tracks.

She peered up at Ned, the boy clinging to her skirt.

"How bad is it?" Ned asked. Ned had noticed the boy's eyes—one was black and blue, the other surrounded by a fading bruise. His face was drenched in fear and sadness.

"Mama, I don't want to go home."

Ned felt a vein pulsing in his temple as the woman removed her bonnet, revealing bruises on her long, white face. *My God,* Ned thought. She looked to have been battered by a club.

Frida Lomax looked up at Ned with ravaged eyes. They were eyes with no life or fight left in them, eyes that cried for help.

"You and the boy can stay with me until other arrangements can be made." Ned surprised himself with his words, but he had no intention of going back on them.

"I don't know ..." Frida looked around as though lost at sea.

"Mama, please. I don't want to go back to Stepfather." Tears streamed down the boy's face as he tightened his grip on his mother's skirt.

"Oh, Daj ..." Frida put an arm around her sobbing son.

She looked at Ned Fallow and nodded.

CHAPTER 31

▼

Ned peeped into the barn and said, "I see you done your share of chores before."

Daj turned from cleaning a stall. He wore a careful smile.

Daj Jorgensen was big for his age, broad-shouldered and sturdy. The boy's silence reminded Ned of himself, and he figured that the longer Daj stayed away from Lomax, the more he would come around.

Ned didn't mind the living arrangement: he slept in a bedroll in the room off the front door, and the mother and boy slept in his bed. Frida was an uncomplicated woman, capable of doing a day's work that would make most men proud.

Living with the woman and boy brought back good memories of Ketchum.

Folks had seen them ride out of town in his wagon two days ago. Ned figured that Lomax would come at night, and he kept his loaded rifle near where he slept. He had never killed a man before, but realized that it could happen—he would kill Lomax before he let him have them back.

Ned heard a wagon rattling at a good clip into the yard and wished he had stashed the rifle in the barn. He walked to the barn door and motioned to the boy. "Daj, go to the house." Ned walked into the yard to face his enemy.

Lomax sat in his wagon, a rifle across his lap. Daj ran to his mother on the porch. "You gone too far, Fallow." Lomax pointed to Frida and Daj. "Get in the wagon."

"They ain't going anywhere, Lomax."

Lomax raised the gun, and Ned ran for cover. Before he made it past the barn's double doors, he heard the report of a rifle and felt a stinging sensation in his left shoulder. The bullet's impact thrust him forward. He scuttled through the door and to his right.

Ned grabbed a pitchfork off the wall. The pain in his shoulder ripped up into his head; he knew that he had little time to act before he passed out.

Ned looked through a knothole and saw Lomax coming toward the barn with the rifle at his hip, pointing forward. "I told you, Fallow: I got a long memory. Time to meet your maker."

Frida shouted from the porch, "We'll go. Don't kill him!"

Lomax ignored her as he stopped just short of the entrance. Ned crept out of his cover, being sure to stay out of Lomax's line of sight. He raised the pitchfork behind his right ear, took two quick steps, and turned toward Lomax, who fired a shot that Ned felt graze the hair on the side of his head. He hurled the pitchfork hard and true.

The tines hit Lomax square in the throat. He dropped the gun, and a look of shock settled across his dying eyes. Before his hands could reach his throat, he fell flat on his back. Blood spurted from his neck.

Ned fell to a knee as Frida and Daj rushed to him.

The last words he remembered before passing out were Frida's. "I will get doctor."

Ned struggled to wake up. It felt as though he were in some dream world from which he couldn't escape. Finally half awake, he saw the room come into blurred view. A vision of his Aunt Lorrayne scrubbing the farmhouse walls in Ketchum rose in his mind as Ned sniffed the unmistakable scent of lye and ammonia.

A figure sitting in a chair said, "I scrub house good."

"How long did I sleep?"

"Two days." Frida took a damp cloth and placed it on Ned's forehead.

"Lomax?"

"He dead." She put the back of her hand on Ned's cheek and left it there.

"Thank you."

Ned tried to sit up, but a shooting pain in his shoulder brought him back down.

"Doctor come today. You want soup?"

"Yes, thank you." Ned heard the front door open, and footsteps approached his room from the kitchen.

"Well, I see you finally woke up." Doc Auld stood at the door, holding his medical bag.

Frida got up from her chair. "I warm soup," she said, walking out.

Doc took Frida's seat and rested his gaze on his patient. "You gave us a scare. Lost enough blood to kill a grizzly. Damned if you're not just too ornery to die."

"Was I worth saving, Doc?"

"You've always been worth saving. Now, let me get a look at that shoulder."

Ned awoke groggy and a bit confused. A large figure sat in the chair beside his bed.

"How are you, Ned?"

Ned blinked. "Bill? Well … I guess it could be worse."

"Look, Ned, I arranged for Jim Cotton to come by in a few days to bind your winter wheat and have him thresh it afterward." Etheridge's worried eyes questioned Ned.

"Oh … my wheat," Ned said, struggling up to a sitting position.

"Now, everything is taken care of, Ned. I'll look after the binding and threshing, and Mr. Tharrington will send Wilson to take the grain to town."

Ned's first inclination was to protest, but he buried the thought.

"Thank you … neighbor."

Bill Etheridge clucked at the mare in Ned's front yard and pivoted the buggy, turning toward the south fork and home. He didn't tell Ned about the deputy marshal who was coming to investigate Lomax's death. It should just be a simple procedure, he thought—Frida Lomax had told anybody who would listen that it had been self-defense. Her husband had come to kill Ned Fallow and almost succeeded. But he had lost his own life instead.

Still, Etheridge heard the talk in town: Ned had never given folks the time of day; he was now living with that woman and her son; some even said that Ned Fallow was an impudent, immoral man. And then, there was the feud with Lomax.

Etheridge raised his shirt collar against a gust of air that blew through a row of cottonwoods. Turning into the dirt road leading up to his house, it came clear that a change was coming over Ned.

CHAPTER 32

▼

Lily sat in the sunroom holding an envelope addressed to her, which she had found at the front door. She could not imagine whom it was from. She opened it and began to read:

My dear Miss Thomason,

I thought long and hard before writing this letter, and finally came to the realization that it was my duty to do so. The matter involves Mr. Theodore Riggins.

Since I have provided my services to your lovely family over all these many years, and look forward to your visits, I have grown fond of the Thomasons. Were the matter I'm about to relate inconsequential and subject to the healing powers of time, I would be inclined to dismiss it. However, I believe that a pattern of deceit and dishonour has befallen you. It is with great sorrow that I must tell you of it.

Mr. Riggins, although always the gentleman in your family's company at the Sycamore, leads a secret life. He consorts with unescorted women of ill repute at Emerson's, a place I occasionally visit for my nightcap. I have never spoken with him there, and, if we encounter each other, he chooses to ignore my presence unless it is to direct some snide remark toward me. Though he attempts to keep these liaisons discreet, the company he keeps is not always so inclined.

I have spoken with of one of his companions, and she has informed me that she has not been wholly comfortable with her relationship with Mr.

Riggins since the announcement of your engagement to him. She is, however, unaware that I am reporting this matter to you. I have given no indication to her that I find Mr. Riggins's behaviour abhorrent. She sees me as someone whose ear she can bend, so to speak, and to whom she can relate her problems. If you need confirmation of my report, I believe that she would confirm that all I have stated is true.

This matter does weigh heavily on me, but I confess that it is with much relief that I do what I believe to be the right thing and bring this unfortunate affair to your attention.

I am truly sorry that my communiqué is of this distressing and sordid nature.

Respectfully,

Edward J. Sims

PS I will be working tonight at the Sycamore, if you need to speak further with me on this matter.

Lily entered the Sycamore Hotel and found Sims waiting on a group of ladies in the tearoom. She caught his eye, then went to the lobby to wait.

The letter, although a shock, had also come as a relief. It had been confirmed to her that Ted Riggins was not whom he had presented himself to be.

After Sims verified that he had indeed written the letter, Lily left the Sycamore and walked up to the north side of town. She stopped at a small house at the end of a street lined with trees that provided shade over the sidewalk. She had never been inside this little A-frame, but this was no time for demureness or any other nonsense that her mother would advise. No—she would meet this directly.

Lily knocked at the front door.

"Who is it?" said an aggravated voice.

"Lily."

"Lily!"

"Ted, open the door. We need to speak."

"Yes, give me a moment, and I will be out."

Lily heard a woman's muffled voice, stepped off the stoop, and turned to leave.

At the front gate, she heard the door open.

"Lily, wait!" Ted Riggins, his shirt tail out and his hair in disarray, ran to Lily. "I never expected to see you here, Lily."

"You're not the person I thought you were, Ted." Lily raised her chin toward the house, where she saw a blind close shut. "Don't lie to me, Ted."

The bravado left Riggins' face. His cunning eyes searched Lily, as though they were trying to ascertain how much she knew. "Lily, you must understand ..." Riggins raised his thumb over his shoulder. "That is nothing. Once we're married—"

"What type of woman do you think me, Ted Riggins?" Lily turned to go.

Riggins grabbed her arm. "Don't be a fool, Lily!"

Lily broke free of his grip. "Not anymore, Ted. Not anymore." Lily walked away as Riggins shouted after her. "Lily, come back. Don't be a fool."

She did not stop or look back and walked directly to the Western Union office.

Lily found her parents in the sunroom. "Father ... Mother ... I have come to a decision. Two days ago, I contacted the superintendent of schools, and I've been offered my old job teaching in Midland next term. Also, the Groves will put me up and can use my help at the store. I'm leaving the day after tomorrow." Never had Lily been so bold with her parents.

Sarah Thomason brought her hand up to her gaping mouth. "Lily, no!"

Vernon Thomason said sharply, "Sarah." He then softened his tone. "Are you sure, Lily, dear?"

"Yes, Father. Midland is where I belong."

Her father's large, protruding eyes moistened. "We only want you to be happy. Don't we, Sarah?" Vernon leveled his gaze on his wife.

Mrs. Thomason drew in her sharp chin. "It's that Ned Fallow, isn't it?"

"Mother, please understand. It is *my* life."

Sarah Thomason's face grew ashen. "You will rue the day, daughter."

Lily looked out the French window at the sunlight splintering through the branches of the old birch tree. Never had it looked more majestic.

Abilene sank into the distance, giving way to rolling prairies and tree-lined streams. Lily looked out the train window at a meandering tributary and wondered how Mother Nature had decided what path it would take. Would it be the right one? Further along came stretches of checkered farms with their freshly painted farmhouses and wooden windmills that whirled incessantly.

Hooray. Lily thought. *This is my life to live.*

As the long whistles announced Lily's return to Midland, she waved out the train window to Hank and Henrietta Grove, who stood on the depot platform.

Lily rushed to greet them. "Hello, hello."

Mrs. Grove's faded eyes lit up. "Oh, Lily, it's so good to have you back."

Hank hollered "Giddyup." to the team and drove Lily the roundabout way home through town.

Lily took in every sight and sound: the Grange Hall anchoring the south end of Main Street, the livery, the majestic bank with its limestone face and wooden cornices, Grove's General Store, and the gentle pace of folks who hollered hello and welcomed her back.

Hank put the last of Lily's bags in her room and joined his wife and Lily in the den. "Store hasn't been the same without you. What say, after we get you unpacked, that you and I go by the store and say hello?"

"That sounds wonderful."

Bo Fielder and Shorty rushed to greet Lily as she entered the store. "Miss Lily, w-welcome back."

"Well, hello, Bo. It's wonderful to be back."

Lily smiled at Shorty, who stood back a little. She stepped toward him and extended her hand. "Hello, Shorty."

Shorty's cheek twitched twice, then flushed crimson. After lightly shaking Lily's hand, he took a step back. "Hello, Miss Lily." Shorty looked down at the floor. "Hope you'll save a dance for me at the threshing party at the Grange."

"Why, Shorty, I look forward to it."

After saying hello to folks, Lily walked back to the Groves' house. In the den, Henrietta Grove was sitting in her chair, reading a book. A pot of tea and cups sat on the table in front of her. She peered up from her wire-rimmed glasses and smiled. "Have a seat, dear, and join me in a cup."

Lily sat on the loveseat across from Mrs. Grove and said, "Thank you again for having me back." She felt her eyes welling up. "It's ... so good ..." Tears streaked down her face as she surrendered to the life-altering events of the past few months.

Mrs. Grove put down the teapot and sat next to Lily, putting an arm around her shoulders. "It's all right, dear. You go ahead and have yourself a good cry. That's right, let it all out."

Lily buried her head into the comfort and safety of Mrs. Grove's soft bosom. She cried herself dry, then lay still in the older woman's arms and fell asleep.

Lily looked out her bedroom window as the dawn broke clear, spreading the first light over the prairie. How sad and pale—and how beautiful—the light. A morning wind, hinting at a mild day, ruffled the curtains and rousted her from a daydream.

After breakfast, Lily and Mrs. Grove sat in the kitchen, drinking coffee.

Henrietta Grove idly stirred cream and sugar into her cup, then let her spoon linger for a moment before looking up at Lily. "There have been plenty of things going on since you left, Lily ..." With a sharp eye on Lily, Henrietta Grove proceeded to tell her in detail about the death of Tino, Ned getting shot, that horrible Lomax's death, and Mrs. Lomax and her son staying with Ned while he recuperated. "Some folks don't like it one bit, and some believe that there's a romance going on—and with a child staying there, no less."

Lily took a final sip of her coffee. "Oh my goodness." she said, and stood up. "Could I borrow the buggy today? I need to drop off some schoolbooks."

The corner of Henrietta Grove's lip curled down then pragmatically rose up, her eyes searching Lily for a reaction to her gossip. "Why, yes, dear, that would be fine."

Lily steered the buggy out of the Groves' yard and headed toward the schoolhouse, mulling over what she had just heard.

Ned and another woman? It hadn't dawned on Lily, but she decided that it was possible—very possible. She could see how a woman would find his good looks and intimidating presence compelling. After all, hadn't she?

Lily thought back to their first meeting at the train station. *Yes,* Lily thought, *Ned Fallow is certainly a compelling man.*

Lily rolled along on the crooked trails, as free as the long, puffy clouds floating lazily in the great azure sky. A gust of wind came over a rise and blew into her face. Oh, how good it felt to be back in Midland, Kansas.

Sparrows, darting about in the mulberry hedges along the river, greeted her as she approached a farmhouse. After a warm hello from the family and dropping off books to be read before classes began, Lily set off for another farm.

Back on the trail, she noticed the acres upon acres of land that had been turned and tamed, its rich, black soil yielding great long stretches of shocked wheat in the late summer air, which hinted at autumn and change. *This is where I belong,* Lily thought as she crossed over a stretch of prairie. All sorts of plants and flowers surrounded her: sunflowers, larkspur, wild oats, and a tangle of weeds, forming a medley of purples and yellows. Butterflies danced above a field of clover, past which Lily spotted the corner of a farmhouse.

Coming closer, it dawned on her whose farm it was, and she came to a halt. She noticed how everything seemed in proper order and in its place—the skillfully constructed well, the garden, the house, and the barn. Anybody who could create all this had beauty in his heart.

A stretch of wheat in a field rippled in the golden light; chickadees sang their two-note song and fluttered about in the lonesome blue sky. A man stood at the well with his back to her, his left arm in a sling and his right cranking the pulley. His shock of dark hair ruffled in a gentle breeze. *Hello, Ned Fallow.*

A woman and a small boy emerged from the house. The boy ran over to Ned and took the water bucket. Together, they joined the woman and went inside the house.

Lily slackened the reins and headed toward Ned's place. Halfway there, she stopped. *What will I say to him?* she thought.

Taking a deep breath, she clucked the mare forward into the yard. She heard a man's laughter coming from the house. It dawned on her that she had never heard Ned laugh before.

Lily felt like an interloper. She had begun to pivot the mare about when Ned came out of the house.

Lily pulled back on the reins.

They stared at each other. Finally, she said, in a soft voice, "Hello, Ned."

"Lily," Ned said, nodding. "Welcome back." Lily tried to hide her surprise at the flat tone that greeted her.

"Thank you. I've missed it so around here." Lily felt her face flush and her heart pound. "I see that things have changed for you."

"Oh, this is temporary—just until Frida and Daj can get back on their feet. I suppose you heard about the trouble."

Lily jumped in her seat when the front door clattered opened and Daj tumbled out. Frida stood at the door jamb but did not greet her.

"Hello, Miss Thomason. Are you comin' back to teach us?"

"Why, yes, Daj."

Daj offered a weak smile to Lily, then turned back to his mother's side. Mother and son, with frosty eyes, stared at Lily as though she were an invader.

Lily felt her shoulders sag. "Well, I just wanted to say hello. I'd better get back."

Ned came off the porch and walked over to the buggy.

There was tranquility in his gaze—it seemed as though he had come to some sort of peace with himself. Lily raised the reins, and Ned grabbed her hand and held it; then he stepped away from the buggy and raised his hand to wave good-bye.

Ned watched the buggy until it disappeared around the south fork. He turned to Frida, who was still standing at the door. "Frida, what's for supper?"

CHAPTER 33

▼

Everything about Deputy U.S. Marshal A. J. Patterson said that there was no hurry. He rode into town at an easy trot, his long body dwarfing his sorrel mount. Bill Etheridge left the front window of the Grange and waited in the entryway.

Patterson scratched a match on an oak post and lit a thin cigar. "I need to talk with a Frida Lomax."

"I can take you over to see her, Deputy." Etheridge had seen Ned earlier in town and knew that he was on his way to the Mercantile. *Thank goodness,* he thought.

Patterson drew on his stogie, then turned to face Etheridge. "You'd be, again ...?"

"Bill Etheridge. I'm a neighbor of Frida Lomax."

"Just give me directions, and I'll be on my way."

Etheridge felt a knot twist in his stomach. He remembered Patterson from the shooting of the Mexican, and he didn't trust him a bit to do the right thing. Plus, he might have had it in for Ned, after their run-in. Bill wished that the sheriff hadn't handed over these investigations to this sorry excuse for a lawman. "Now, Marshal, I bet you're tired after riding all day. Why not let me take you on out in my buckboard?"

Patterson bit down on his cheap cigar and drew back his head. "All right, then. Let's get to it."

Frida sat with her arms folded, facing the marshal across Ned's kitchen table. Etheridge sat next to Frida.

"It was self-defense," Frida blurted.

"We'll see about that. Why haven't you and your son returned to your place?" Etheridge cut in. "She's been tending to Ned's—"

Patterson shot a glare at Etheridge, silencing him. He leveled his hollow-boned gaze on Frida once more. "Now, why you still here?"

Frida looked lost.

"What were your feelings toward your husband … and toward Ned Fallow? They'd been feuding for years, isn't that right?"

"Ned *had* to kill him. He was going to shoot him dead." Frida put her hand to her mouth and looked at Etheridge, who placed his hand on her shoulder.

"Your husband beat you?" Patterson leaned forward, his great, beaky nose sniffing ever so slightly, as though there were a foul odor in the room.

"Yes, yes, he beat me. But what—"

"That's all." Patterson stood up and motioned to Etheridge that they were leaving.

As Bill Etheridge pulled the wagon up to Grove's with Patterson aboard, he noticed black, shadowy clouds tumbling out of the western sky.

Inside, Shorty Swanson and Bo Fielder were stocking shelves. The place seemed eerily quiet to Bill. Everywhere Patterson went, a dull emptiness seemed to swallow up the air.

Patterson motioned for Shorty and Bo to come to the counter. "Need a word with ya."

"W-we be r-right there, Marshal." Bo's voice seemed ready to crack with excitement.

Shorty stood between Bo and the deputy. "What you want?"

"You know anything about a feud between Pete Lomax and Ned Fallow?"

Shorty turned his back to the deputy and frowned at Bo, his eyes telling him to hush up. Shorty turned back to the lawman and said, "I don't go by rumor. I ain't seen nothin'."

"W-why, I h-heard they had a couple of run-ins." Bo stepped around Shorty and faced the deputy.

"Shut up, Bo." Shorty looked over to Etheridge.

"Now, Marshal—"

Patterson pounded his fist on the counter and looked hard at Etheridge, then at Bo. "Go on."

"W-why, Ned Fallow almost killed Pete Lomax a c-couple of times with his b-bare hands."

Deputy Marshal A. J. Patterson straightened himself and took a long sniff of air, as if something had just pleased him. He then turned and walked out of the store. Etheridge knew that an inquiry was coming.

At the storefront window, Etheridge watched Patterson ride west toward the blackening sky. For the first time in his life, Bill Etheridge wished for bad fortune to befall a man.

Ned saw a horseman canter around the south fork. From the dappled coloring of the mount and the size of the rider, Ned knew who and what was coming.

"Ned Fallow?" Deputy Marshal A. J. Patterson's slit eyes questioned Ned.

"Yeah."

Patterson brought the horse alongside the porch and handed Ned an official-looking document. "There you go, sodbuster." Patterson pivoted the horse around and rode away.

Ned looked at the paper, his eyes skimming over the text and seeing only his name and Lomax's in bold lettering. Ned crumpled up the paper and threw it into the yard.

CHAPTER 34

$\blacktriangledown$

A tall oak bench anchored the far wall of the Grange Hall. Behind it sat a county judge, and facing him were the district attorney at one table and Ned and his lawyer at another. Next to the bench was a witness chair, and off to the side were twelve chairs for the jury. Behind Ned and the attorneys was a packed house of murmuring seated citizens and others standing behind.

The judge pounded his gavel. "Order."

A hush fell over the room.

"Mr. Fallow, please rise."

Ned stood and faced the judge.

The judge leaned forward. "For this inquiry, there is a twelve-man jury, and a majority of seven is needed for charges to be filed." The judge sat back and raised a sharp eye at Ned. "Do you understand?"

"Yes, sir." Ned looked over at the jury. Bill Etheridge was the only one of them he really knew—some he knew by name, and others only by face. Ned now realized what a poor neighbor he had been.

"You may be seated." The judge looked over a sheet of paper. "First witness to be called: Frida Lomax, step forward."

Frida sat in the witness chair next to the judge and faced the district attorney. "Did you leave your husband for Ned Fallow?"

The courtroom broke out into a loud buzz. The judge pounded the gavel.

"My husband beat me, and Ned take me and my son in."

The DA approached Frida. "Isn't it true that Ned Fallow tried to kill your husband with his bare hands?"

Frida brought her hand to her forehead. "They fight in barn, and Ned win. That is all."

"How many days before Ned Fallow killed your husband had you been living with Mr. Fallow?"

"Two days."

The DA tapped two fingers on Frida's chair. "And why didn't you go to the sheriff if you were so worried about your husband?"

Frida looked up at her accuser, then down at the floor. In a soft voice, she said, "I did not know what to do."

After a few more questions in this vein, the DA said, "No more questions, Your Honor."

Ned's attorney poured water into a glass and handed it to Frida, who took a nervous swallow.

"Mrs. Lomax, how long had your husband been beating you?"

"Your Honor." The DA stood. "This has no bearing on the death of Mr. Lomax."

Frida blurted out. "Since we marry."

The judge pounded his gavel. "Strike that answer from record." He leaned forward toward Frida. "Mrs. Lomax, please."

Ned's attorney, a young fellow from Abilene whom Hank Grove had hired, turned to the judge. "Your Honor, I am trying to establish the character of Mr. Lomax. It will explain why Ned Fallow had no other option."

"Fair enough, but we need to follow proper procedure."

"Objection." The DA approached the bench. "Your Honor, what does Mr. Lomax's character have to do with his death?"

"This is an inquiry, not a trial," said the judge. He pointed to Ned's attorney. "Proceed."

"Tell us, Mrs. Lomax ... what happened the day of your husband's death?"

"I said we go with him, but his eyes full of murder, and he shot Ned."

"So, Mr. Lomax was going to kill Ned Fallow." The lawyer let the last three words roll off his tongue real slow.

After a few more questions and objections, Frida left the stand.

The judge looked at his sheet. "Next witness: Lily Thomason."

"Miss Thomason," said Ned's attorney, "tell us about the day Mr. Lomax and Mr. Fallow had an altercation at Grove's General Store."

Lily folded her hands in her lap and recounted every detail of that nightmarish day. There was plenty of gasping from the people, pounding of the gavel, and objecting from the DA, but, in the end, Lily told of her assault by Lomax, as well as of the day she and Shorty had brought the schoolbooks to Lomax's farm.

"Next witness: Samuel Swanson."

Ned took a deep breath as Shorty took the witness stand.

Ned's attorney said, "Tell us about the day Mr. Lomax tried to kill one of Ned's workers."

"Lomax put a knife to the other Mexican fella's throat, and said that the only good Mexican was a dead one. Everybody knows Lomax shot that other boy."

The courtroom erupted in a thunderous roar. The judge pounded his gavel for order as several men jumped to their feet and cheered Shorty on.

Ned never thought he would have such support from the people after his brusque manner for all these years. But it was the little man's hour—his time to show the townspeople that, although he was a drunk, he cared about his town and the folks in it.

The judge frowned at Shorty. "Mr. Swanson, just answer the questions. Do you understand?"

"Yessir, Your Honor."

"Are you dead certain, Mr. Swanson," the DA said, "that Pete Lomax was dead earnest in doing harm to this Mexican fellow, and not just trying to frighten him?"

"Lomax had a mean streak in him, and everybody in this town knows that for a fact."

"He picked on you, and now you're trying to return the favor?"

"Yeah, he picked on me. But I'm not returning any favor, as you put it. I'm just telling the truth. He was threatenin', like Miss Lily testified, when I rode her by to drop off some schoolwork."

Shorty's face began to twitch, then he straightened up so abruptly that it appeared that he had left his seat. "Pete Lomax deserved what he got. It's one thing to attack Fallow or me, but he was a threat to Miss Lily, and *that*, I wouldn't stand for. Pete Lomax was a bad man, plain and simple. Everything he touched, he spoiled … like a plague."

The judge pounded his gavel as men stood up again, cheering.

"Lomax had murder in his eyes with that Mexican in the store, same way I 'spect he did at Fallow's place. And Ned Fallow ain't no friend of mine, neither," Shorty piped in before leaving the stand.

Ned sat in the witness seat.

"You've been trying to kill Mr. Lomax for years," the DA suggested, pausing for effect as he looked at the jury with palms upturned, "and finally you succeeded, with his family living in your house for two days before you killed him."

Ned nodded.

"Let me get this straight … after years of trying to kill Mr. Lomax, you took his family from him, and then, when he came to bring them home, you put a pitchfork in his throat. Why are they still living with you?"

"'Cause they want to."

"Let's cut right to the heart of the matter," Ned's attorney said. "Did Mr. Lomax shoot you in the back on your property?"

"Yes."

"And you killed him when he came to finish you off with his rifle?"

"Yes."

"No further questions, Your Honor."

Bill Etheridge sat in a conference room at the Grange, amongst eleven other jury members. Over the past two days, they had heard from various citizens about the years-long feud between Ned Fallow and Pete Lomax.

Etheridge had noticed his fellow jurors' expressions drop and the sympathy in their eyes as Frida had explained, in her stoic manner, how Lomax had come to Ned's place. But a lot of folks didn't care for Ned's standoffish manner, and this jury could very well have repaid his rudeness with a vote to go to trial.

The foreman was a good man, about thirty-five years old, from the eastern end of the county. "Let's go round the table, take a vote, and see where we stand."

"Wait a minute … if I could …" Etheridge aimed his folksy smile toward the foreman. "I'd like to say a few words before we vote."

The foreman looked around the table and saw that no one disputed the request. "All right, Bill."

"Now, I know that Ned Fallow hasn't always been the friendliest person, but I've known him since he came to Midland." Etheridge raised a forefinger for emphasis and continued, "He is a good man who just wants to grow wheat—the best wheat ever seen in these parts.

"He isn't the type of man to go looking for trouble, but when it comes to his door, he's not gonna turn tail and run. He's the kinda of fellow who'll help make Midland a better place.

"I know what you're thinking—wondering why he's so unfriendly and all—but he's turned a corner in that regard, and he's been coming round for supper on occasion. Mildred and I are beginning to look upon him as the son we lost all those years ago …" Bill Etheridge bit his lip as he felt the emotion rise in his throat. He ran his hand across his mouth. "He didn't do anything that anybody else in this room wouldn't have done."

Etheridge looked at his fellow jurors and wondered how he did.

"Well, let's start on my left, and say trial or no trial." The foreman pointed, and they went around the table.

By the time it was Etheridge's turn, the vote was eleven to nothing in Ned's favor. Pete Murray looked at Etheridge and said, "Well, I guess we already know *your* vote, Bill. Let's go tell the judge."

The jurors sat in their seats, and the judge said, "Mr. Foreman what do you say?"

Etheridge tried to catch Ned's eye, but Ned stared straight ahead. The foreman stood up. "We find that Ned Fallow acted in self-defense."

Ned bowed his head, then looked over to Etheridge and nodded his thanks.

Etheridge looked at Ned and smiled. *I wasn't gonna let them take you, son.*

CHAPTER 35

▼

Bill Etheridge tied his reins to the hitching post outside of Grove's and saw Ned crossing the street from the smithy.

Etheridge waited for him, and they walked into Grove's together.

"Hey, Ned, there's a telegram for you over at the depot," Hank said from behind the counter.

The words stopped Ned in his tracks. "Telegram? For me?"

Hank pulled a pencil off his ear to add up an order. "That's right. You. Ned Fallow."

Ned walked out.

Hank ran a dust rag over the cash register. "Bill, notice a change come over Ned lately?"

"He's comin' around some, but there's a ways to go."

Hank finished ringing up an order, and the door jingled open again.

"That didn't take long." Hank said. "See you got that telegram all right, Ned."

Ned paused for a moment, looked at the telegram, and nodded.

"Well, we're not trying to be nosy none, Ned, but who's it from?" Etheridge asked.

"My cousin in Colorado. He's visiting me next week."

The wheels were spinning in Etheridge's mind. "He's the one you grew your first wheat crop with?"

"Only cousin I got."

"Bet he can handle a scythe. I'd like to meet this fellow."

A grin creased the corner of Ned's mouth, a grin that said *You never quit, do you?* He nodded at Etheridge and started to leave.

"Ned, what about your order?" Hank asked.

"I'll pick it up Saturday." Ned walked out.

Etheridge looked at Hank. "I'm gonna save a spot for him and the cousin in the scythe competition. I got a good feeling about this. I do believe there's a higher power at work here."

After the evening meal, Lily went to Mrs. Grove's piano and sat at the edge of the stool. Her mind ran back to her first introduction to the piano at her Aunt Esther's house. My, when that woman played, it had been as if the angels had come down from the sky and touched her face, it glowed so—it was the only time she had ever seemed happy. Lily thought about her first lesson on her spinster aunt's Steinway upright. Lily had never seen anything more lovely—the fancy scrollwork on the front and the red velvet behind it.

She ran an index finger back and forth across the ivory keys, lost in the idle movement.

Whenever she wanted to think over a situation, the piano was her retreat. She swung her leg over the stool and faced the piano. She flexed her fingers and began playing her favorite song, one her grandfather had written for her. She sang softly as her fingers glided across the ivory.

"When the sun sets just over Green Mountain,
When shadows of blue grow and cover the lane,
'Tis then that I wander, my memories unfettered
Calling me back to that home on the plain.

And when the sun rises, blessing Green Mountain,
When the day's labors are long and a strain
'Tis well to remember, to pause and be thankful,
The strength from Green Mountain will meet and sustain."

It came to Lily like thunder on the prairie: *Midland is my Green Mountain.*

Lily finished the song, then started it again. Never had she felt such power in its words.

Finally, she played herself out and retired for the evening.

Falling fast asleep, she dreamed of herself and Ned. They were dressed in formal evening wear at the edge of a moonlit mountain lake lined with tall pine trees. He offered his hand, and they stepped out of the shadows into the moonlight, gliding across water as still as glass.

The dark cloud lifted from Ned's countenance as the music flowed all around the lake. The smiling trees on the shoreline sang out the words:

Over Green Mountain
I remember it still,
Blessed Green Mountain,
Your bounty, our fill

She felt so safe and sure in his arms, dancing ever so lightly under a great, shiny moon in a pitch black sky. A voice came clear, and it was her own.

Listen to your heart, it said.

CHAPTER 36

▼

Ned paced up and down the depot platform. Peering down the west end of the tracks, he spotted Vern Swensen, Frida, and Daj coming up the steps. A stranger might easily have mistaken them for a family.

Ned hadn't seen much of the woman or the boy since Vern had started coming around every day to work his rental land and help Frida around the place. *They have such similar personalities,* Ned thought. *Just hard-working folks without a lot of fuss about them.*

Once Frida had moved back to her own place, Ned's yearning for her faded, and he realized that he'd never had any notion of loving her. He felt glad that Frida and Daj would be in good hands with Vern, and he played a part in helping them.

Daj ran up to Ned. The boy wore high-spun overalls and a bright red flannel shirt. "My uncle Thor is coming!" His eyes, no longer sad and downtrodden, sparkled.

"That's good, Daj. Hello, Frida, Vern." The thought of having killed Lomax brought not a whit of guilt, but much satisfaction that he had freed a mother and son from a monster.

"My brother." A great smile spread over Frida's face, creasing her red cheeks. "Thor, he come on train."

Vern tipped his flat-brimmed hat in greeting. "The brother and I will cut wheat in competition."

"Is that right?" Ned looked past Vern for a sign of the train.

Daj smiled up at Ned. "Ned, who are you waiting for?"

Ned noted how Daj's happy, curious eyes reminded him of Tom as a child. "My cousin is on the train."

Ned heard the faint sound of a train whistle. Down the tracks, past the grain elevator, a thin, white plume of smoke rose and separated over a stretch of cottonwoods.

Thoughts of Ketchum raced through his mind. The bond he and Tom O'Brien had forged during childhood could never be broken, no matter the time or distance.

Ned knew it to be Union Pacific Mixed Train #544 that was clanking around the corner with long, loud blasts announcing its arrival. The long, black engine with a red smokestack came creaking to a halt. The deafening noise seemed not to register in Ned's ears, but to rumble in the pit of his stomach as he realized that his best friend—his only friend—was aboard.

The passengers debarked, and a man in a checkered gingham shirt and dungarees tucked into high-top boots with pointed toes walked toward Ned.

"Tom!" Ned waved to his cousin. "Damn, if you don't look like a cowboy."

Tom dropped his suitcase and shook Ned's hand, and then they embraced.

"Good to see you, Ned." Tom O'Brien grinned. "How long has it been?"

"Too long. Too long."

It was Tom, all right—not quite as tall as Ned, but with big shoulders anchoring a sturdy frame. He was a little older, to be sure, but those sparkling eyes still hinted at mischief, and that same, wide, bright-as-a-sunrise smile let a person know that here stood a good and decent man. Square jawed, with a finely turned nose and his black hair longer and wavy, he had grown into a handsome man.

Tom said, "We got a lot of catching up to do. We kinda lost touch."

"Yeah … I should have tracked you down," Ned said. "Well, what you been up to in Colorado?"

"I'm married with two boys—Thomas and William. Own a cattle ranch west of Denver."

"Married. With boys named Thomas and William. Well, I'll be … How long?"

"Nine years. How about you, big cousin?"

Ned shook his head and looked down. "No."

Tom picked up his suitcase and said, "Say, Ned, anyplace about where I can pick up a tin of tobacco?"

Ned motioned and said, "Follow me." Turning around, he saw Vern, Frida, and Daj standing with a great boulder of a man. There was a placid ruggedness about Frida's brother that brought to Ned's mind Nicholas, the great Ukrainian wheat grower.

Walking over to Grove's Store, Ned thought; *Yes, that man looks familiar with hard work.*

"Ned. Come on over and introduce us." Bill Etheridge poured himself a cup of coffee at the potbellied stove.

"Tom, meet Bill Etheridge, Jim Cotton, and Doc Auld."

Tom shook hands with the men.

"It's a pleasure to meet you, Tom," Bill Etheridge said through his folksy grin.

"Thank you very much. This is a nice little town you got here."

Doc Auld gave Tom the once-over. "What brings you this way?"

"Gonna look at some cattle in Abilene, and thought I'd pay old Ned a visit."

The front door jingled open and Shorty Swanson shambled over to the group. "Just got a look at Frida's brother," Shorty cackled. "That man's put together like a dang-gum threshing machine."

Etheridge's ears perked up. "Him and Vern Swensen are gonna scythe a patch on Frida's place." Bill shifted his gaze to Ned.

Ned saw the glance and knew what was coming.

Shorty walked over to the group at the stove, then snuck a peek over toward Ned and Tom. "I imagine there ain't two men in these parts gonna stand a chance against the likes of that big Norwegian and Vern Swensen." Shorty's cheek twitched as he let out a short, nervous laugh.

Ned looked over at Shorty, but couldn't get riled up enough to muster much of a sneer.

"Some folks probably too chicken to even enter." Shorty's droopy eyes widened with glee. "I reckon a fella who ain't entered in the past sure ain't gonna want no part of it this year."

Hank Grove came up to the counter. "What can I do you for, Ned?"

Ned looked at Hank, then at Shorty. He knew they had him.

"Now, Ned," Doc said, fighting a grin, "Shorty's just having a little fun with you."

"Ain't nobody around here gonna be able to hold a candle to that big Norwegian, including you, Ned Fallow." Shorty looked dead-on at Ned and Tom. "This here must be your cousin. You two best stay away from the competition. No reason you two wanna get whupped." Shorty feigned laughing.

"Competition? What competition is this, Ned?" Tom lowered his brow and leveled his gaze at Shorty.

"Scything wheat for three days—"

Shorty cut in. "But your cousin here has never wanted any part of it." Shorty thrust out his jaw for good measure. "He sure don't want no part of it this year. I guarantee *that.*"

The room grew silent.

Tom looked at Shorty, then Ned, his gaze sure and confident. "What's this yahoo talking about? A little work?"

"Yeah, a little work." Ned turned to face Etheridge. "Where do we sign up?"

Etheridge looked right at Doc Auld. His eyes brightened and a smile cut across his face that said, *I told you so!* "Over at the Grange Hall—today."

"All right."

Ned and Tom left the store.

As they walked down the boardwalk, a grin creased the corner of Tom's mouth. He nudged Ned's shoulder with his. "Ain't been in town twenty minutes, and you're turning me into a sodbuster."

"Just want to make sure you haven't gone soft on me."

Tongue in cheek, Tom nodded at Ned. "I see you still bring out the best in folks."

"I see you're still a wiseacre."

"Somebody had to get out of Ketchum with a sense of humor, and it sure wasn't gonna be you."

Tom O'Brien saw a large sign with bold red letters hanging over the entrance to the Grange Hall: "Scythe Competition Registration Inside."

"Damn, Ned—folks take this thing serious."

"I can't believe I just got snookered into this damn thing."

"Come on, Ned. It'll be like the old days in Ketchum."

"I came here to get away from those old days."

"Well, big cousin, there's no turnin' back." They entered through the double doors, and Tom took in the spacious area in front of him.

An enormous green threshing machine was on display near the entrance. It stood roughly twelve feet high and was eighteen feet in length. Four large wheels supported a carriage that had intake and outtake chutes.

Stationed at the rear of the hall was an enormous oak table on a platform; behind it, a blackboard listed the two-man teams, along with the names of those assigned to monitor the competitors.

Tom looked over at Ned, who had a scowl running from cheek to cheek. "Ned, they *really* take this serious."

Ned sighed. "Let's register."

A young farmer approached the cousins. "Ned, you're not registering, are you?"

Ned stared at him as if looking at a pesky fly.

The young man looked at Tom. "Howdy."

Tom smiled and nodded hello.

The young man looked back at Ned for some response; seeing none coming, he walked away.

Tom watched the friendly fellow slink off. He looked around the room, now filling with farmers fresh from registering. Many of them lingering just a bit to socialize and size up the competition.

"I don't need your lecture," Ned said, anticipating Tom's disapproval.

"Ned, no need to be unfriendly to folks."

"Did you come all this way to lecture me?"

"What good has it ever done? All I know is that I've only been in town an hour, and I see that you still got that chip on your shoulder."

"Any more advice?"

"Grandpa used to say, 'This life's a journey, and it's about the people you help along the way.'"

"Yeah, well, I did help a woman and her son get a new start in life."

"There's more to it than that. It's how a man treats his neighbor—rich or poor, big or small. You need to take it to heart and start acting on it. Otherwise, this land, no matter how rich it is, will turn you sour as Ketchum did, maybe more."

Bill Etheridge approached the cousins. "Say, Tom, I guess you didn't plan on cutting wheat for three days."

"Can't say I did, Bill. How many teams entered?"

"Twenty. Now, I hope you're staying for the hoedown afterwards."

"The big cousin here hadn't told me about it, but, after cuttin' wheat for three days, I reckon that sounds like a good idea."

"Great. Now, I'm holding you responsible for bringing ol' Ned along with you." Etheridge winked at Tom.

Tom, fighting a smile, looked at his cousin. "If I got to drag him kicking and screaming, he'll be there."

"Well, good luck to both of you, and I'll be seeing you during the competition, 'cause I'll be spot-checking you."

"See you then, big fella." Tom nodded at Etheridge and couldn't miss the note of approval passing between them that hinted that, together, they could bring Ned around.

A loose-limbed man wearing a wide-brimmed hat approached the cousins.

"Ned," the man said, tipping his hat. His eyes seemed uncertain.

He seemed to want to ask something, but his shy nature fought against it.

"Vern, I want you to meet my cousin, Tom O'Brien. Tom, meet Vern Swensen, one of the best wheat men in these parts."

Tom shook hands with Vern, and his hand was engulfed by long, sinewy fingers. "Nice to meet you, Vern."

Vern's eyes questioned Ned. "You cut wheat, Ned?" He gaped in disbelief as Ned nodded.

A man came toward them, looking like he had been chiseled out of a mountainside. His short blond hair lay on a massive head that rested on a thick, cruel neck.

Vern turned an upturned palm toward the man. "This is Frida's brother."

Ned extended his hand. "Ned Fallow."

The man looked at Ned, his pale Nordic eyes holding an icy reserve. "Yah, Thor Jorgensen here." He shook Ned's hand, then Tom's.

Tom felt the power of the strongman's grip.

"Thor …" Vern paused and raised a forefinger. "He runs his own farm single-handed, like you, Ned." Blood rose to Vern's cheeks, and a sparkle invaded his placid eyes. "Born in Norway like me, and come to North Dakota with his family back in '77."

Tom noticed Ned stealing glances at the impassive Thor—he knew right then and there that they were in for the competition of their lives.

The wagon bumped and clattered over the dirt road as Tom took in the acres and acres of black earth and golden wheat.

He looked at the endless land in the waning sunlight. The crimson-streaked horizon stretched on and on. "I see how you'd take to it here, Ned."

"First time I laid my eyes on it, I knew."

"I remember Grandpa saying how land can swallow up a man." Tom glanced at Ned, noticing his clenched jaw and uncompromising eyes. *My God, he's got a hardness about him*, Tom thought.

Ned sat silent, his face set in sadness.

"Ned, most folks seem real hospitable in Midland."

Ned nodded.

"Appears like they all know about hard work."

"Some do." Ned shifted his gaze to the northwest sky. A lone vertical cloud resembling a man's profile faced an assembly of cumulus clouds huddling to the east. "Plenty more have no idea."

"Something tells me that big Norwegian does," Tom replied.

"Maybe so." Ned had a far-off look. It seemed as though he were trying to find a missing part of himself.

"Plenty of these folks struggled greatly to make this life for themselves."

Suddenly, Ned's Belgian horse reared up and snorted, shying away from a large coyote that bounded out of a patch of bluestem grass. The animal scurried across the trail, stopped, and looked back. It focused its keen eyes on Ned, then darted into a thicket.

"That was a big ol' male loner," Tom said. "Acted like he knew you. Probably wondering where the prairie went. Remember, Grandpa said that the Indians believe the coyote to be the spirit of the prairie."

The horse remained spooked, snorting and rocking its head up and down.

"Easy there, big fella," Ned commanded. The horse settled down, and they continued.

"How's your farm doing, Ned?"

"Doin' good. I have a threshing machine and binder come twice a year. Had some Mexicans that helped out, but one of them passed ..." The words died in Ned's throat.

"How'd it happen?"

"Heatstroke."

"I've lost two men on my ranch, Ned. You can't let it get to you. Nobody ever said this was an easy life we cut for ourselves."

Ned looked at Tom, then back to the road ahead.

Tom let the silence settle between them for a bit, then said, "Ned, that Norwegian's one big son of a bitch."

CHAPTER 37

▼

At first light, Tom stood with Ned at the corner of a patch of Red Jerusalem wheat. He shielded his eyes from the sunlight that streamed over the eastern bluff, casting long shadows in the yard. A light breeze blew from the west, signaling that it would be a good day to cut wheat.

Tom thought of the old Ukrainian wheat grower, Nicholas, teaching them how to flail wheat, his voice booming, "Is good, boy, is good." And now, Tom stood on Ned's farm, in Ned's wheat field, getting ready to cut Ned's wheat.

Tom could see the same hungry look in Ned's eyes—the same look he'd had in Ketchum, in his first field of standing wheat. Tom said, "Like Grandpa used to say, 'What are we waiting for? That wheat isn't getting any younger.'"

Ned smiled at his cousin. "Always liked Red Jerusalem for its durability." Ned took a kernel from the head of a stalk and snapped it with his fingernails.

"Old Nicholas would say, 'Just right, boy.'" Tom said.

For a second, Ned had that far-off look, and Tom reckoned that his cousin was seeing himself and Nicholas in Ketchum, in a wind-swept field of wheat.

Ned cradled the scythe handle in his big, rough-hewn hands, then wrapped his fingers around it. "Yeah, looks like we might have some competition, little cousin."

"Work always brought a joy to you, Ned."

"Well, what are we waiting for? This wheat ain't getting any younger."

Their scythes swept through the stalks with a rhythm forged out of sweat and tears on the Ketchum prairie. They were a team once again, swinging their large shoulders in cadence. The familiar sound of the hissing blades striking the stalks brought back childhood memories.

"Ned, it ain't even noon, and I'm bettin' we got an acre of wheat cut and shocked."

"There'll be a harvest moon tonight, Tom." They paused to sharpen their scythes with fieldstones at the north end of the field. To their left, the west field lay barren.

Tom said through a grin, "Well, we're gonna work nonstop, like the old days in Ketchum, and give that big son-bitch Norwegian a run for his money." They turned toward the south end. Just beyond sat Ned's barn, brimming with livestock and farm implements.

Ned tilted his head to one side. "Why not, cousin? I got plenty of kerosene lamps in the barn for night work."

"We best be careful—don't want to burn your field."

"Haven't yet."

Tom searched Ned's face. "I see Bill Etheridge gonna spot-check us. That there's a good man. You're lucky to have him for a neighbor."

"A little windy, but he is a good man and a good neighbor." Ned looked away. "I learned that much, anyway."

Tom saw a buggy approaching. "Well, speak of the devil. Who's riding with Bill?"

Ned dropped his scythe and stood frozen in place.

"Hello-o-o, neighbors." Etheridge waved his old straw hat at the cousins, and his silvery hair shone in the sunlight like a sea beacon in one of Grandpa's stories.

Ned regained a bit of his composure. "Folksy as ever."

"And he's thinking you're as grumpy as ever." They exchanged a look, the years passing between them back to when they were boys.

"I'm tryin', little cousin, I'm tryin' …" Ned's voice trailed off as he stared at Etheridge's companion.

"There they are—those threshermen cousins." said Bill. "Tom, this is Lily Thomason, our schoolteacher who returned to us from Abilene."

Tom absorbed the sight of the beautiful young woman. She wore a white blouse with frilly lace around the collar, and a blue skirt. Her golden face seemed to glow.

"Pleasure to meet you," Tom said, feeling like he had just seen a beautiful sunrise for the first time.

"Nice to meet you, Tom," Lily said. She then looked at the dumbstruck Ned. "Hello, Ned." A hint of red rose to her cheeks.

Ned stood blank-faced. "Hello."

Etheridge looked like the cat that had swallowed the canary.

No one spoke; then Tom said, "What brings you out this way?"

"I made some sandwiches and lemonade," Lily said, keeping her eyes on Ned.

Ned remained planted in his tracks, seemingly unable to move or speak further.

Etheridge straightened himself, as if to break the awkwardness. "Was at Frida's farm earlier today. That Jorgensen fella cuts wheat like a house afire, and ol' Vern ain't no slouch, neither."

Tom smiled and said, "Well, now, we'll just have to work straight through. Right, Ned?"

Ned snapped out of his stupor. "We didn't enter this thing to lose."

Etheridge dropped his chin, his expression allowing a little beyond amazement. "That'd be two nights straight without sleep."

Tom noticed Ned sneaking looks at Lily, who seemed as cool as a cucumber. "That it would, Bill. But don't you fret none—old Ned and I will see it through."

Etheridge handed Tom a basket of sandwiches and a jug of lemonade. "We won't keep you boys. I'll be checking on you, and don't forget, I'll be by the morning after to take measurements." Etheridge clucked to the mare, which pivoted around. "Also, I 'spect to see both of you at the hoedown."

Lily turned and raised a hand toward Ned, the way an Indian would in offering the peace sign. Her face showed so little, yet revealed so much.

Ned watched the buggy until it turned past the south fork and out of sight.

"Big cousin, I do believe that pretty young thing has taken a liking to you."

"We gonna yammer all day, or we gonna cut wheat?"

Tom raised his scythe. "Let's cut some wheat, and you can tell me all about you and the lovely schoolmarm at the same time."

Under the deep blue twilight that shrouded the land, the cousins placed the last of the kerosene lamps along the perimeter of the field. Then, they grabbed their scythes and resumed cutting, side by side and six feet apart.

Tom said, "Remember? Oh, it must have been back in the fall of '84. You were twelve, me eleven. Grandpa had us work through the night."

They continued to cut the wheat, and they approached the back swath.

Ned kept his head down and stroked the scythe blade. "Oh, yeah, pulling all those vegetables—turnips, carrots, okra … everything, and having us store them in the root cellar. Said his left knee ached, and that meant a big storm was a-comin'."

"Damned if he wasn't right," Tom said, pausing as they reached the north end. "One helluva twister come through. Just missed the house and barn, but tore right through that vegetable patch. Remember? Grandpa had a feel for that sort of thing. Said he saved a Pawnee medicine man's life back in '46, and that the Injun taught him all he knew about the Spirit in the Sky. Said that men could never conquer nature, but that nature could conquer men, and in ways you couldn't expect."

Ned struck a match and lit a kerosene lamp that a gust of wind had blown out. He looked up at the starry sky. "I can't see why we stayed in Ketchum. That land wasn't fit for anything." Ned attacked the standing wheat with his scythe and remembered a morning long ago …

The wheat had put up its first "joint," which contained the tiny head that would later emerge and develop. William O'Connor gazed at the giant, orange sun resting on the horizon, strewing light over the wheat field.

"Ned, Mr. Tennyson has a description I always liked: 'The scarlet shafts of sunrise.' Every time I see the break of dawn, I'm amazed all over again. Such a beautiful thing."

Ned looked at the landscape below the sun: it was stark, almost barren, save for some spear grass and an occasional scrub tree.

"Grandpa, how come we never left Ketchum for a place with more fertile land?"

William O'Connor paused for a moment, running his hand through his thinning white hair. "Packin' up and movin' is for younger folks. 'Sides, everything I am or ever was is right here in Ketchum. Met and fell in love with your grandma not far from here—she's buried beyond the berm—and your and Tom's pa's were lost out yonder. Sometimes, I feel their spirits in the wind. Ketchum holds the hand the good Lord dealt me, and I reckon I'm gonna play her out to the end. For this land takes more than it gives."

Ned paused from cutting. The full moon shimmered high in the sky, and the lamps around the field flickered like giant fireflies. A line from a passage of Tennyson that William O'Connor liked to read aloud came to mind. "A land of old … where fragments of forgotten peoples dwelt."

A stark sun rose over a pale horizon, daring a cloud to enter its realm. The sky had the look of shimmering heat, and the warm, humid morning air clung all around, confirming that it would be a scorcher.

As the morning wore on, the air grew hot and sticky. Back and forth across the field, the cousins scythed. Late in the afternoon, Ned left the field, barely able to keep his head up. His denim shirt was soaked with perspiration. Tom looked weary to Ned, but seemed in better condition.

Ned had little appetite, but would try to eat.

Doubt crept into his mind. Would he be able to continue for two more days without sleep? The sight of Lily had done something to him.

So much had happened in the last few months: he had harvested his winter wheat; Tino had died; he had killed Lomax; he had lived with Frida and Daj; the trial; he had harvested his spring crop ... and Lily had returned. *Yes, she has returned,* he thought. *And what have I been waiting for?*

He felt torn between working with Tom and rushing into town to see her. Images of his family in Ketchum and Lily all rose in his mind, clouding his thoughts. He felt his once-inexhaustible energy being sapped from his body.

"That sun was some kinda hot," Tom said, looking across the table at Ned.

Ned noticed the sun sinking behind the catalpa tree, its damage done. "Yeah." Ned heard the weariness in his voice, and he lowered a forkful of cold beans back down to his bowl.

"Ned, why don't you get a couple hours rest, and I'll head back out?"

"Nah, I'll be all right."

Tom shook his head. What was the use?

As darkness fell over the western horizon, gathering in the waning sunlight, a light, cool breeze blew in from the north. It had come too late for Ned, who struggled to light the kerosene lamps. Working into the night, Ned's movements became slow and deliberate. Then, while raising his scythe, he collapsed, face-first.

Dazed, he smelled the rich, dark soil, which brought back memories of Ketchum and a glimpse of an October day, late in the afternoon, when Ned and his grandfather had tilled the vegetable patch. The hazy, purple sky; the crisp autumnal air; the safety and comfort of William O'Connor's presence—the touch of his leathery hands; the feel of his unshaven face; the unconquerable twinkle in his eyes. God help him, how Ned had loved that man. "Love heals all wounds, boy ... Follow your heart," were the only words Ned remembered from that day with his granddad. It had been a quicksilver moment of a childhood that felt so close, yet so far. He struggled to regain consciousness.

"Ned, are you all right?" Tom yelled to his motionless cousin lying on the ground.

Ned rolled onto his back and forced himself up into a sitting position. "Had better times."

"Come on, Ned, I'll help you inside."

Ned grabbed Tom's hand and pulled himself up. His shoulders slumped forward. He placed his right arm across Tom's shoulders and stumbled to the farmhouse, where Tom took him to his bed.

"Ned, you get some rest. I'll head back out."

Ned's sleep was fitful and included a nightmare in which he was a wheat stalk rooted deep in fertile soil. As his stems and leaves waved majestically in the Kansas sun, an uneasiness ran through him. He didn't belong to the soil anymore; he was unfit. He saw his grandfather William as another stalk of wheat.

"Ned ... Don't reject your roots, son."

Ned felt his grandfather's sadness and ached to embrace him.

The earth drew Ned's roots down deeper.

His grandfather cried, "I love you, boy."

Ned desperately tried to free his roots, to get near his family. Deeper he sank into the soil, until only his spikes remained above ground. Panic ran through him.

The moist earth then swallowed him whole. His consciousness began to dissolve. He felt himself disappear into nothingness.

At first light, Ned looked out the kitchen window; down in the field, Tom continued to cut wheat. So much had passed in the years since he had last seen his cousin, but so little had changed.

Ned stuck his head out the window and hollered, "Loafin' on the job, cousin?"

"What else you expect from hired help?"

"Come on in for breakfast."

Ned watched his cousin walk toward the house. Tom's curly black hair was matted down with sweat and dirt. Specks of soil flecked his handsome face.

Ned stood at the stove warming a pot of oatmeal as Tom came in from the porch. "Well, little cousin, we'd best eat this porridge and get back to the field." Ned felt a smile curl at the side of his mouth. "As Grandpa used to say, that wheat ain't getting any younger."

CHAPTER 38

▼

Around midmorning, the Grange Hall was alive with loud whoops and hollers as boisterous farmers roamed about, wagering and swapping stories. Many also sipped corn whiskey from mason jars. This conduct had become a tradition during the competition; town teetotalers and fussbudgets had given up on cleaning it up a while back. The competition had taken on a life of its own.

Shorty Swanson burst into the Grange Hall, twitching like crazy. He went over to a group of men sitting on barrels in a corner.

"Is it true?" Shorty's big saucer eyes whirled with excitement.

"What's that, Shorty?" Etheridge asked, trying to keep his best poker face.

"Hank said you told him that Ned Fallow keeled right over in his own wheat field." Shorty removed a red bandanna from his back pocket and wiped his brow.

Doc Auld scratched under his chin, pondering Shorty's words. "Seems like Mr. Fallow just got knocked down a peg."

"Think you ought to check on him, Doc?" Shorty asked.

"Nah, Bill says he's just a little overworked. Bet he gets back into his field more determined than ever. Think Mr. Fallow's learning a little humility, Bill?"

"Too early to tell, Doc, but I'm a-bettin' he'll be a better man, win or lose." Bill stood up. "Well, I better head on home. Tomorrow's gonna be a big day. Let's all meet up here tomorrow."

Hank said, "Now, where *else* would we be?"

Bill smiled. "You got a point there, Hank." He waved so long and left the Grange Hall.

Driving out of town, Bill wondered what tomorrow would bring out of Ned Fallow and his cousin; he reckoned that it might be a sight to behold. He could hardly wait.

Rattling along in his buggy on the dirt trails, Bill Etheridge headed back into town after spot-checking his entries on this, the final day of competition. The air was windy and warm, but dry. He always liked dry, warm days for cutting and threshing wheat. The wind he could do without, but you rarely got everything going your way when it came to wheat. At times like this, he couldn't imagine another life for himself.

Pulling up to the Grange Hall, he heard the shouts and laughs of good, hard-working folks letting their hair down a bit.

Lord knows, they deserved it. They had been through some difficult times, surviving drought and pestilence. These were strong and resilient men of wheat. Bill had just left Ned Fallow's place, and, goodness gracious, those two cousins were cutting some wheat.

Ned Fallow was the purest wheat farmer Bill had ever seen. Nothing, but nothing, would or could stop him from growing his wheat. Bill thought that Ned's and his cousin's upbringing had made them strong and enduring.

And now, the end result of that upbringing was a display of cutting wheat the old way—a way fading faster than a setting sun in January.

Bill spotted Doc Auld and a few other men talking in a corner. As he walked over, an idea popped into his head, an idea he would throw out at the right moment.

Bill leaned his big shoulder on a post and said, "Ned Fallow's cuttin' wheat like a man possessed. Lord have mercy. Yesterday, he appeared half dead, and now … Whew, this is some competition."

Doc pointed his pipe at Etheridge. "I told you to never count that man out. Hard to the bone, yessir." His eyes widened and his body bristled, dissolving his steady demeanor. "Shorty, I could use a swig of that concoction in your flask."

"Certainly, Doc." Shorty handed over the flask. "I hear them Brockway boys are holdin' their own." Shorty's cheek quivered out one good twitch.

"They're doin' good, but this is a two-horse race." Etheridge heard the excitement rise in his voice and all around the noisy Grange.

"I got a thought." Doc Auld took a swig and handed the flask back to Shorty. "Let's hitch my team to the courtin' wagon; a bunch of us could head up to Fallow's and Vern's farms tonight and see them in action."

"Great idea, Doc." Shorty looked up at Etheridge. "How 'bout it, Bill?"

"Don't that beat all. Why, I was thinkin' the same thing."

Doc nodded. He liked what he was hearing. "We're just a couple of old birds who aren't in such a hurry about progress."

Promptly at six o'clock, Doc Auld pulled the courtin' wagon up to the Grange.

"Hey, Doc," Bill Etheridge said in greeting. He tried to climb up into the wagon, but couldn't manage it. "Whee, this is a big ol' wagon."

Shorty and Hank Grove helped Etheridge up to the front seat, then stepped up and sat on long benches anchored to the back bed.

Doc slackened the reins. "Let's head west and see how Vern and that big fella are doin'." He hollered to the horses, and off they rode.

At dusk, they approached Vern's farm from a small bluff. Below, kerosene lamps flickered in the wheat field adjacent to the farmhouse; overhead, field moths fluttered in the ethereal light.

A faint whooshing sound broke the stillness of the night—*Shoo, Shoo*. Thor Jorgensen—shirtless and bigger than life—scythed the wheat.

Shorty wiped his brow with his trusty bandanna. "Lord have mercy," he said, twitching three times. "Would you look at that."

The huge Norwegian's muscular body glistened with sweat and wheat.

Walking in long strides from the farmhouse, Vern waved to the wagon.

Vern shot a glance at Thor, who continued to mow down the wheat. "We work through night." He raised his scythe and resumed cutting the wheat, his long arms like two pendulums.

Doc Auld nodded in appreciation. "Yessir, Ned always admired old Vern's work."

Bill Etheridge took a swig of Shorty's corn liquor and wiped his lips. "Let's go to Ned's and see how he's doin'. I do believe this is going to be a night to remember."

Doc Auld wanted to hold onto every moment as he drove the big wagon that rattled across the diminishing prairie in the cool night air. A canopy of huge, black sky chock full of shining stars and a fat, yellow moon added to the night's magical quality.

"Gentlemen, this is a special night—one we may never see the likes of again." He steadied the team as his side of the wagon rose up and rolled over a big stone, bouncing him up and back down.

"Yee-haw." Doctor Richard Auld shouted. For one night, he wanted a piece of his youth back.

"Shorty, I believe I need another swallow of your Kansas sheep dip," Bill Etheridge said.

Shorty slid up his seat and handed the jug to Etheridge.

Etheridge took a swig, his face full of confidence and a hint of whiskey in his cheeks. "This competition reminds me of how it used to be in Midland." He handed the jug back over his shoulder.

Hank Grove took it from Etheridge. "Memory's a funny thing. The good times are remembered fondly, and the bad are tucked away in the back of the mind."

Doc peeped back at Hank, who cradled the jug in his hands, his face marked by the wonder of it all.

Doc knew Hank's words to be true, and, soon enough, the old ways would only be a memory. But tonight, he was going to bury that thought and let the nostalgia flow through his veins.

They pulled up at the edge of Ned's field and found the cousins working almost as one. Stroke after graceful stroke, no motion was wasted. Their shoulders swung in perfect rhythm, and they were as light on their feet as fireflies dancing in the moonlight.

"Don't ever forget this night, boys. Them there are men of wheat." Etheridge's grand, mellow voice strung out the words. "The way the good Lord intended it to be."

Doc Auld hollered, "Come on, Ned. Come on, Tom. Cut that wheat."

The rest of the men let out a unified roar straight from their bellies and hearts toward the two men in their field of wheat.

Ned heard the cheer from the wagon. He straightened and paused, which was so out of character that a look of surprise came over Tom.

"What's wrong, Ned?"

"Nothing. But I need to cross a bridge. Come on." Ned shouldered his scythe and started across the stubble toward the big, white wagon with its side lanterns lit, sitting at the field's edge like a great ghost.

"You fellas wouldn't be sharing a nip, now, would you?"

"Shorty's got us covered in that department, Ned." Etheridge's flushed face reminded Ned of a happy Hallowe'en pumpkin.

"This is some fine-lookin' wagon. Don't remember seeing it around town."

"Belongs to me, Ned," Doc said. "I keep it packed away for special occasions. Reminds me of the Conestoga I rode out to Oregon from way back in Baltimore. Goodness, that was nearly half a century ago."

"Think of that," Tom said, smiling at Doc, "This country was wild as the wind back then."

"It was somethin', I tell you. By the time we hit the Mississippi, Manifest Destiny was in my veins."

Tom held out a tin cup, and Shorty poured. "You saw the big herds, then?"

"We saw the big herds, son, rumbling and thundering across the plains, yes indeed. Hunted some, too. Had a skirmish or two with Indians along the way. Got all the way to Oregon, and the place was just too wet. I'd liked the looks of this country, so I drifted back this way. Almost lost a child along the way. It's been a hard life, but one I wouldn't have traded for any other."

Tom raised his cup to the moonlight. "Here's to the men of Manifest Destiny. If not for them, none of us would be here today."

"Hip, hip," the men chorused, and all raised their cups in a toast to Doc Auld.

"Gentlemen, to the old ways. I never swung a scythe, but, tonight, we are all men of wheat." Doc took a healthy swallow. "And tonight, Dr. Richard McGuire Auld is proud to be among you."

Ned put his hand on Doc's shoulder. "This country owes you and your kind a lot, Doc."

"I did what I could."

"You did more than your part, Doc." Shorty tipped the jug to Doc's cup.

"Shorty," Ned spoke up, and everyone turned toward him. "Why don't you take the reins from Doc and drive us to that bluff over yonder? I'd like you all to see something."

"Hey, cousin, don't we have some wheat to cut?"

"Tom, I'm listening to your advice right now, so jump on up."

The wagon came to a stop where the moon and sky seemed but an arm's length apart. "Over there," Ned said, pointing. "The moon's a bit too bright, but that yellow light is shining from Frida's place. I never noticed it until the night after my trial. I started seeing things different after that."

The men kept silent, their eyes on Ned.

"Far as I'm concerned, that's where something good happened. When Shorty Swanson tore into Lomax with both fists 'cause he had disrespected Lily." Ned paused and cleared his throat. "I want to thank you for that, Shorty, and for coming to my defense at the trial. You had no reason to, the way I've treated you over the years. I hope someday you can find it in you to forgive me. You're a good man, Shorty."

Shorty sat up, a tear streaming down his reddening cheek. "Let's shake on it." Shorty extended his hand, and Ned shook it.

"Let's have one last toast." Bill Etheridge stood and raised his cup. "To the old ways, and to new beginnings."

Ned leaned back in his chair on the porch and saw the moonlight streaming through the catalpa tree, casting long, oblique shadows across the yard and up the barn walls, shadows that looked as though they belonged to some fairy tale.

"Um …" Tom took a bite of his sandwich, and his cheek swelled. "Ned, I gotta say, this is the best ham sandwich I ever did eat. That pretty schoolmarm gonna make some man a good wife."

Ned shook his head as he felt a grin crease the corner of his mouth. He looked up at the sky. "Remember how Grandpa taught us to find the North Star and make a wish? He said our dreams would come true."

Tom gazed at the sky. "The year before he died, Grandpa told me he wished on that star every night that you and I'd have a better life than he had. Think we lost anything going after that life?"

"Know *I* did. I had so much inside me from Ketchum that I took it out on folks around here."

"Never too late to make amends, big cousin."

"Did tonight. And I promise you, cousin, that I'll keep at it until I get it right."

As the night wore on, Ned felt a freedom working the scythe, gaining strength even as Tom slowed. He thought about the meaning of his small place in the universe, about the values his grandfather had taught him, and about how ashamed William O'Connor would have been of him. He returned to a spring day in Ketchum, a few months after his father had passed …

William O'Connor plowed a field with mule and harness as young Ned walked by his side. Taking a break, William gave an apple core to the mule and sat down with his grandson in the upturned soil.

"Grandpa, how come we're not seeding this field?"

"This field needs to lie fallow for a season."

"Like my name?"

Grabbing a chunk of soil, William O'Connor placed it under his grandson's nose.

"You smell that? She's startin' to go stale. Mother Nature needs to nurture this field for a while. We work her too hard, and she'll lose her substance."

As the dawn broke clear over the eastern bluff, Ned dropped his scythe and wondered how long he had gone on without his substance. He longed for one last meal with his family in Ketchum—one last meal to tell William O'Connor and his progeny how much he missed and loved them.

Ned walked up to Tom and put his hand on his shoulder. "Don't know if I've ever told you this, but there isn't any man on this earth I'd rather work with than you. Let's go on in and have some breakfast. I'm famished."

Ned handed the last dish to Tom, who dried it and hung the rag on a peg.

"Ned, I got something I think you might like. Wait here a minute."

Tom returned with his hands cupped.

"What you got there, Tom?"

Tom opened his hands, and there was their grandfather's corncob pipe. "It's brought me good luck, and, well, I figured it was your turn to have it."

Ned felt it in his hands. The rough texture of the bowl and the feel of the pipestem flooded Ned with memories of those mornings long ago when William O'Connor had sat on a bucket in the yard and drawn on his empty pipe.

That had been his time alone—a time when Ned figured William had thought about *what if:* What if Jim Fallow and Thomas O'Brien hadn't died? What if they hadn't settled on that godforsaken land? What if he had never left for the west at all?

"This means a lot, Tom. Thanks."

"Ned, I'm gonna stick my nose in one more time. You in love with the schoolmarm?"

"All the way, cousin."

"I don't know what all passed between you two, but I know when I see two people in love. What do you intend to do?"

"She turned me down twice before. Guess you could say I'm a little gun shy."

"Tell her you're changing.... No, *show* her you're changing. No woman should be burdened with Ketchum. Maybe you could show her that new, charming side ..." A big grin spread over Tom's face, and Ned couldn't help but join him.

"You're reminding me of Grandpa."

"His humor helped get us through Ketchum, and it'll help you right here in Midland, Ned. What do you think he'd say?"

Ned studied the floor until he could no longer see it. "Follow your heart."

Ned looked through the kitchen window and saw Bill Etheridge struggling to get out of his buggy. *Ol' Bill needs a bigger buggy,* he thought.

Ned came out to the porch.

"That's a mighty fine piece of work you and Tom did in the competition," Etheridge said, pointing to the west field, where the shocked wheat stood.

"Not bad for a couple days, I reckon."

"Reason I come by, Ned, is to let you know that the hoedown has been set back a week, 'cause Frida and Vern are gettin' hitched today at the Grange Hall." Etheridge nodded hello to Tom, who had joined them on the porch.

Ned said, "I'm real pleased for the both of 'em."

"Bill, is there a train leaving for Abilene today?" Tom asked.

"Yes—if you hurry, you can catch it."

Tom lifted an eye toward Ned as a knowing grin spread across his face. "How 'bout I go to Abilene, take care of business, and get back in time for the hoedown?" Tom raised a finger at Etheridge. "Bill, I've *never* been one to miss a good time."

"Get your gear together, Tom, and I'll get you to the depot." Ned hadn't gotten the words out before Tom had hustled into the house.

"Ned, Frida and Vern wanted me to make sure you were coming to the wedding. They got the new preacher marrying them today at two o'clock at the Grange Hall." Etheridge's eyebrows rose, and his face brightened with hope. "Can I tell them they can count on you coming?"

"I'll be there."

Tom came out to the porch, holding his leather satchel. "Ned, let's get me to Abilene. Bill, I'll see you at that hoedown. I 'spect you to save a cold beer for me."

Pivoting his buggy around, Etheridge grinned out of the side of his mouth. "Don't you worry none, Tom, we've never run out yet."

Ned watched the Abilene train disappear around the bend. Then, he decided to take a chance. He walked up Main Street and took a seat at the gazebo steps at the end of town and waited. He ran his gaze down the empty street and reckoned that folks were getting ready for the wedding.

He thought of how good it had been to spend time with Tom, and he promised himself that they would see more of each other.

Ned thought about Lily in Etheridge's buggy the other day. Yes, she was beautiful, but there was something else, too. There was a tranquility about her now that he hadn't seen before; she wasn't so skittish, and seemed to have turned a corner without looking back. But what about himself? Was *he* peeking around that corner, too? And was anyone there, waiting for him?

He looked past the Grange Hall to a rise where a little cottonwood tree stood at the top. He wondered whether there were a spring nearby, for the tree would need some help, being so small and alone. Somehow, bravely, its tiny, bare branches reached upward. Someday, it might be a great tree a hundred feet tall, with many strong limbs stretching high and thick roots sunk deep into the earth.

But now, it was small and alone on top of a grassy hill surrounded by those giants, the sky and the earth. It needed the water and light from the sky and the nutrients from the earth to prosper and grow the thick, green leaves that would work in harmony to replenish the giants.

Ned peeked over his shoulder and saw what he had been waiting for—Lily was coming down the boardwalk. She wore a blue skirt and a white-and-red-checkered blouse; a shawl was draped over her shoulders.

"Hello, Lily."

Lily stopped and smiled at Ned, her olive skin making the smile seem even brighter. "Hello, Ned. Are you going to the wedding?"

Ned approached her, his heart pounding. "Yes. May I escort you there?" Ned offered his arm and realized that this was his first social engagement with Lily Thomason. He hoped it wouldn't be the last.

Inside the Grange Hall, wooden seats were set up in rows, with an opening down the middle, facing a planked platform. A murmur started and grew as folks elbowed one another in disbelief at Ned and Lily arriving and sitting down together.

A stranger in a dark suit with a crease down the middle of the pant legs came out onto the platform. Ned figured him to be the new preacher. He was of average height, with a sharp chin and nose, and his long forehead ended at a shock of brown hair parted down one side. His cheeks had a light pink hue, which added a bit of life to his prim, pale face. His small, pouched eyes gazed seriously over the audience. The general feeling was that he could resort to fire and brimstone, if it were called for.

"Today, I have the pleasure of bringing together Vern Swensen and Frida Jorgensen in marriage."

Ned noted that Frida was using her maiden name. *Good for her,* he thought.

Vern came down the aisle dressed in a long, black jacket and string tie. His hair, oiled and combed straight back, accentuated his long, angular face. He stepped lightly, without the usual underlying woe. Vern got to the platform, where Dan O'Hurley, his best man, stood.

Frida then came down the aisle with her blond hair in pigtails. Dressed in a blue organdy dress with long sleeves, she was escorted by her brother, Thor. Ned felt a warm glow in his chest as she turned and looked at him for a moment, her pale eyes shining.

Ned reached for Lily's hand and held it throughout the ceremony.

Dan O'Hurley stood on the platform as everyone gathered around. "I would like to wish the best of times for Vern and Frida. Never were two people more deserving." He raised his glass of punch. "To Frida and Vern."

Folks clapped and cheered, and someone yelled, "Vern. Speech."

Vern ambled over and shook Dan's hand. His face flushed red as he put his hand to his mouth, trying to find the words. Dan put his hand on Vern's shoulder. "This is a happy day; tell the folks how you feel."

Vern looked at Dan as though asking what he should say. He exhaled for so long, one wondered where all the air came from. "Thank you ... I never thought I would feel this way again. Thank you for coming."

As folks clapped, Vern reached his hand over to Frida and helped her onto the platform.

She stood next to her husband. "I would like to say some words." She paused and took a deep breath. "Like Vern ..." Frida looked up at her new husband with smiling, happy eyes, "... I never thought ..." A tear streamed down her cheek as folks sighed in unison.

"I must thank one person." Frida opened her hand toward Ned, who stood in front, next to Lily. "Thank you, Ned Fallow." Frida bowed her head toward Ned.

Fighting his emotions, Ned returned the gesture.

Dan O'Hurley put his arms around Vern and Frida. "Been a change in plans. Vern and Frida want to celebrate the threshing contest tonight, along with this fine wedding. The beer's on the way, compliments of Bill Etheridge."

A thunderous cheer came from the men.

Dan raised his arms and pointed at the big oak table. "Hank, are you ready with the results?"

A hush fell over the room as all eyes focused on Hank.

"I'll announce the top three scores, in reverse order." Hank took a sheet of paper off the table. "Finishing third, with seven and a half acres, are Nick and Sean Brockway." The room fell silent. "Finishing second, with fourteen and a half acres, are Ned Fallow and Tom O'Brien."

Ned shook his head and thought of how next year's results would be different.

"Finishing first, with fifteen acres, are Vern Swensen and Thor Jorgensen." A great cheer rose from the crowd.

Lily turned to Ned. "Will you excuse me, Ned? I need to help set up the food."

"I'll be around," Ned said.

Lily gave Ned's hand a squeeze and joined a group of women rushing around placing platters of food on the big oak table.

A quartet dressed in red-and-white-striped jackets and bow ties, warmed up in a corner. Hank Grove stroked his fiddle, trying to find the right pitch, while the other three worked on harmonizing their voices over the din of boisterous, thirsty men rolling kegs of beer past them. Ned felt the excitement in the air, and also a pang of guilt for having missed past evenings like this.

Ned saw Thor sitting alone in a corner.

"That was some competition."

"Yah. Frida and Daj happy we won."

Ned extended his hand to Thor.

Thor stood up; looking straight at Ned, he grabbed his hand and shook. "Frida tell me about your help." Lowering his brow, a frown came over his broad face. "Lomax no good. Thank you."

Ned nodded at Thor.

A smile now crept into the edges of Thor's thick lips. "When I see you and your partner at depot, I know threshing competition will be hard."

"I knew, too."

"Yah."

Bill Etheridge rolled a big oak barrel out to the middle of the hall. With some assistance, he stood on the barrel in the middle of the great room and began reciting Thoreau. His voice hung in the air like morning fog, drawing his audience to rapt attention. One passage in particular caught Ned's ear.

"'If one advances confidently in his dreams and endeavors to live the life he has imagined, he will meet with a success unexpected in common hours.'"

I can see it now, Ned thought.

The musicians at the far end of the hall began playing a song Ned had never heard.

He spotted Lily at the punch bowl and walked over.

"Hello, Ned. They're playing a song my grandfather wrote for me."

He noticed the way she held herself straight and true. "Lily?"

"Yes, Ned?"

"May I have this dance?"

Lily took Ned's hand.

The group sang, in perfect harmony:

"When streams flow down the face of Green Mountain,
  When its lush meadow harkens the spring,
  'Tis then that we honor with hearts ever grateful,
  The view from your vantage, the treasures you bring."

Sweeping Lily across the dance floor, Ned caught some of the amazed looks of the womenfolk. He knew what some of them must be thinking, but he would show them that he was a changed man.

Ned wished that Tom could be here, and he thought of the first time he had ever danced. His neighbor in Ketchum, Lars Sorenson, had played his heart out on the fiddle that night. "Music is magic; keep it in your heart." he had hollered as Ned sprang across the floor with Mrs. Sorenson. Ned remembered how alive he had felt at that moment, and how short-lived it was.

Bill Etheridge grabbed his wife's arm gently and pointed to Ned and Lily.

"Oh, my heavens, will you look at that. What a lovely couple you two make," Mrs. Etheridge said as Ned and Lily passed by.

The music seemed to flow right to Ned's heart:

"When the winds blow and snow covers Green Mountain,
  When it lies dormant but keen to renew
  The memories, the promise of eternal springtime,
  That fountain, Green Mountain, will greet us anew."

Ned realized that old Lars Sorenson had been right—music *was* magic. Holding Lily close—but not too close—he looked down and smiled. It wasn't just a little smile, but one as big as the Kansas horizon.

Ned and Lily glided past Doc Auld and Mr. Tharrington, who were standing together. "Well, ain't *this* a sight for my sore old eyes!" Doc said, loud enough for Ned to hear.

Ned saw a trace of sadness in Mr. Tharrington's eyes and remembered the story Etheridge had told him years before of unrequited love, a beautiful girl, and the sea captain who had married her. Ned had once thought that he and Tharrington were kindred spirits.

"Very nice, Ned Fallow, very nice." Tharrington raised his mug of cider. "Yes, indeed," the old man said through a tight smile. His face was marked by melancholy. It was a face that asked, *What if?*

As Ned escorted Lily to a seat, she said, "I had a dream that we were dancing on a moonlit lake to that song. Someday, I must play if for you, Ned." Her eyes shone at him.

He thought he knew those eyes from some other time and place, but it quickly became clear: the other time and place he had imagined was right here and now.

Mrs. Grove came up to them.

"Lily, could you give me a hand with the potato salad?"

"Certainly." Lily smiled at Ned. "I won't be long."

Ned spotted Thor holding a cup of beer in one hand and waving him over with the other.

"Ned, join me and Vern."

Ned walked over.

"Here." Thor poured a cup for Ned out of a pitcher and said, "Is great day." Thor slapped Vern so hard on the back that he almost fell out of his chair.

"You know of Odin and Valhalla?" The beer and festive air had wiped away Thor's stolid demeanor.

"Never heard of them fellas," Ned said between swallows.

Thor began telling dark, foreboding tales of Viking gods and legends.

At the conclusion of "Loki, the Half-Giant, and the Wolf's Joint," Ned asked, "Don't you Norwegian folks have any happy stories?"

"That *was* happy story … for a Norwegian," Thor said, grinning.

All three broke out laughing. Ned laughed so hard that tears rolled down his cheeks.

Ned deadpanned, "Maybe I ought to tell some of my grandpa's Injun stories about the Spirit in the Sky … No, I better not. I doubt they'd be sorrowful enough for old Thor, here."

Again, all three erupted into laughter and backslapping.

After a while, the frivolity died down, and Doc Auld and Etheridge joined the group.

While Ned talked to Etheridge about the architecture of the Sycamore Hotel, Lily came over and sat next to him, holding a small book. Ned grabbed Lily's hand and held it firmly. Folks began to leave the dance, and Ned found himself alone with Lily.

He reached for her book. "Tennyson? He was my grandfather's favorite poet. He used to read passages to my cousin and me." Ned gave the book back to Lily.

"Ned Fallow. How you can surprise a girl."

Ned put his arm around her shoulders and could feel her heart beating against his ribs. She reached over and caressed his hair with a soft, gentle hand. Now he understood what his grandpa had meant by following one's heart.

Ned said, "You know—"

Lily put a finger against his lips. "I want us to remember tonight for the rest of our lives."

Ned lowered his arm to Lily's waist and drew her closer. He felt the book in her hand press against his ribs. "Would you read me a passage?" he asked. Ned saw an image of William O'Connor at his kitchen table, reading Tennyson out loud.

Lily leafed through the book. "Here's something appropriate:

'And on her lover's arm she leant,
And round her waist she felt it fold,
And far across the hills they went,
In that new world which is the old.'

Ned returned home, finished up some chores in the barn, and headed for the house, thinking about the plans he and Lily had made with the Groves at their kitchen table after Vern and Frida's wedding party.

"Two weddings in one month." Mrs. Grove had smiled at Lily and Ned. "Now, don't you worry about your mother, Lily. I'll go to Abilene and talk to her." Hank had then smiled at Ned and said, "She'll listen to the missus, Ned, don't you fret none."

Ned brought a chair out to the front porch and leaned back with his feet up on the rail.

Above the dusky fields of stubble and plowed earth, the sky draped the prairie landscape like a great purple cloak. This land and sky that had held him from the first sight of it had been both his mistress and his enemy. He saw that now.

William O'Connor's story of the Osage Indians came clear in his mind.

"Ned, a person needs to find the true journey of the spirit and keep harmony in his life, or it will be an empty journey."

Yes, now it came clear.

Ned Fallow had turned the corner.

978-0-595-43652-
0-595-43652-8

Printed in the United States
108372LV00003B/310-333/A

9 780595 436521